MY CAPTIVE DUCHESS

THE REEVES OF REEVES HALL
– BOOK 1 –

M.M. Wakeford

First edition.
978-1-7395071-7-6

Cover designed by GetCovers.

www.mw-author.com

THE REEVES OF REEVES HALL

What lies within the walls of Reeves Hall, a grand estate in a lonely corner of Cornwall owned by the mysterious Reeves family?

These steamy romances are set in Regency England—with a subtle science-fiction twist. Follow members of the Reeves clan as each of them take the risk of falling in love while protecting their family's great secret.

Each book can be enjoyed as a standalone, or read in series order for added depth and connection.

Book 1 – **My Captive Duchess**

Book 2 – **My Masquerade With the Duke**

Book 3 – **A Not So Convenient Marriage**

Book 4 – **A Most Reluctant Widow**

PROLOGUE

BROEK

Planet Uvon, in a galaxy far, far away

Keteth approaches me, and I can see at once from his face that the news is not good. I had not expected it to be. Still, I brace myself for what I am about to hear. In a gruff voice, I command, "Speak."

"A unanimous decision," he informs me. "Your mother is to be executed at the seventh hour, the day after tomorrow."

A tightness grips my chest as I nod in understanding. From the moment Mother had set in motion the plot to overthrow the governing body of Uvon, her fate had been inescapable. She has taken the greatest gamble and lost, for there is no other penalty for the crime of treason but a death sentence. I have known this and tried to prepare myself, but it seems I must have harboured some small glimmer of hope, for this news has me overwhelmed with pain.

I manage to choke out, "Father too?"

Keteth looks away, unable to meet my eyes. His silence is answer enough. So, within the next fifty hours, I am to lose both my parents. I take a deep breath and attempt to remain calm. There is one further question that needs to be answered. "What about us?" I grit out. By us I mean myself and my three younger siblings—Liora, Horis and Simor.

Keteth sighs. "I tried, Broek, I really did. I set out all the evidence to show you had nothing to do with any of it, that you are entirely blameless, all to no avail. I do not think they believe you had any hand in the plot, but they are keen to make an example of you."

Do they know about the nanoprobes? Well, Tarla does at any rate, but I would think it is in her best interests to feign ignorance of them. I wonder if it is her influence that is behind this punishment about to be meted out upon us. I would not put it past that traitorous witch to have a hand in this. "Spit it out, Keteth!" I grunt impatiently.

"All four of you are to be banished," he says sadly.

"Where to?" I snap. "Falora?" but Keteth is already shaking his head. "Then where?" I almost roar this time.

He is hesitant in his reply, as if bracing himself for an explosive reaction. "They want you off this planet. In fact, off this galaxy."

I pale, my mind computing the options, which are few. He sees when I reach the obvious conclusion. "Strahmek 2." I whisper it on a breath.

"Yes," he confirms.

"Great Yol, they cannot be serious!"

"I am afraid they are."

I rise to my feet in a burst of energy and begin to pace the room. "We have not shipped people there since the Odoth era," I cry. "Yol only knows what society these felons have formed in over three hundred thousand years of exile. Are they civilised? Do they even speak the mother tongue? Or have they butchered each other into extinction?"

"I have searched the records of our last reconnaissance mission there to find this out and sent you the data," Keteth says placatingly. "But to answer your question, they have formed civilisations, and they speak many tongues, all of which are derived from ours, though unrecognisable now to our ears."

None of this makes any sense. I stop my pacing and glare at my old friend, demanding the truth from him. "Why now? Shipping us there will take years, and it will not be cheap!"

He inclines his head in agreement. "The governing body has agreed to field a ship, the *Nostur*, which was due to be scrapped after seven decades of service." He sees my look of disbelief and hastens to add, "It is still in good working order, and with a few upgrades, can be made ready within the next month for your journey."

I throw myself on the couch and bury my head in my hands. Great Yol have mercy! This cannot be happening to us. And yet, after all the miseries the past few months have inflicted on my family, I can readily believe that a further tragedy awaits us around the corner. I sit up and cast my eyes over the lavish furnishings of this room, which I employed the services of an expert decorator to design. It is my own personal chamber on the grand Reevas estate which has belonged to my family for generations. And now, we must leave all this in order to travel light years away on a ramshackle ship, so we can make our new home on a penal colony we abandoned hundreds of thousands of years ago.

I turn my gaze towards Keteth again. "You still have not answered me. Why now?"

"Do you recall your history lessons about the ancient plan to build a high-speed corridor between ourselves and Strahmek 2?"

I nod impatiently. It is something all children on Uvon are taught about. Hundreds of thousands of years ago, during the Odoth era, a period of our history so called because the greater part of our planet was under the rule of one dynasty, the Odoths, we had made immense strides in our space exploration, searching far and wide for any sign of life on planets beyond our solar system and beyond our galaxy. This extensive search had yielded only one other planet, which we named Strahmek 2, that had the right conditions for life. Like Uvon, it had forests and fertile lands, vast oceans and regions with a temperate climate. In many ways, it was our twin planet, except it was two million light years away and inhabited only by large reptile creatures.

This did not deter Cruls Odoth, who ruled the dynasty at that time. He concocted an ambitious plan to build a high-speed corridor between our two planets, and to begin colonising Strahmek 2 through the deportation of thousands of felons there from our overcrowded prisons. Barely had work on this plan got off the ground than the whole thing fell apart when the Odoth dynasty, bankrupt on its grand ideas, was brutally overthrown. There followed decades of vicious wars, culminating in the destruction of some of our finest cities and death on a scale we have not seen since. We call that period of our history the dark century. In the midst of that chaotic carnage, Strahmek 2 and the first shipment of felons to the colony were forgotten.

After the downfall of a dynasty and the ensuing horrific wars, few subsequent leaders had any further appetite for colonisation of a planet so far from ours. Over the centuries, we have sent the occasional unmanned missions to gather data, but nothing more. I am puzzled as to why such a plan should be resurrected now.

Keteth is quick to explain. "The idea of re-establishing links with Strahmek 2 has been floated for a long time. The governing body is about to launch an ambitious long-term plan that will take centuries to reach fruition, at the end of which we would have a high-speed route to Strahmek 2, based on the creation of a traversable wormhole. We are years away from creating this, but our top scientists are working on it. In the meantime, there is a mission they wish you to undertake on that planet."

He sees the hope on my face and shakes his head. "It will not buy your return home, Broek. Your exile is to be a permanent one. However, this mission will give you an opportunity to atone for the part you played, even unwittingly, in your mother's plot and to rehabilitate your family's name."

"What is the mission?" I ask coldly.

He sits beside me and begins to explain. Once he is done, he concludes, "You will spend the years aboard the *Nostur* preparing for your new life on Strahmek 2. All of you will be properly instructed in the language and customs of its people, from the extensive data we have gathered about them. Once you arrive, in a cloaked shuttle, you will integrate seamlessly into Strahmek 2's society and not disclose your true origins."

I gaze absently at the artwork that adorns the wall across from me. The scheme Keteth has just described sounds preposterous, another grand idea that is doomed to fail. How are we ever to pass for inhabitants of Strahmek 2? I know nothing of them, and it could take us years to learn their ways. Once the *Nostur* departs on its journey back to Uvon, we will be alone and at the mercy of the natives, should they ever discover our true origins. Who knows with what savagery we might then be treated.

Great Yol, what is to become of us? On my next breath, I curse Mother and Tarla for putting us all in these dire straits, and myself for not having put a stop to this when I could have.

A gentle hand squeezes my shoulder. "I know what you are thinking, Broek," Keteth says softly. "But I believe you have the strength and resilience to do this. Your sister and brothers are relying on you to keep them safe, and if anybody can do it, it is you."

I raise my head to face him. "Your belief in me is flattering but unwarranted, Keteth," I murmur sardonically.

He laughs, the first joyful sound I have heard in several weeks. "I disagree, Broek," he says. "You have it in you to turn this misfortune into an opportunity for a fresh start. I shall miss you, my friend, but I know with every fibre of my being that somewhere two million light-years away, the Reevas clan will prosper under your guidance. Do not think of this as the end, Broek, but as a new beginning."

Letting out a long breath, I reply, "I wish I shared your optimism, my friend." I am quiet a moment or two, then ask, "Will they let me see Mother and Father before the end?"

Keteth shakes his head. "I am afraid not, Broek, but you may send them a recorded message."

I sigh and rise to my feet. There is much to be done, and my siblings need to be told the news. "Thank you, Keteth," I say, holding out my arms. My long-time friend steps into my embrace, and for a few moments, I hold him tight before letting go. He represents everything I shall be leaving behind. Then I am all action, getting on with the many things I need to do. My pain is still there, but it is locked away while I take care of my family. Perhaps Keteth is right, and we can make a go of this new life on a distant planet. I sincerely hope he is.

CHAPTER 1

JANE

March 1821, England, ten years later

Once upon a time, an orphaned girl was sent to live in the household of prosperous relations. Her prospects were few, for she had little in the way of fortune or looks. She was not treated unkindly by these relations, but her place in their home was lowly, only a short step above that of the servants. There she lived for some years, playing second, or perhaps more accurately, third fiddle to her cousins, two gracious and gregarious young ladies who had every expectation of making a fine marriage.

Their sights were set on one gentleman in particular, a most sought-after bachelor of their acquaintance. He was none other than the Duke of Coleford, a man endowed with every desirable attribute. He was rich, handsome and well-born. Other traits that might have been considered defects, or at the very least a detriment to his desirability, were eclipsed by this fact of him being rich, handsome and well born. That he was self-effacing and painfully shy was well known, but this was seen simply as a manifestation of the greatness of his mind. That he had a tendency to stammer when in the presence of company was thought to be charming. That he was a poor horseman and preferred sedentary pursuits to sportsmanship was celebrated as one of his delightful eccentricities.

In short, the handsome duke could do no wrong—until the day he committed a most grievous misdeed. And what, one may ask, was this great felony? None other than this. The Duke of Coleford fell in love with me, the orphaned girl who had been taken in so charitably by her relatives. Not only did he fall in love, but he also proposed marriage. The good people in the Somerset village of Coleford, as well as society in the wider world, were all agog at this news. How could it be that such an illustrious personage should align himself with a mousy looking nobody? It was outrageous. It beggared belief. It could only be that the young hussy had used womanly wiles and vile trickery to ensnare the duke.

Numerous wise and well-meaning persons paid visits to him, offering earnest advice. All was done to try to prevent this great misalliance from occurring. But although the duke was of a diffident nature, on this matter he stood firm. He would marry Jane Price, and no one was going to stop him from doing so. And thus, in a small ceremony attended by few, he married me. A year later, we welcomed into the world our daughter, whom we named Chloe.

It sounds like a fairy tale, does it not? And for a short time, it was. Giles, my very own duke, was a gentle, loving husband and father. He rescued me from a lonely life of drudgery and shone a bright light over my world. However, unlike the fairy tales of yore, we did not get to live happily ever after. Our happiness lasted precisely three years, two months and five days.

I think on this now as I sit, wearing my widow's weeds, and wait for Mr Oakley to tell me my fate. He is the Coleford family solicitor, and he has come to discuss matters relating to Giles's estate with me. I barely register his words, for I am too numb with shock and grief. This is the way it has been since the news was conveyed to me of Giles's accident. He had, against his better judgement, accepted an invitation to participate in a local hunt, during which he had been unseated by his horse. Poor Giles had fallen, broken his neck and died instantly. Those are the dry facts which my mind cannot grapple with just yet. Instead, I stare at a glittering piece of lint on the shoulder of Mr Oakley's jacket. Perhaps I should call Simms, Giles's valet, to run a brush over it. Or would the gentleman mind so very much if I leaned forward and flicked the offending item away?

I am so preoccupied with this that I almost fail to grasp the import of Mr Oakley's words. "The Coleford estate is subject to an entail, which requires it to be passed in its entirety to the next male heir, along with the dukedom. That would be the late duke's cousin. I have written to inform him of the duke's passing, and he has written back to say he shall arrive at Coleford Hall on 3rd April to take possession of his inheritance."

My sluggish mind is slow to take in the ramifications of this statement. I am conscious of one fact only—that in less than two weeks' time, Coleford Hall shall no longer be my home. That is not a bad thing in and of itself. I have never felt truly comfortable in this great mausoleum of a house. And without Giles's cheery presence, it is a cold, unwelcoming place. Absently, I mumble, "We shall have to move to the London house."

I catch a pitying look upon Mr Oakley's countenance before he quickly schools his features to make it disappear. "I am afraid not, Your Grace," he says gently. "The London house is also part of the entail."

"I see," I murmur, though I do not really see. Where are Chloe and I supposed to live now?

As if in answer to my silent question, Mr Oakley goes on to explain, "Ordinarily, as dowager duchess you would be entitled to live in the Dower House. However, that house has been rented out and is not available."

Of course. Had I been thinking clearly, I would have known this. A sense of doom engulfs me. I cannot quite keep the tremor from my voice as I ask, "Then where are we to go?"

Mr Oakley interlaces his fingers and directs his gaze at me as he speaks, "There is one house which does not form part of the entail, for it belonged to the late duke's mother. It passes now to you, Your Grace."

"What house is this?" I ask, for I have not heard of it.

"Penhale Manor, Your Grace," replies the solicitor. "It is located in Cornwall, a few miles east of Newquay."

"Cornwall," I repeat blankly. I am not at all familiar with that county.

Mr Oakley smiles kindly. "Yes, Your Grace. I have not been to see it, but I understand it is of good size. If you wish, I can write to request the house be prepared for your arrival."

I nod my assent, not trusting myself to speak, and feeling overwhelmed at this sudden change in my circumstances—coming at a time when all I wish to do is grieve. The solicitor clears his throat. "There is one further matter to discuss," he says ponderously. "It is to do with your funds. Your Grace will understand, of course, that all income from the land on the Coleford estate now goes to the new duke. However, the late duke's mother also left him a lump sum, a part of her dowry, which is invested in the funds. It yields an income of around £400 a year. It is no great fortune, but that sum now goes to you, Your Grace. I was surprised there are no other funds for you, however, I believe it should provide a sufficient income to live on in reasonable comfort."

"I am sure it will be more than sufficient for our needs," I say softly. Giles and I had been used to living a quiet life, neither of us predisposed for grand balls and the great gatherings of the ton. Our pleasures were simple—walks in the park, sketching and of course, a great deal of reading. This new life at Penhale Manor will suit me and Chloe very well, I tell myself, though our surroundings will be foreign and new to us at first. I let my mind wander, emerging briefly from the numbness of grief to imagine a characterful and cosy house where I shall spend the rest of my days. We shall live simply but comfortably, away from the gossip of the ton. There, I shall raise my daughter, instil in her good Christian values, undertake her education, and in the fullness of time, see her married to an upstanding local gentleman. A trickle of hope begins to banish some of the dull, aching gloom that has beset me. We shall start anew, Chloe and I, and everything will work out.

CHAPTER 2

JANE

Two weeks later

We are near our destination at last after two long and wearying days of travel. At least, I hope we are not too far from Penhale Manor. I cannot be sure, for I am new to these parts. We were told, on setting out this morning from the inn on the outskirts of Exeter where we had stopped for the night, that Penhale was an easy day's journey and that we should reach it well before sundown. I am beginning to doubt the truth of this. Outside my carriage window, the twilit sky is spreading darkness over the flat, grassy landscape we are traversing.

Ever since we stopped in the town of Bodmin to refresh our horses earlier this afternoon, we have been travelling through the moor on a rutted and mostly deserted road. We have passed the occasional farmhouse or hamlet, but for the most part, all I have seen through the window is a vast heathland covered in stubby shrubs, the only sign of life being the occasional flock of grazing sheep.

Chloe's head rests in my lap, her even breaths assuring me that she is fast asleep. In her small, dimpled hands, she grasps Nessie, the rag doll she is loath to ever part with. Over the course of the journey, she had grown restless and fractious, her young body more accustomed to energetic activity than sitting still in a carriage all day. Much as I adore my daughter and delight in her youthful exuberance, I must confess to having grown weary of the need to placate and soothe her these past few hours. I am thankful she is finally resting.

The only other occupant of the carriage is Betsy, my maid, though she too has given in to lassitude. Her chin has dropped to her chest in sleep, rousing with the occasional jolt of the carriage before dropping down again. It is only me and the coachman that are alert in this empty and rapidly darkening landscape. My worried gaze flits once more to the window, searching for any building or turning in the road that would indicate proximity to Penhale village. Nothing but shrubland greets my eyes, a vast carpet of long grass dotted with the purple and yellow of spring blooms.

And then, I see it.

To my left, I catch sight of a stone wall, at least ten feet in height. My pulse quickens as we begin to drive alongside it. Could this be Penhale Manor? I frown in concentration, trying to make out the road ahead. The wall stretches out before us, and I cannot see where it ends or where the entrance gates might be. All I can deduce is that there must be a sizeable estate behind the wall, enclosing far more land than I was led to expect. A sense of unease trickles through me. Perhaps then it is not Penhale Manor we are reaching but a neighbouring house.

By now, the carriage has slowed its pace, allowing me to make out a painted wooden sign affixed to the middle of the wall, the message on it stark and unwelcoming: INTERLOPERS BEWARE. I cannot help the shiver that runs through my body at reading those words. Whoever it is that lives in this house evidently wants to be left well alone.

It is another half mile before we finally come to a stop in front of imposing iron gates. In the gathering dusk, I can narrowly discern the name engraved on a large slab of grey stone set into a tall pillar by the gates, beyond which I can see a small lodge, presumably housing the gatekeeper. I gently remove Chloe's head from my lap to push open the carriage door and peer out, hoping to get a better look. With an effort, I manage to decipher the words: Reeves Hall.

Just as I suspected, this is not Penhale Manor, but perhaps we may enquire here about directions. It seems the coachman has the same idea, for I see him jump down from his perch and go to ring a bell set into the stone pillar. The sound of it ringing is an eerie echo in the quietness of the gathering night. We wait at least a full minute before the lodge door opens, and a man wearing a deep scowl strides towards us. He is in shirtsleeves, the top buttons undone and revealing dark swirls of hair on his broad chest.

"Yes?" he barks.

For a moment, I am taken aback, but I quickly gather my wits, rushing forward to where the man stands behind the gate, hands on hips. As I near him, I can see that he does indeed have a hostile countenance. "Good evening, sir," I say in my most genteel manner. There is no need for my standards of courtesy to be compromised, even when confronted by such a blatant show of rudeness.

He does not respond but directs his glowering stare at me. I continue, trying to sound brave, "I wonder, sir, if you would assist us with directions to Penhale Manor. Is it very far from here?"

Still, the man stares, no hint of softening in his expression. Up close, I can see he is tall—a few inches above six feet—and powerfully built. The taut muscles of his arms strain against the fabric of his shirt as he continues to hold his stance, hands on hips. He exudes menace, firmly reined in but ready to be unleashed at any given moment. Quite clearly, this is not a man that one would ever want to cross. I feel tremors run through my body, and it takes every strength I have not to step backwards or show any fear.

Finally, the man deigns to respond. In a low voice, he grunts, "What business have you at Penhale Manor?"

"My business, sir, is that it is my home, and I am come to live there," I answer smoothly, proud that my calm voice does not betray the inner turmoil I feel.

"And who might you be?" he bites out.

I gather myself up to my full height, which admittedly is not very high at just two inches above five feet. "I am the Dowager Duchess of Coleford," I tell him, "and Penhale Manor was left to me by my late husband. I would appreciate, sir, given the lateness of the hour, if you would kindly direct us to our destination."

His eyes rake over me, from the top of my black silk bonnet to the tips of my boots peeping out from under the bottom of my cloak. Then, with a dismissive huff, he turns to my coachman and instructs him, "Keep going another quarter mile. You'll then see a turning for Penhale Manor on your right." Without another word, he turns and strides back to the lodge, closing the door behind him with a resounding clack.

I take in a deep, shocked breath. I do not think I have ever felt so humiliated—and that is saying something, thinking back to how I was treated at my aunt's. And by whom? A mere gatekeeper? A rush of anger quickly replaces the shock I had been feeling. My cheeks burn with it. How dare that man speak so to me, a duchess, and dismiss me so casually? If his master is anything like him, then I would be well advised to maintain my distance from whatever family resides behind those walls. I send out a silent prayer that this is the last I ever see of this rude man, then I turn to face my coachman. "Let us be on our way," I say crisply. "We have only a short time until darkness falls." Determination in every step, I return to my carriage and snap the door shut with a satisfying clack of my own.

CHAPTER 3

BROEK

"What are we going to do about it?" asks Liora. Her legs and feet are bare as she reclines on the healing couch and receives an invigorating rub to the lower part of her body. I cast her a fulminating glance, annoyed that once again, she has beaten me to it. My body aches with tension, and all day, I have been promising myself a session on that couch.

Once upon a time, this would not have been a problem, for each room of our palatial home back in Uvon was equipped with all the creature comforts we required. Here on Strahmeck 2—or Earth, as the natives call it—there is but one such couch, salvaged from the ship before it took off for our home planet. Instead I am sitting on a chair next to the console, with Horis and Simor lounging by the window.

With an angry huff, I consider my sister's question. What indeed are we to do about the rumours circulating that our family is part of a pagan cult that practises a form of witchcraft? It is a view held by the more ignorant members of this society, though I fear that some of these opinions are spreading into the wider world. I am not too worried that a justice of the peace will come knocking on our doors with an arrest warrant. It has been over three quarters of a century since the crime of witchcraft was abolished. Laws may have changed, however, but attitudes linger, and superstition is still rife in this part of the country.

We chose this land to settle in for the sparsity of its population and the vast acreage we could acquire at a reasonable cost. It is not fertile land, which would account for why we were able to purchase it so cheaply. No matter to us.

We grow the crops we need in our glasshouses; the rest we purchase from the nearest towns. What we wanted, more than fertile land, was a place devoid of nosy neighbours, where we could maintain our way of life within the enclosure of our secure walls.

What in the name of Yol are we to do about these pesky rumours? It is not as if I wish to befriend the English populace—they are a backward and primitive people. We have been careful though to keep up the appearances of their society, even attending church service every Sunday, which I consider the dullest hour of every week. It seems that is not enough. Still they talk about us, damned halfwits with nothing better to do. A part of me wishes we could simply ignore them, but I know that rumours can escalate and become ever more outlandish unless they are nipped in the bud. Something will have to be done, but what?

Before I can speak, my middle brother, Horis, observes, "People fear what they do not know. The more we keep to ourselves, the more suspicious they become of us."

"What would you suggest?" I bite back acidly. "That we invite them into this settlement so they can gawk at our screens and marvel at our 'magical' lighting?"

Simor, the youngest of us at five and twenty years of age, sits up with a gleam in his eyes. "That idea is not half bad," he pronounces. At my frown, he hastily adds, "Not the gawking at our technology, but the invitation to our house. We could host a dinner party for a select number of guests. Wolkan is the chief of security and can ensure none of the guests venture where we do not want them to go."

"Hmm," murmurs Horis. "You could be onto something there. We would have to set up the dining hall and drawing room so none of our technology is visible, as well as put in some props—candlesticks and such like."

Strangers in my home. Marvellous. I cannot help the scowl that takes residence on my face, especially when my sister throws at me, "Grumps, what do you think?"

"Do not call me that!" I growl menacingly, but Liora merely chuckles in amusement. I do not particularly care for this nickname my siblings have given me, although I cannot deny that with each passing year of our exile, I have become increasingly more irascible in disposition. I almost forget the merry person I used to be before our lives took this dark turn over a decade ago. In that first year aboard the ship bound for Earth, we were all numb with grief, as well as filled with rage at what had been done to us. But then, one by one, my siblings picked themselves up and recovered their spirits. All except me.

Perhaps it is because my sense of loss and betrayal was greater than theirs. On Uvon, I had been in my element, distinguishing myself in my studies and rising up the ranks to lead a multibillion-Krosor business empire. My successes had not only been in the field of business. I had had my pick of beautiful women in my well-spent youth, eventually settling down with the most beautiful and talented of them all—Tarla. Even after these many years, the thought of her, and her treachery, makes my chest ache with pain. But I must not think of her. With an effort, I direct my thoughts to the matter at hand. A dinner party.

"We shall have to invite the most influential people we know," I muse. After a moment's reflection, I suggest, "Sir Nicholas and Lady Calthorpe with their two daughters." Sir Nicholas is a baronet whose estate lies some three miles from here, not far from the port town of Newquay. I have only met him on a handful of occasions. He is a self-important, blustery gentleman with a placid wife and several children, the eldest of which are two young ladies, out in society.

"Their two marriageable daughters," says Liora knowingly.

"What of that?" I bark in annoyance.

She raises a brow but humours me with an explanation. "It occurs to me that merely holding a dinner party will not be sufficient to stamp out the rumours. What we need is a visible union between us and a respectable, well-regarded family." We all stare at her in shock. Surely she does not mean… but yes, Great Yol, she does. "One of you, dear brothers, ought to marry into a family such as the Calthorpes," Liora goes on to say.

"Have you taken leave of your senses?" exclaims Horis, echoing my thoughts exactly. "Setting aside why it should be one of us to marry and not you, how in heavens are we to have one of them live among us without our secret being discovered?"

"I will have you know, Horis," quips Liora with a smug grin, "that since I have reached the grand old age of one and thirty, society considers me unmarriageable and on-the-shelf, so of course, I cannot be the one to marry."

"That is beside the point," I grit out, my patience with my sister at an end. "Marriage with an outsider is out of the question for all of us. We cannot be inviting any of the natives to live among us."

"Hear me out, Broek," Liora retorts. "I agree with you. We cannot invite an outsider to live here, but what if one of us were to marry and live elsewhere nearby?" She rises to her feet and pads over to a side table on which rests a copy of *The Times*. She picks it up and flicks to the obituary page, pointing with her finger at one of the notices. "It says here that the Duke of Coleford has passed away from an accident, leaving behind a young widow, one who will no doubt inherit Penhale Manor. This may finally be our opportunity to purchase the property."

Penhale Manor is a nearby house that has lain empty ever since we moved here seven years ago. Only a groundsman lives there, a drunkard who spends most of his time at the village tavern—which suits us very well. The less people around us the better. For some time now, I have been keen to purchase Penhale Manor to afford us a greater measure of privacy as well as to enlarge our settlement, for in addition to myself and my three siblings, a crew of thirty-six people—all of them loyal family retainers—joined us on this exodus from Uvon. Already, several of them have entered into unions, even going so far as marrying in the local church to keep things official. With their growing families, we will soon need to expand our settlement.

Three months ago, I sent a letter to the owner of Penhale Manor, the Duke of Coleford, expressing my interest in purchasing the property, but my generous offer was rejected. It is unfathomable to me why this nobleman would wish to keep a nearly derelict house with land that earns him little income, which he never uses, even for a fleeting visit. The ways of these humans are still a mystery to me.

I take the paper from Liora's hand and read the notice, thinking rapidly. We must strike fast and make the widow a generous offer she cannot refuse. Once Penhale Manor is in our hands, we can make the necessary refurbishments and have one of us live there with his bride, effectively acquiring a veneer of respectability and downplaying any rumours about our family. Of course, we would not be able to install much Uvonian technology at Penhale Manor and that person would have to live there as the natives do, perhaps trusting her enough to reveal our secret in due course. It cannot be me, I conclude. I have sacrificed enough for this family already. It is surely time for Horis or Simor to step up.

As my glance finds my brothers, they both instantly catch the drift of my thoughts and raise their hands in protest. "Not me," says Simor hurriedly. "I am far too young to marry."

"You are not!" I declare with a satisfying thump of my fist on the table.

"Well, but it will seem very odd that I should marry before either of my two older brothers," he says smoothly, not the least bothered by my show of anger.

My eyes dart towards Horis, who wears a horrified expression on his face. "Great Yol, do not look at me!" he exclaims. "I am the least handsome of the four of us, as you all well know. It would take a miracle if I were to get any young lady to accept my suit."

I let out an aggrieved sigh. It is a fact that Horis has not been as blessed as we have in terms of looks, but he is not ugly by any stretch of the imagination. The goodness of his heart shines through and renders his countenance most pleasing, in my view. Any young lady should count herself lucky to be his bride, but he does not realise this. I do wish I could instil some confidence in him. When all hell broke loose a decade ago, he had barely entered adulthood and was still gawky and shy. Then, with the upheaval of our banishment to Earth, he was denied the opportunity to spread his wings and to sow his wild oats—as the English saying goes.

Oftentimes, I feel keenly the weight of the responsibility that was thrust upon me when I shepherded my siblings and servants into this exile on Earth. The life I have lived here has been a far cry from the pleasurable existence I had on Uvon. For more than a decade, I have acted as protector and provider, ensuring we have sufficient wealth to live comfortably, settling squabbles and stepping into the role of leader—one that I never wished to take. On my darkest days, I have thought of leaving it all behind, setting out alone to sea for some far off destination, but of course, I have never done so. It may be arrogance to believe it, but what would they all do without me? Instead, day by day, I have sunk into gloom, turning into the morose person I am today. Perhaps I do deserve the nickname of Grumps after all.

As for me, I have no need to marry. Whenever I feel the urge, I seek pleasure with Catana, a young female who had been a servant in our household back on Uvon and who elected to come with us to Earth. She works now under Wolkan, helping to ensure our settlement is kept safe from curious eyes. Every so often, Catana and I spend some salacious time beneath the sheets, but I am careful not to take it any further than that. I have suspected, once or twice, that she harbours an ambition to form a union with me, and that can never be. After Tarla's betrayal, I do not think I can ever give myself to another in that way.

My wandering thoughts come to a standstill as I notice three pairs of eyes directing their hopeful gaze at me. "Oh no," I grumble. "I am *not* getting married."

"Well, one of us will have to, and it may as well be you," declares Liora with a shrug.

My mood, already sour, darkens considerably. "I am not getting married," I repeat.

"How about this?" interjects Horis, ever the peacemaker. "We host our dinner party and see which of us garners the most interest from the ladies or gentlemen present." He says this with a pointed look at Liora, who laughs good naturedly.

"I have no issue with that," she says.

All eyes turn to me once more. "Hmph," I grunt, then walk out of the room without another word.

I am restless, and it is not yet dark. Without thinking, I throw on a coat and head out of the house, striding briskly in the direction of the lodge. I know Catana is on duty there, and I am sure she will not mind if we snatch some moments of carnal pleasure together.

A few minutes later, I am at the door, giving it three knocks before I enter. Catana looks up from her console and smiles. "Broek," she says, her voice low and husky.

I lean against the doorframe and give her a smouldering look. "Catana," I respond. I say nothing more, letting my gaze wander over her voluptuous figure before returning to stare into her eyes. My invitation is loud and clear. She stands and approaches, hips swaying seductively, coming to a stop inches from me. She places a hand to my chest and feels the beating of my heart. I breathe deeply but otherwise stay still. It has been several weeks since I have fucked, and lust has my cock swelling uncomfortably in my trousers. Slowly, she removes my coat and throws it to the floor. Then her hands are at my throat, untying my cravat and undoing the ties of my shirt. She drops a kiss to my chest as she does so. I am about to grab the vixen and hurry things along when a loud clang interrupts us. Someone is at the gate.

"Damn," I mutter in annoyance. In two quick strides, I am at the console, looking at the visual feed. A carriage has stopped outside the gates, and two persons are standing there waiting. "I'll go," I tell Catana. I open the lodge door and walk towards them. "Yes?" I ask, not caring if my tone is unfriendly.

A lady steps forward and asks for directions to Penhale Manor. I stare at her for a few moments, my mind trying to work out who she might be. She does not have the look of a servant. What business does she have at Penhale Manor? I grunt out a question, and she responds, "My business, sir, is that it is my home, and I am come to live there." Surely this could not be the widow? My eyes land on plump lips and big brown eyes in a pale face that looks innocently seductive.

"And who might you be?" I ask sharply.

She straightens her posture, and with a regal voice announces, "I am the Dowager Duchess of Coleford, and Penhale Manor was left to me by my late husband. I would appreciate, sir, given the lateness of the hour, if you would kindly direct us to our destination."

Hell and damnation, she is the widow. Have we left it too late to buy her off? Though perhaps she will take one look at the decrepit house that has been left to her and run away in fright. I examine her from head to toe. She is a diminutive little thing, no older than five and twenty. I cannot imagine her living alone in that draughty and dilapidated house. Tomorrow, or the day after, I will pay her a visit and make a generous offer she will surely not refuse.

With a huff, I turn to the coachman standing at her side and give him directions. Then without another look, I head back to the lodge and shut the door behind me. Catana awaits, hands on hips. "Well?" she asks.

I gaze at her pensively, my mind elsewhere. Finally, I say, "Penhale Manor's new owner has arrived." All desire has evaporated as I bend down and pick up my coat. "Excuse me, Catana, but I have much to discuss with my siblings." With that, I turn and walk out of the door.

CHAPTER 4

JANE

At last, we have arrived. My pulse beats rapidly at my temple as we trundle over the cobbled stone path that leads towards Penhale Manor. I press my nose to the carriage window, straining to catch my first sight of what is to be my new home. Chloe, remains fast asleep on my lap. Across from me, I sense Betsy's worried regard.

In the murky shadows, I glimpse a rectangular-shaped, two-storied structure with twin chimney stacks on either side. Soon, we come to a stop, and without any further ado, I gently ease Chloe off my lap, open the carriage door and hop down. It is then that I take my first proper look at the house, and my heart sinks. The building itself is of good size and characterful in appearance with grey-coloured brickwork and tall, mullioned windows. However, even a cursory glance reveals that the house has been sadly neglected.

Several windowpanes are cracked, with one missing altogether. Great clumps of ivy cover the whole east side of the building, obscuring some of the windows. As I raise my gaze to the top of the building, I spy a few gaps in the tiles on the roof. Has water leaked into the house? If this is the state it is in on the exterior, what condition will it be in on the inside? There is only one way to find out. With a determined step, I hurry to the door and ring the bell.

As I wait for a response, the coachman begins to bring down our trunks. Betsy remains in the carriage with a still sleeping

Chloe, but I feel her worried glance follow me. After what seems an eternity, I ring the bell again, but there is still no answer. The house is evidently deserted. I huff in frustration. Mr Oakley has informed me that there resides at Penhale Manor a housekeeper named Mrs Treen and a groundsman named Pedrick. He has written to inform them of my arrival. They should be expecting me, but there is no sign of either of them. I turn the handle on the door, hoping against hope that it will open, but the door is firmly locked.

I turn and walk back to the carriage, a heaviness in my chest. Night is about to fall, and it is imperative that we find shelter very soon. I have no knowledge as to how much further the village of Penhale lies, nor if there is a respectable inn there at which we may stay. There is nothing for it. We shall have to brave it at Penhale Manor. But first, we must get inside.

I study the house once more, my eyes going to the broken windowpane. It is on a ground floor window on the far side of the house. An idea takes shape in my mind. "Evans," I call to the coachman. "Do you see that broken glass over there?"

He looks to where I am pointing and replies, "Yes, Your Grace."

"Would you be able to reach inside to unlock the latch on the window and lift it open enough to climb inside?"

He considers it for a moment, then nods. "I will try."

Quickly, he goes to the window in question and reaches his arm through the gap, looking for the latch. Then with a loud creak, he lifts the sash window up a few inches. The resulting aperture is small, certainly not large enough for his bulky frame to fit through. My spirits take another dive.

There is only one other possibility. I look down at myself. I have often been teased for being a small slip of a thing. Many have been the times I have dreamed of growing an extra inch, or filling out a little more at the hips, all to no avail. For once though, my diminutive frame may present an advantage. I hurry towards the coachman and speak with as much authority as I can muster. "Evans, you will have to lift me up high so I can get inside."

He looks at me doubtfully, unused to the idea of a gentlewoman clambering through a window. It is not, admittedly, something that I have ever done before either. This entire situation is new to me, but I have never shirked from facing up to any predicament. One must do what one must. I peer through the window at the dark room within, trying not to think about what I may encounter inside. I make out a ghostly-looking shroud to one side, and my heart quickens. Then I remind myself that it is only a dust sheet protecting the furniture. This is not the time to panic. Chloe needs a bed tonight, and we need to get inside. Before I lose courage, I chivvy him, sharpening my tone, "Quick. There is no time to be lost."

I see the moment he makes his decision. With a huffed breath, he kneels on the ground and interlaces his fingers for me. Carefully, I set one foot on the inside of his hands and hoist myself up, gripping the window sill to propel myself forward through the gap. Head first, I tumble inside, feeling a painful burn on my thighs as I slide over the sill. A moment later, my head hits the wooden floor with a thump. For several instants, I lie in a heap on the floor, too dazed to move. Then, I force myself to my feet.

The room is dim, only a very faint light streaming in through the open window. I stand for a moment, trying to get my bearings and to fight the rising fear in my breast. Glancing to my right, I catch sight once more of the white shrouded furniture that has the look of a ghostly apparition despite all the rational words I tell myself. Slowly, my eyes begin to accustom themselves to the gloom. I take a deep breath. With a nervous flutter in my heart, I step towards the door, but a sudden creak underfoot has me pause. Standing still, I take another deep breath, willing myself to stay calm. This is not the time to panic. Chloe needs a warm, safe bed for the night.

I start again and reach the door, feeling my way to the knob and turning it. The door opens with a creak into a darkened hallway. There is no light at all now, only an impenetrable black. I step blindly forward in the direction of where I think the main door might be, but I cannot help a whimper of pain as my toe stubs into the clawed foot of a side table. The pounding of my heart is loud in my ear as I force myself to resume my journey. I take small steps, a few inches forward at a time. Finally, I enter a large open space which I feel sure must be the main hallway. In the shadows, I perceive the front door.

I go to it quickly and pull at the iron bolt that forms a bar, the thick end of which is burrowed into a slot in the adjacent wall. Evans is on the other side, helping to pull the door wide open. He goes then to retrieve our trunks while I search for a taper to light. I am in luck! On a side table stands a large candlestick, and inside a drawer, I find a tinderbox. I manage to pry it open and with shaking hands, strike the steel to the flint a few times until it sparks, setting alight the tinder cloth inside the box. I am thankful then that my many years living as little more than a servant in my aunt's household have taught me well. I do not think either of my cousins would know what to do were they faced with a similar situation, so coddled is their life. Emboldened by my success, I quickly light the candlestick, then search for more candles to light.

Under their glow, I am finally able to take a good look about me. The hallway is covered in fine dust, and there is a musty smell in the air, but the room is dry. In spite of my previous misgivings, I feel a small burgeoning of hope. Dust can be swept. Rooms can be aired. Matters are not so very bad.

The hallway is rectangular in shape, the floor covered in large slabs of polished grey stone. On my left, I spy a fireplace, above which hangs an ornate gilt mirror. I give it a cursory glance, for my attention is on the wide staircase that lies before me. It is time to explore the rooms upstairs and find suitable bedchambers. I take another deep breath and head towards it, holding the candlestick in my hand. Something scuttles in the shadows, a mouse no doubt. My heart jumps, but I force myself to keep going.

Up the stairs I go. On the landing at the top, I pause and look around. On either side of the staircase are six sets of doors. I go to the first one and open it. I find a bedchamber, furnished with a sturdy four-poster bed. My exploration of the other doors yields three further sleeping rooms, a washroom and an upstairs parlour. There is a small side staircase that leads to the eaves, where no doubt the servants' rooms are located. The larger of the four rooms is obviously the master and mistress's bedchamber. The air is stale in there, and the bed linen though clean, has a musty smell to it. It will have to do. Putting the candlestick down on the dressing table, I go to the window, and with some effort, manage to open it so I can air the room. As I turn back, I catch sight of cobwebs on the ceiling, but for now, I let them be. My daughter and I need a bed for the night.

With a determination borne from need, I pull the bedcovers and shake the dust out of them. I pound the pillows and mattress, airing them as best I can. Before I head back down to Betsy and Chloe, I light a fire in the hearth but keep the window open for now, to chase out the mustiness. I take a last look around. This will have to do, I tell myself firmly.

I go back down the stairs on legs that are steadier than before. *Nothing has more strength than dire necessity*, as the saying goes. I see that Evans has placed our various trunks and bandboxes in the hallway. Betsy sits on a chair with Chloe asleep in her lap. She looks about her in evident dismay. A quick glance outside tells me Evans has taken the carriage and horses to the stable and is busy settling them down. I turn back to my maid. "Follow me, Betsy," I say, injecting authority into my voice.

Eyes wide in her round face, she does as I ask, holding Chloe in her arms. In silence, I lead her to the bedchamber I prepared, and together, we get Chloe ready for bed, removing her shoes and dress. She stirs but does not come fully awake. Betsy finds the chamber pot, and together, we help Chloe do her business before settling her under the covers. I go to shut the window, though leave a sliver open, just to ensure some fresh air in the room.

Over the next hour, Betsy and I work away with gritted resolve, sweeping, airing and unpacking the most necessary of our belongings. I send her to look for fresh water, and after some time, she returns with a filled jug, which I direct her to leave for me in the bedchamber. Night has now fallen, and there is not much more we can do until morning. I am about to retire to bed when I hear a commotion outside.

I hurry down to the front entrance and find a grizzled looking man of uncertain years talking loudly with Evans. My coachman turns to me. "Your Grace, this is Pedrick, the groundsman," he says. "I found him asleep in the kitchen. I believe he is a trifle bosky," he adds severely.

I turn my gaze to the groundsman, who is swaying a little with inebriation. "Pedrick," I address him sternly. "Where is Mrs Treen and why has the house not been made ready for us? We sent word of our arrival over a week ago."

Pedrick scratches his head, clearly befuddled. "I got a letter, aye, but I carn't read. Mrs Treen be the one for that."

"And where is she?" I demand.

"Gone to meet her maker, Your Grace, last winter it be."

I sigh in frustration. The situation is becoming clear. With the housekeeper gone and a drunkard groundsman, it is no wonder the house has fallen into disrepair. It will not be a simple matter to redress the situation, but I do not think I have the strength to think about it now. I am bone weary and in need of sleep. Curtly, I tell him, "Pedrick, help Evans put up for the night. Tomorrow, bright and early, we shall talk." And with that, I make my way back inside, bolting the door securely.

A short time later, I get into bed, shifting Chloe aside to make room for me. I say a silent prayer and close my eyes, willing sleep to come, but though I am weary, it is not quite so easy to lose myself in slumber. Thoughts jumble in my head. Worry and grief tumble painfully in my chest. It has been almost two months since I lost Giles. I miss the quiet reassurance of his presence and how he would run a gentle hand over my hair late at night before we settled into bed. Over and above my sorrow and my worries about the future, I have one nagging thought. I am alone now. There is nobody but myself on whom I can rely. How I wish I could fall into eternal sleep and never have to wake up to the overwhelming burden of this solitude.

Unbidden comes a vision of the man I met this evening at Reeves Hall. His face was handsome, the features strong and regular. All this handsomeness had been belied, though, by the piercing menace of his stare. A shiver runs through me as I remember. How am I to manage with a terrifying man for a neighbour, a drunkard groundsman and a run-down house in need of expensive repairs? It is too much. A tear then two slide down my cheeks. I cry silently, not wanting to disturb Chloe.

It is a long, long time before I finally fall into a fitful sleep.

CHAPTER 5

BROEK

Two days later

I finish knotting my cravat with a flourish and glance at myself in the mirror with satisfaction. Cravats have been the bane of my existence these past several years. Once we emerged from our ship and began to live among the natives of Earth, we had to dress like them. Gone were the comfortable shirts and stretchy long pants of Uvon. In their stead were tight trousers, starched shirts, cravats and fitted tailcoats. For months, I chafed at the constriction of my new garb, though I eventually grew accustomed to it. Cravats, however, have continued to bedevil me. Not today though.

Today, I am in fine spirits, which is quite something for grumpy me. It does not take much effort to discover the reason for my good humour. Penhale Manor is within my grasp. I am sure of it. That fragile little thing will not last a day alone in that run-down house, let alone two. Last I saw it, the house had broken windowpanes and was overgrown with ivy. No doubt it is damp in there, rodent infested too. The housekeeper is gone, and the little duchess will be hard pressed to find a replacement in the village. Now that the gravity of the situation has been borne upon her, I can swoop in with my generous offer. She is bound to accept. Even though, for the past two days, my memory has kept on replaying how brave the little duchess looked in the moonlight, I cannot imagine that she will be brave enough to stay on in that wreck of a house.

In the dining room, I join my family for breakfast, where I partake in an excellent breakfast of Uvonian pancakes and eggs, together with a fresh brew of coffee—one Earth beverage I have found surprisingly enjoyable. I even smile as I pass the butter dish across to Liora before she even asks for it. She studies me in perplexion. "You are strangely cheery today, Grumps," she observes.

"Maybe then it is time to consign that nickname into oblivion," I reply.

"No, it is much too soon for that, but enlighten me. Why are you in such fine spirits?"

Horis laughs, stirring his own coffee. "Is it not obvious? He is going to Penhale Manor today where he will browbeat that little slip of a duchess into selling it to him."

I sit back in my chair, feeling pleasantly full. "I do not think there will be any need for browbeating," I point out. "Mark my words, she will jump at the chance to cast aside that ruin of a house. And with the generous sum I am willing to pay for it, she may easily afford a comfortable cottage somewhere else. I cannot think that she has decided to live at Penhale Manor permanently. She must be there merely to inspect the property with an aim of selling."

And once the house is in our name, I think to myself, it will make a good home for Horis and his potential bride—after we make improvements to it, of course. The longer I have reflected on the matter, the more certain I am that his marriage will solve several problems in one go. It will allow him to emerge from his shell of reserve and grow in confidence while bringing him the joy of procreating his own family. And in addition to all that, it will achieve our objective of putting a stop to the rumours about us.

There is a knock at the door and Wolkan walks in, bearing a sealed missive for Liora. We watch curiously as she takes it from him and breaks the seal. We are not in the habit of receiving much in the way of correspondence. "Ha!" she says, upon reading it, then looks up with a victorious smile. "It is from Lady Calthorpe, accepting our invitation to a dinner party next week."

"Who else are we inviting?" asks Simor. He is sitting opposite me spooning jam onto his pancake.

"It would only be proper to extend an invitation to Edmund Horton, as he is our local vicar," I respond.

"And how about Timothy and Verity Drake?" suggests Liora.

I nod in approval. The Drakes are a family whose modest estate lies some two miles to the south east of Reeves Hall. I have kept an eye on them, and other local families such as the Calthorpes, with the use of my nanoprobes. I know that Timothy Drake has a sister of marriageable age who could also be considered a possible bride for Horis. Yes, it would be a good idea to include them in our dinner party.

"And of course, we must invite the Duchess of Coleford," adds Horis with a gentle smile.

"Whyever would we do that?" I growl. My interest in the duchess is simply to get her to agree to sell Penhale Manor. It would be pointless to get to know the young widow socially, since she will be gone from the house before we know it.

Horis takes a sip of his coffee before replying, "Simple courtesy would dictate that we include our nearest neighbour, not to mention the fact that we need another female guest to make up the numbers."

"And of course, there is the cachet of her being a duchess," pipes up Simor.

I feel a strange unwillingness to have her here, though I could not say why. There is something about this duchess that has me feeling a trifle unsettled. Perhaps it is guilt at the fact that I am conspiring to rid her of her house. I shrug uneasily. "I doubt she will still be in residence at Penhale Manor by next week," I say, "but I see no harm in extending an invitation to her as well." I stand. "And now, if you will all excuse me, I had best go visit this duchess."

A few minutes later, I am astride my horse and galloping in the direction of Penhale Manor. Horse riding is another thing I have had to grow accustomed to here on Earth. No longer can I get into my own personal drone and program in my destination. No indeed. Nowadays, travel is on these curious four-legged beasts. It was not an easy thing to learn, though out of the four of us, Simor was the one that took to it as if he had been born to ride. I have made my peace with this mode of transport. On fine days such as this April morning, it can be quite a pleasant sport.

It is not long before I reach the turning for Penhale Manor. I guide my horse there and approach the house in a fine mood. As I get close, my exuberance falters. I stare at it in surprise. The ivy that had once covered a good half of the building is nowhere in sight. The broken windowpanes have been sealed with wooden boarding, and the overgrown weeds that had sprouted along the front yard are gone. A scowl forms on my face as I take in this unexpected sight and begin to wonder if I have come too late. Does the duchess mean to stay after all?

I jump down from my horse and tie the reins around the trunk of a nearby tree. In several quick strides, I am at the door and ringing the bell vigorously. Some minutes pass before it opens. A timid maid looks up at me and mumbles, "Yes, sir?"

"I am here to see your mistress," I state firmly. "Tell her Mr Brook Reeves has come to pay a call." Brook is the English name I have given myself. It is close enough to my real name that I do not mind it too much. And we decided Reeves would make an appropriate family name for us, similar as it is to our real name of Reevas.

The maid bobs a curtsy and steps back to let me inside. My quick gaze notes the cleanly swept hallway as I am led towards the drawing room. This room too is impeccably clean, the air fresh with the aroma of cut flowers artistically arranged in a vase that has been placed on a side table. "I will fetch Her Grace," mutters the girl and beats a hasty retreat. I take my seat on a well sprung settee and look around me in dismay. Were it not for a crack in one of the windowpanes, one would hardly credit that as little as two days ago, this house had been a wreck.

I scowl in annoyance at the charming display before me. This could throw all my plans into disarray. Such effort as has been expended to spruce up this house can only indicate one thing. The duchess means to stay. At the same time, I wonder how that small slip of a thing managed such a transformation in only two days. I cannot help but feel an unwilling spark of admiration.

For several minutes I wait, my mind working at speed to reassess the approach I will need to take with the duchess. Soon, the drawing room door opens, and I am on my feet at once, pasting what I hope is an ingratiating smile on my face—smiling is another thing that no longer comes naturally to me. As my eyes meet hers, she comes to an abrupt halt. "You!" she says accusingly.

I sketch a bow. "Brook Reeves, at your service, Your Grace."

She continues to stare. "But you are the gatekeeper," she sputters. She looks me up and down, evidently confused by the smartness of my clothes.

"Pardon?" I feign a puzzled glance.

She tightens her lips and addresses me haughtily, "Who are you, sir, and what business have you here?"

My response is equally cold. "I am Brook Reeves, esquire, of Reeves Hall, and I am here to pay a courtesy call on my neighbour."

She stares at me in confusion. "I—I do not understand. I thought you were the gatekeeper."

I snort. "No, indeed I am not. I was merely taking care of some business at the lodge when you rang. I apologise if I have given you an incorrect impression of me."

"I see," she says quietly and with great dignity. "Then I too must apologise for jumping to the wrong conclusions, though you can understand my confusion after the manner in which we met. Please, Mr Reeves, do take a seat."

We sit down, me on the settee and the duchess on a chair opposite. She links her hands in her lap and looks down at them, a becoming flush painting her cheeks. Silence reigns for several moments. I take advantage of it to study her once more. She is small, at least a foot shorter than me, and fine-boned. I do believe I could span the entirety of her waist with my two bare hands. Her light-brown hair is swept into a bun at the back of her head, but several strands have escaped and curl over her rosy cheeks. She looks up then and meets my eyes. Hers are large, a curious shade of hazel brown, and fringed with long lashes.

"It is an honour to make your acquaintance, sir," she says in a stilted voice. Then for lack of anything else to say, she adds, "May I offer you some refreshment?"

I wonder what is going through her mind. Do I intimidate her? Or is she still feeling affronted at the rudeness of my manner towards her last we met? There is one other, tantalising consideration. Could it be she is sensing my growing attraction to her—perhaps also reciprocating it? Absurd thought!

"No need," I say, then gentling my voice, "I was sorry to hear of the duke's passing. Please accept my deepest condolences."

"Thank you."

Are those tears forming in her eyes? She blinks them back rapidly. I look away, suddenly uncomfortable. This emotion is a painful reminder of my own experience of grief after Mother and Father passed. Scrabbling around for something else to say, I grunt, "I am full of admiration at the great changes you have wrought on this place in such a short time. Do you mean to stay on here?"

She raises her chin. "Yes, of course. It is my home."

"Please pardon the indelicacy of the question, but have you no other home? I had understood the duke to be a wealthy man."

"Yes, he was," she says on a breath. "Only his estate is entailed and now passes on to the next duke. This house is all that is entitled to me." Ah yes, male primogeniture, another aspect of the backwardness of English society. For a moment I hesitate, not caring to deprive this strangely dignified creature of the only home she possesses. To be thrown out of one's home is an experience I know only too well. But then I remind myself that she will surely be more comfortable in a tidy village cottage somewhere closer to her relatives. After all, my family adapted, and I shall be doing her a great service with my generous offer.

"I am not sure if Your Grace is aware of this," I venture, "but some time ago, I wrote to the late duke, wishing to make a purchase of Penhale Manor. I am still very desirous of making this purchase and would offer a generous price for the house."

The duchess stiffens. Her eyes flash as she says sharply, "The house is not for sale, Mr Reeves." There is something curiously appealing about her fierceness.

Nevertheless, I persist. "As it borders my own lands, I am particularly desirous of it and would pay above the market value. I am willing to offer £3,500 for the house and grounds, which I am sure you would agree is a more than generous amount. I urge Your Grace to consider it."

She bites her bottom lip. I notice it is lush and full. "Your offer is generous," she agrees, "but once again I must tell you, Mr Reeves, the house is not for sale."

I sigh, frustrated but not yet ready to concede defeat. I narrow my eyes at the duchess. Despite her strength of will, she is surely too young and pretty to live here unprotected. Rallying together the arguments I had formulated in my head while I waited for her, I say brusquely, "Your Grace, there are only two houses in this vicinity—Penhale Manor and Reeves Hall—and the nearest other habitable home is at least two miles distant, in the village itself. Forgive my forwardness for saying this, but I do not think this place is at all suitable for a gentlewoman living alone, without the protection of a husband." I speak in earnest, for the safety of this small wisp of a female is growing in importance. I wish her to sell Penhale Manor not just for my own purposes, I realise, but also as a way to protect her from harm.

But then her eyes widen at my words, and I curse my indelicacy for reminding her of her recent loss. Nonetheless, I push forward with my argument, though irritation has me glower at the duchess as I growl, "Your Grace, you will be well served to accept my offer and use the funds to purchase a home more in keeping with your needs. It is simply not safe out here, so far from the village. There are highwaymen on the roads and unscrupulous men who would take advantage of a lone female. Truly, setting aside my own reasons for wanting this property, I do believe it to be a most honourable thing for me to take it off your hands. I urge you to reflect further on this matter."

I have barely finished my speech before she stands, hands held stiffly at her sides. "Mr Reeves," she says, "if the reason for your visit today is to convince me to sell Penhale Manor, then I believe you have wasted your time, for I am not selling. This is my home, and I am here to stay. Now, if there is nothing further to discuss, I will bid you good day."

I too am on my feet, towering over the little slip of a duchess. My eyes take in the pleasing rise and fall of her delicate bosom. I sense her instinctive desire to step away and put some distance between us, but she stands her ground and glares at me with fierce determination. A peculiar feeling overtakes me—a strange craving to kiss her. What can I be thinking, wanting to embrace one of these primitive Earth people? "Duchess," I rasp in a low voice, dispensing with formality. "There *is* another matter. I am holding a dinner party at Reeves Hall next Thursday, and I wish you to attend. My carriage will collect you promptly at seven. Good day." Without another word, I take my leave.

CHAPTER 6

JANE

I am shaking as I watch Brook Reeves stride out of my drawing room. The air around me still holds a remnant of his scent—a curious spicy aroma that invades my senses and heightens my tremors. His presence was powerful, intimidating and not a little terrifying. I feel my heart hammering in my chest as I take in deep breaths to try to regain my composure.

That is next to an impossible task, for no sooner have I recovered from my reaction to his overwhelming presence than I am beset by anger. How dare that man try to chase me from my home! Two days I have spent, from the break of dawn to the darkness of night, trying with Betsy to make the house liveable. I summoned Pedrick, the first morning of our arrival, and had stern words for him. Then I bade him clear the ivy from the house and the weeds from the garden. I sent Evans to the village to find another housemaid and fetch a carpenter for the most urgent repairs. Throughout these two days, one thought has been constant in my mind. This is my home now; I have no other place to go.

And this arrogant Mr Reeves thinks to drive me from it? His offer was generous. For an instant—a very short instant—I was tempted. But no. I have not come all this way and put in all this effort, only to give up. Penhale Manor is not for sale. As for this invitation to dine at Reeves Hall next Thursday—I have no wish to break bread with that ogre of a man, especially, as I assume, he lives alone. But if he has a wife, or family, they will undoubtedly be objectionable too. Besides which, I am still in mourning. I had almost forgotten this in my anger.

On this last thought, I stride over to my bureau and take out a sheet of paper. I then dip my quill in the pot of ink and begin composing a letter which reads as follows.

Mr Reeves, esquire,

Reeves Hall

Dear Sir,

I thank you for the invitation to dine at Reeves Hall this coming Thursday. However, I must decline, since I am in my period of mourning.

I pause, thinking back angrily to his words. *Your Grace, you will be well served to accept my offer.* The arrogance of that man! Perhaps unwisely, I dip the quill in more ink and add the following:

Besides, your ungracious behaviour has me conclude that it would be best not to continue our acquaintance.

Yours sincerely,

Jane Cavendish, Dowager Duchess of Coleford

I summon Evans and hand him the missive, asking him to deliver it as expeditiously as possible, after which I resume my work around the house. Chloe is being seen to by the young maid that arrived from the village this morning, a girl named Mary, though my daughter is proving to be quite a challenging charge. With the resilience of youth, Chloe has settled into her new home and taken great joy in running about the house to explore its many rooms; and escaping her young minder. I shake my head in amusement as I hear my daughter's shrieks outside the door and Mary's pleas to "Come back here!" What a hoyden I am raising.

I turn my attention back to my task. I have one more trunk of books to unpack, then I shall rejoin my daughter for our luncheon—a simple affair of soup and bread, for we have yet to fill the kitchen larder. As I kneel by the trunk and carefully take out each book, dusting it with a cloth before placing it on the book case in the drawing room, I catch myself humming a familiar old tune, one by the name of *Black-eyed Susan*. I stop just as soon as I realise what I am doing, sitting back on my heels in dismay. Could it be that already, the pall of grief is fading away? I summon an image in my mind of Giles. Good, kind, gentle Giles. He was my saviour, my gallant rescuer from menial poverty, and I did love him so. I smile as I think of him.

Earlier this morning, when Mr Reeves expressed his condolences for my loss, I had felt my eyes fill with unbidden tears at the reminder of my bereavement. I had valiantly held those tears back, for I had no wish to cry in front of that man. So it is strange that now, as I busy myself with the business of settling into my new home, I feel a sense of hopeful cheer—enough to have me humming. What could possibly have changed in the few hours since then?

I do not have far to ponder this question. It is to do with that man—Brook Reeves. My encounter with him has lit a fire in my belly. It has awoken a streak of contrariness in my character, one that has appeared a time or two before. When my family implored me to distance myself from the Duke of Coleford and reject his improbable advances, I ignored them all. Truth be told, they partly spurred me to encourage Giles's suit, for I had not at first paid him much heed. After all, I thought his frequent visits to our house were in order to court one or other of my cousins, certainly not me, the poor relation.

And just as those many admonishments had stoked a stubborn wilfulness in me to resist, so too have Mr Reeves's entreaties for me to sell Penhale Manor awoken a determination in me not to do so. A sensible moment's reflection would have me conclude that a sum of £3,500 is not one to be sneered at. It would allow me to purchase a suitable house in a village or town, perhaps back in my home county of Somerset, and leave a tidy amount to spare which I could put away for Chloe's dowry. And yet I know that I will not sell. It is that contrariness again. But I am glad of it, for it strips away my grief and gives me a bold sense of purpose. Moreover, I think I might enjoy the challenge of restoring this house to its former glory.

I resume my task, taking the next book out of the trunk, and start humming again, this time with the lyrics to the song.

All in the downs the fleet was moor'd,

The streamers waving in the wind,

when black-ey'd Susan came on board:

Oh! where shall I my true-love find?

Tell me ye jovial sailors, tell me true,

if my sweet William sails among the crew!

I am interrupted mid-song by Betsy's arrival, bearing a letter for me. I take it from her and hurriedly break the seal. It is a note from Mr Reeves, terse and lacking the usual preambles.

Duchess,

Nonsense. I will come fetch you myself Thursday at 7.

BR

Well, if that isn't the outside of enough! He expects me at this dinner does he? "We shall have to see about that!" I exclaim to a much startled Betsy.

MY OPPORTUNITY PRESENTS itself on Sunday, as I attend church service at the quaint little church in Penhale village. It is my first foray into the village, which is small, consisting of the church, a row of shops on the main street and a handful of modest stone cottages. All eyes are upon me as I enter the hall and look for a suitable pew to perch on. I hear the buzz of whispering voices, no doubt discussing the appearance of a stranger in their midst. I lift my chin haughtily, for I am no stranger to whisperings about me. The early days of my marriage to Giles were education enough into the gossiping ways of the world, and I soon learned not to mind them, or at least make a semblance of not minding them.

With Chloe's hand clasped in mine, we walk down the central aisle. I nod a regal smile here and there, but my eyes are fixed on a pew mid-way down, which blessedly seems to be unoccupied. I am about to take a seat when a harsh voice calls out to me, "Over here." I look up and catch sight of none other than Mr Brook Reeves. He beckons me over, and after a moment of hesitation, I guide my steps towards him. My usual stubbornness, it seems, has deserted me.

"Mr Reeves," I say in greeting as I reach him, performing a stiff little curtsy. I am immediately surrounded by his spicy scent, something about it setting my pulse racing.

"Sit here, Duchess," he barks, making space for me beside him. I have little choice but to obey, sinking down on to the wooden pew that is covered in a long, purple cushion. I settle Chloe in my lap, and she turns her curious gaze upon the man beside me.

"I am Chloe," she says simply.

"I am Brook," he responds, just as simply.

"You are big," she says earnestly.

He nods his head in agreement. "And you are small," he says in reply.

I hear a snicker of laughter and turn to the man sitting on the other side of me. He smiles and bows his head. "Your Grace," he says. "I am pleased to make your acquaintance. I am Harry Reeves." He makes a gesture with his hand towards the two people sitting on his right. "And this is my sister, Laura Reeves, and my younger brother Simon."

I nod to them in acknowledgement. There is no need for them to tell me that they are brothers and sister to Brook Reeves, for the resemblance is there for all to see. Harry Reeves is equally tall as Brook, but of a leaner build. His hair and eyes are of the same rich brown, but his features are sharper. One would hesitate to call him handsome if not for the kindliness of his expression, which gives him a friendly, open demeanour, nothing like the scowling intensity of his older brother's countenance.

"I was so pleased to hear that you will be attending our dinner party," Harry now says with a shy smile. "You will have to forgive us though, for we are a trifle rusty with regards to entertaining. We live a quiet life you see."

I smile, immediately put at my ease. "I am used to a quiet life myself," I assure him, then remember that I am not planning to attend. "However, you will have to excuse me from your dinner party on this occasion, for I am still in my period of mourning."

His face falls. "Oh, of course," he mumbles. "That is quite understandable."

"Nonsense," a now-familiar voice growls at my side. "You are coming, Duchess. No arguing about it."

I open my mouth to retort, but just then, the organ begins to play the first chords of a hymn as everyone rises to their feet. Throughout the ensuing church service, I am disconcertingly aware of Brook Reeves's towering presence beside me in the crowded pew—the warmth of his large body, pressed much too close to mine, his scent, the frequent glances he sends my way. I try my very best to pretend I am unaffected by his proximity, putting on that cold, haughty look that I wear like armour.

Chloe is heavy on my lap. Soon, she grows restless and fidgety. "Settle down," I urge her quietly.

"Want to play," she says plaintively.

"Soon," I promise.

She sticks out her bottom lip petulantly. "Now," she demands.

As I try to quieten her, strong arms reach towards us and lift her away. Brook Reeves makes a mock scary face at Chloe that has her giggle in response. Next instant, I see him untie his cravat and give her the two ends of it, instructing her to tie it into a knot again. She takes the starched fabric and begins to play with it, tying it this way and that. In such manner, she is diverted until we reach the concluding part of the service. It is then I take Chloe back into my arms while Mr Reeves effects some repairs to his appearance, with mixed success.

After the service is over, I am kept busy with greetings and polite chit chat with all manner of people wishing to make my acquaintance. By the time I finally return to my carriage where Evans waits patiently, I have lost sight of Brook Reeves and of my opportunity to once more inform him that I am not, under any circumstance, attending his dinner party.

CHAPTER 7

JANE

Thursday dawns and with it my continuing resolve not to let Brook Reeves browbeat me into attending his dinner party. If he does show up to fetch me, I shall merely tell him he has made a wasted journey.

The day passes in busy endeavour, as I continue to set Penhale Manor to rights. I send Evans on an errand to the nearest town, asking him to find a glazier to fit new windowpanes and a tiler to repair the broken tiling on the roof. All the while I am mindful of the rapidly dwindling guineas in my purse. I shall simply have to live frugally until the next payment of my allowance is due in July, perhaps foregoing meat on a Friday—a very Christian thing to do.

Evening soon comes, and I go to bid Chloe goodnight. I settle her in bed and read Puss in Boots, her favourite story. Once I am done and putting away the book, she surprises me by mumbling sleepily, "When will we see Mr Brook?"

"Mr Brook?" I query.

"I like him," she murmurs simply.

I make a noncommittal response and kiss her cheek. "Goodnight, Sugar plum," I whisper softly. Then I stand and tiptoe out of the room, hesitating on the landing before I head to my bedchamber. I tell myself it is so I can read quietly by the light of a candle rather than be wasteful by lighting several of them in the drawing room. I must be frugal after all. I go to my wardrobe and look through the dresses. There is not much of a choice to be had while I am in mourning and must wear black. I have four muslin morning gowns in black and one lone evening gown in black silk satin. I caress the soft fabric with my finger, hesitating. No, I decide. I will not.

I push the wardrobe closed with a firm hand and go to sit on my bed. Reaching behind me, I untie the laces on the bodice of my gown and pull it over my head. I shake the gown out and place it over a chair, then my fingers go to my petticoat, preparing to remove it as well. I pause. Slowly, almost without my volition, my feet take me back to the wardrobe. I do not question why I do so, but I take out the satin gown and quickly pull it on. I stare at my reflection in the mirror as I tie the laces and arrange the bodice so it is snug on my figure. The cut of this gown flatters me, and the silky folds of the satin relieve the austerity of its dark colour. It is a welcome sensation to feel attractive again. I take out a few hair pins and rearrange my curls under the lace cap. Pearl earrings and a dab of cologne complete my toilette.

The front doorbell rings just as I am pulling on a pair of long kid gloves. The sound of Brook Reeves's deep voice reaches me. As promised, he is here to fetch me for this dinner party, and fool that I am, I have made myself ready for him. A muslin shawl in hand, I close the door behind me and tread softly down the stairs. With every step I feel a rising sense of… what exactly? Is it fear or is it excitement? I think perhaps it may be a bit of both.

I catch sight of Brook Reeves standing in the hallway just as his eyes land on me. He watches me fixedly as I descend, a customary frown set into his handsome face. Clad in a massive greatcoat, there is something dark and menacing about him. My heart skips a silent beat. I am walking into the lion's den, or so it seems to me. And yet I keep walking sedately, each step taking me closer to him. "Mr Reeves," I say, and bend my knees in a curtsy.

"Duchess," he replies, ignoring etiquette and addressing me as if we are equals. "Let us go. Our guests await."

Quickly, I take my pelisse, which hangs on a peg under the stairs, and button it up securely. As we walk out into the chill of the night, I bid Evans to keep watch on the house. Then, I allow Brook Reeves to help me up into his carriage. The door closes upon us, and soon, we are on our way. Mr Reeves sits beside me, the heady scent of him enveloping me. We do not talk much on the short drive to his home. He asks me how the works are getting along on the house, and I paint a brief picture of the improvements that have been made over the last few days.

"I must take my hat off to you, Duchess," he says in a deep voice, laced with a touch of amusement. "I did not think a little slip of a thing like you could take on the challenge of bringing that house back into good use."

"It is a sad fact that many a person has judged me by the slightness of my figure rather than by the strength of my will," I say with a touch of asperity.

"It is not a mistake I shall make again," he rumbles in response.

I turn to him. "So I take it, you will no longer try to convince me to sell Penhale Manor?" I enquire with a raise of my brow.

"Oh, rest assured I will," he promises. And with that, our conversation ends. It is not long before we reach the gates of Reeves Hall which are opened for us by a tall, heavily-set man— the gatekeeper for whom I had mistaken Brook Reeves. We drive along a winding avenue and in the light of the moon, I see before us a vast three-storied building. Our carriage comes to a stop.

"Duchess," says Mr Reeves, holding out his hand to me. I allow him to escort me down. The front doors of the house open, revealing a brightly lit main hall. A butler takes my pelisse and Mr Reeves's greatcoat, then I am ushered through another well-lit corridor—the Reeves do not stint on wax candles it seems—and into a spacious drawing room.

There I am met by the Reeves siblings and a number of other guests, of which I recognise Reverend Horton, the vicar of Penhale. Introductions are made. I make the acquaintance of a florid looking gentleman named Sir Nicholas Calthorpe, his wife and their two daughters who seem to be newly out into society. There is also a younger gentleman of around thirty, a Mr Drake, and I meet his sister who looks to be of a similar age to me. They greet me with great civility, and I begin to hope that I may, in the fullness of time, make friends here in my new home. If Mr Brook Reeves thinks he can compel me to sell Penhale Manor, he can think again.

We converse for a short while before we are called to the dining room. I find myself on the arm of Mr Brook Reeves by no design of my own. Presumably it is so he can interrogate me again, though I can't help feeling a frisson of excitement at the outlandish notion that he wishes me close for other, more personal reasons. He leads me through another well-lit corridor—what a great number of candles they must have burning tonight—and to a generously sized dining room with a long, rectangular table laid out with twelve place settings. My host seats himself at the head of the table and guides me to his right. On my own right sits Harry Reeves and opposite me is Lady Calthorpe.

A footman walks in and pours the wine as well as glasses of water for all the guests. I am unused to seeing water drunk at the dinner table, but I take a refreshing sip of it. It is cold and clear, with a pleasant taste to it, making me wonder what sort of well is kept at Reeves Hall that produces such fine water. The first course is brought in, a cream of vegetable soup that is so velvety that I marvel how long his cook must have slaved to achieve such a smooth consistency. Around me conversation flows, though Brook Reeves says little, contenting himself with listening to and observing those around him. Despite his silence, his presence looms large in the room. I cannot help but feel a tingling awareness in every inch of my body.

It falls to Harry Reeves to take on the burden of discourse with me. He gives me his kindly smile and remarks, "I am very glad that you decided to join us tonight, Your Grace. This dinner party is much elevated by your presence."

Brook Reeves makes a harrumphing sound deep in his throat at his brother's civilities. I flash the man a stern glance as I reply to Harry, "Thank you, sir, though I must point out I was not given much of a choice in the matter."

Another huff from the man on my left. I studiously ignore it.

"My brother can be a trifle forceful," Harry says in amusement. "I have learned over the course of my years the ways to manage his forcefulness."

"Do please share your wisdom with me, for I shall need it if Mr Brook Reeves continues to harangue me about selling Penhale Manor," I say with great feeling, but Harry merely shakes his head.

"I cannot give away my secrets, but in any case, I do not think you are much in need of help when it comes to managing my brother." His tone is wry as he looks across the table towards the man in question.

Unwillingly, I turn my gaze to Brook Reeves. He raises a sardonic brow, then asserts with perfect confidence, "She will sell. It is the only sensible course of action and well she knows it."

My back stiffens in annoyance. I do not at all appreciate being spoken of as if I am not present. However, I will not deign to take the bait. Instead, I smile pleasantly at Harry Reeves and move the conversation to a different subject. "Tell me, Mr

Reeves," I begin. "I am most curious to know. I detect an unusual intonation in your speech. Is it a Cornish way of speaking or is your family originally from other parts of the country?"

He hesitates, once again exchanging a glance with his brother. "Your Grace is most perceptive. Although our family is of Cornish descent, we have for many years been abroad in Brazil. That may account for the slight difference in our speech." He says this last in a rush, almost as if it is something he has rehearsed, though I do not see why that should be. Perhaps he has been asked about it often and has evolved the same response. In which case, I am sorry to have brought the matter up. One never likes to be singled out as different to the rest of society.

I smile. "You are fortunate indeed, sir, to have lived abroad. I myself have never left these shores. In fact, until my marriage, I had never even travelled further than my home county of Somerset."

"Yes, I am fortunate indeed," he responds laconically. His relieved expression has me steer the conversation to safer waters. We turn to discussing the local area. I enquire about landmarks worthy of a visit and the shops to be found in the nearest town of Newquay. In this manner, we while away the rest of the meal.

In my periphery, I am conscious of Brook Reeves listening in to our discourse like a hawk studying its prey. I hear his occasional grunted responses to Lady Calthorpe's polite civilities but mostly, he is a silent presence at my side. Once or twice, I cannot help throwing him a quick, curious glance. Each time, his gleaming brown eyes hold mine. I do not quite understand it. For some unfathomable reason, something about me has excited his interest. It must be to do with Penhale Manor and my determined refusal to accept his offer for it.

As the repast comes to an end, the ladies adjourn to the drawing room while the gentlemen remain in the dining room for their port. Feeling the need to refresh myself, I make my excuses and go in search of the water closet. Outside the drawing room door, I am accosted by a stiff-faced footman who demands to know where I am going. "Please would you be so kind as to point me to the retiring room," I respond loftily.

With a bow, he escorts me through the well-lit corridor, refusing to leave my side until he sees me to the retiring room door. I give him a regal nod, then enter the room. Again, it is surprisingly well lit, though I do not know how that can be, for I see only one lone sconce on the wall. I cast my eyes around the room, looking for a commode or chamber pot. I spy an oval-shaped receptacle made of a darkly polished wood. I lift the lid, which feels curiously light. Perhaps, I reason, this is some exotic wood brought over from Brazil. The small aperture inside the bowl confirms this is indeed a commode, though of an unusual design. I lift my skirt and swiftly do my business over it, finding on a table nearby a square of linen to dry myself with. The linen is very fine and soft to the touch. It seems everything here is luxuriously appointed. The Reeves must be very wealthy indeed.

As I stand and arrange the skirt of my dress, my eye is caught once more by this strange-looking commode. I run my finger over the glossy smoothness of the wood and along the back panel, where it comes to some slight hollow no larger than my thumb, not immediately apparent to the eye, covered as it is with a satiny black cloth. My fingers explore this hollow, pressing down on it slightly. All of a sudden, a gush of warm water rushes up at me from the depths of the commode. I cry out in alarm and step back, but I am not quick enough to avoid getting wet.

I glance down at myself in dismay. The top of my bodice is damp, and droplets of water are trickling down from my collar to my chest. I look for some more linen cloths and use them to dry myself as best I can. I very much hope that the water was clean, seeing as it came out of the commode. What a bizarre contraption it is! I give myself a little sniff to make sure I have not been sprayed with a noxious liquid.

To ensure I am clean, I pour some fresh water from a jug into the bowl that sits by the stack of linen cloths. There is a small bar of soap there too. I dip a linen cloth into the water and rub it with a little soap, then wipe my chest with it, as well as the top of my bodice. I rinse it out and wipe again, to be doubly sure. I have achieved a modicum of cleanliness, but at the expense of making my dress even wetter than before. I cannot return to the drawing room in such a state as this. I take another linen cloth and try to mop myself dry, but it is no good. In the mirror set in the wall above the table, I can see clearly the dark and damp patch on my bodice. So will others.

I think quickly of what I may do. With relief, I remember the muslin shawl I brought with me. I can drape it around my shoulders, claiming to be cold though in truth this house is wonderfully warm, and hope to cover the visibly damp patch. The shawl, however, is not with me here, for I left it on the back of my chair. I sigh in vexation and think some more. The men will be at their port for a while longer, so maybe I could pass the time exploring some of the rooms in the house, and hope that the dampness of my bodice will have lessened in that time.

I go to the door and edge it open slowly, casting a look along the corridor to see if there is anyone there. The punctilious footman has his back turned to me. Quickly, I slip out and make my way further along the corridor, in the opposite direction from whence I came. On soft feet, I approach a large wooden door and put my hand on the knob. It turns easily, and the door swings open without a sound. I hesitate on the threshold, knowing I should not be wandering about these rooms without the express permission of my hosts. But my curiosity is greater than my need to be bound by propriety. Something about this house, about this family, feels different. And I would like to know more.

On cautious feet, I step into the room. It is large and unlit, though there is enough luminance streaming in from the corridor to make out the various shapes in the room—some armchairs, an odd-looking chaise longue, a low round table with a handful of books strewn over it. This is some kind of parlour, I conclude. My curiosity satisfied, I turn to retrace my steps. I am nearly at the door, when something strange catches my eyes. On the far wall, at waist height, a curious light is flashing green and then red.

My pulse quickens nervously. Some instinct makes me want to run far away from it. And yet, contrary as ever, I find myself walking to the far side of the room, wanting to know what it could be. I reach the wall with the flashing light and stare at it in bewilderment. It is a small square of light, no more than two inches in length, flashing so rapidly that I can barely make out when it is green or when it is red. I stare at it for several moments, trying to make sense of what I see. There is no candle there, no lamp. Could it be a glass panel enclosing some hollow space in which a candle is flickering? How very odd.

I reach out my fingers to touch it then jump back in fright. At my touch, a buzzing energy had flooded my fingers with a tingling warmth. I shake out my hand, still feeling a tingling sensation in the tips of my fingers. What in great heavens is this? After a while, my curiosity gets the better of me, and I reach out my hand once more, feeling that curious buzzing warmth on my fingers.

"Just what do you think you are doing?" booms a voice behind me.

I pull away quickly from the wall and turn in trepidation to face Brook Reeves. He stands at the threshold, the light from the corridor casting his great hulking frame in an ominous shadow.

"I—I, nothing," I say, stumbling on my words. "I took a wrong turn on my way back from the retiring room."

"Come away from there," he barks furiously.

On unsteady legs, I make my way to him. He takes my hand and places it firmly on his arm, hurrying me away from the room with the curious flashing light.

"W—what was that in there?" I ask breathlessly.

"Nothing that should concern you," he responds, his tone brusque. He marches me down the corridor but stops abruptly as we reach the drawing room door. Turning to me, his face cast in the grimmest of scowls, he grits out, "If you know what is good for you, little Duchess, you will put whatever you saw in there from your mind. My house is none of your business."

"And *my* house is none of your business either," I strike back, my anger rising to the fore.

His hands grip my arms, pulling me flush with his chest as he glowers down at me. I am caught in his stare, my breaths coming short and shallow. The blood rushes to my heated cheeks. Then slowly, his furious face bends towards me. My lips part on instinct. It must be so that I can gulp much needed air into my lungs. It cannot be for any other reason. His face is so close to mine now I can feel his breath feather my nose. Oh Lord! Is he about to kiss me? I should resist, demand he unhands me, but all I do is stare dazedly as his parted lips stop a hair's breadth from mine. We stay fixed in place, neither of us moving to close the remaining gap between us. I inhale his warm breath and feel as if it is igniting a raging fire in my entire body. And then suddenly, he is gone. He steps back without a word and strides away, entering the drawing room.

I am left reeling, gulping in air as I watch him go. What in the world just happened? Gracious Lord, I nearly let that man kiss me. That he did not must be a relief, though my body is shaking in disappointment. I take a few moments to compose myself before following him into the room, any worries about my damp dress forgotten. For the rest of the evening, I sense Brook Reeves stewing with leashed fury next to me. We do not address each other. I barely register what is said in the conversation around me, though I believe I make the appropriate responses when I am spoken to.

Soon, the dinner party comes to an end, and we all rise to leave. The Calthorpes depart in their carriage, the vicar riding with them. The Drakes take their leave too, and then it is just me that is left. As I button up my pelisse, Brook Reeves approaches me. "I have urgent business to attend to, so I shall let Simon see you home," he says in a cold, clipped voice. "Good evening, Duchess." With a perfunctory bow, he leaves me at the front door. I wonder for a moment if this urgent business has anything to do with me and what I saw in that room, but I am not left to wonder long as Simon Reeves appears, fixing the ties on his long cloak.

With a smile, he holds out his arm to me. "Your Grace, it is an honour indeed to be escorting you home," he says, the warmness of his tone in sharp contrast to his brother's coolness. He assists me into the carriage and perches beside me as we begin the journey.

"You are too kind, Mr Reeves, and I do thank you," I venture to reply. The strangeness of the evening weighs upon my mind, and I am unable to converse any further. We sit in silence, the only sound the rattling of the carriage wheels as we sway gently from the motion. I ponder all the strange occurrences, from the commode that sprayed me with water to the curious flashing light in the parlour. What was it that had caused Brook Reeves's fury? Of that almost kiss, I resolutely do not think.

"Do not mind my brother, Your Grace," I hear Simon murmur beside me. "His bark is very much worse than his bite."

"I seem to have angered him tonight, and I am not entirely sure why," I say tremulously.

"Angered him? No, Your Grace, he is not mad at you, truly." Simon sighs, "Ever since we lost Father and Mother, Brook has taken it on himself to be responsible for all of us. It is this responsibility, and the worries that come with it, that often make him seem surly. He is mistrustful of others."

I nod, though I do not quite understand. "And this dinner party tonight was one of those worrying responsibilities?" I enquire, a little doubtful.

He laughs softly. "You could say that." He grows serious and goes on to say, "There are matters of which I am not at liberty to speak, but suffice it to say that Brook carries the weight of these matters on his shoulders. I am sure he did not mean to discomfit you tonight. Do please accept my apologies on his behalf."

"Of course, Mr Reeves," I murmur. "There is no need to apologise."

The carriage draws up before the front steps of Penhale Manor. Simon hops down and holds out his hand for me. I let him assist me out of the carriage and up to my door, which Evans holds open. "Thank you, Mr Reeves," I say quietly. "I shall bid you goodnight."

He smiles, a genuine and warm expression on his young countenance. "Goodnight, Your Grace." With a tip of his hat, he takes his leave.

Wearily, I bid Evans goodnight, bolt the door and head up to my bedchamber. As I prepare myself for bed, my mind keeps turning over the events of the evening, not finding any satisfactory answers to my questions. All I can conclude is that something strange is going on at Reeves Hall, and Brook Reeves is in the thick of it.

CHAPTER 8

BROEK

I pace up and down the room in fury. "How in the name of all that is holy, was the duchess allowed to stray into this part of the house?" I demand. Nobody answers. I turn to face Wolkan, whose job it is to ensure our security. "Well?" I ask. "What have you to say?"

He returns my gaze, his eyes not faltering. "I walked her to the retiring room, and Great Yol, any sane person would have known the way back from there to the drawing room," he says by way of explanation, adding, "How was I to know she would slip out, get lost and walk in the wrong direction?"

My lips curl. "Mark my words, the duchess was not lost. She turned this way so she could pry about the house." That damned slip of a woman did the opposite of what anyone would expect. I sense in her a lively curiosity—a dangerous inquisitiveness. She could be the downfall of us all if we are not careful.

"So, she found this room," Horis reasons. "It was in darkness though, and I doubt she saw the screen. Even if she did, she would have no idea what it was. No irreparable harm has been done."

"I saw her touch the charging panel," I say flatly.

"Ah."

"How are we to explain away a flashing red and green light which zapped her hand with energy? The work of the devil?" I ask sardonically.

To this he has no answer. It is Liora that replies in his stead. "We do not explain ourselves or say anything, unless the little duchess brings the matter up with us," she says decisively. "To do so would make it seem as if we have something to hide and would only invite more curiosity."

"She has enough curiosity about us as it is," I snap, wishing everyone here would grasp the true peril of our situation. And furthermore, something in the way Liora just called Jane *the little duchess* is grating fiercely on my nerves. I may call her by this nickname and think of her as a little wisp of a thing, but nobody else should get to do so. I give my sister the blackest of scowls.

"I do not doubt her curiosity," continues Liora, undeterred. "But even so, what is she, a newcomer to these parts, to do about it? Should she speak of seeing a flashing green and red light to anyone, they would think her mad. The wisest course of action for her is to keep the incident to herself, and she strikes me as a sensible female."

"Liora is right," concurs Horis. "We must hold our nerve and trust that the Duchess of Coleford will not speak of what she saw to anyone."

What if we are wrong, and she speaks of it in the village? A cold wave of fear hits me at the thought, increasing my fury. "No more dinner parties," I bite out.

"For now, no more dinner parties," agrees Liora, "though I think tonight achieved more than you realise, Broek."

All it achieved was to kindle dangerous curiosity in the duchess's head about us and to shatter my peace of mind. A magnificent evening's work indeed.

It is as if Liora reads my thoughts, for she continues, "The Calthorpes were greatly impressed with our home and our hospitality. As for their daughters, they were undoubtedly charmed by my handsome brothers." Liora fixes her eyes on Horis as she says this, but he turns away, hanging his head, as if certain he is not included in this praise. I stifle an irritated sigh. When will my brother hold his head up high and realise he is our equal in every way that matters? Great Yol it pains me to see him put himself down. If we had not been banished from our home, I think bitterly, he would have grown out of this timid phase and blossomed. Not for the first time, I curse Mother for bringing this misfortune down upon us. The years have not softened my resentment at our exile.

"So," Wolkan now says, a hopeful tilt to his voice, "putting everything into perspective, it does not seem as if tonight was an unmitigated disaster."

I snort my disgust. Much does he know! Everyone here is keen to downplay the danger of Jane's discovery tonight. Not me. I have begun to discern the features of her character, and I cannot forget her words to me earlier this evening. *It is a sad fact that many a person has judged me by the slightness of my figure rather than by the strength of my will.* Jane Cavendish, Duchess of Coleford, is a hazard to be reckoned with.

"I will rest easier when the duchess sells Penhale Manor and returns to where she came from," I grunt morosely.

"How well this project fares with you," remarks Liora with a hint of a sneer. I glare at her in response.

"She will sell," I state with more confidence than I truly feel. Somewhere in the back of my mind is a suspicion that the little duchess will hold on to that house merely to spite me.

Liora creases her brow in thought. "There is another way for us to get hold of Penhale Manor," she muses. At our questioning glances, she elucidates, "Through marriage rather than purchase." Then, addressing Horis, she says, "I saw that you got along well with the duchess tonight and spoke easily with her, showing none of your usual reserve. Would she not make an excellent bride for you?"

Now, that is going beyond the beyond. The very idea of Horis marrying Jane is preposterous, and I say as much. "Quite clearly, you do not know what you speak of, Liora. The duchess is far too wilful to ever make a good match for Horis. Do not mention it again or I shall lose all patience with you." And with this last speech, I storm out of the room.

I go to my usual haunt in the evenings, descending a set of stairs to the basement. There, beyond a door that is discreetly hidden behind a rack of wine bottles, is our operational centre. I stand before a small gap in the wine rack and let the security system scan my face. As it does so, I cannot help but imagine what would have happened if Jane were to have explored this far into my house. Would she have seen the wine rack as the innocuous looking decoy it is, or would she have poked and prodded, her inquisitiveness coming to the fore?

The door now opens to allow me through, and as I walk inside, I determine grimly that at all costs, the duchess must not be allowed back into Reeves Hall. She must not marry Horis either. In fact, the only solution is for her to sell Penhale Manor to me and leave this county far behind. I stride down the corridor and open the third door to my left, which requires an additional security scan before it lets me in. The door slides silently shut behind me as I go to my console. With one touch, I power it up, instructing the computer to send my nanoprobes to Penhale Manor and display the visuals on the screen.

Now as I watch her house, I see our carriage draw up in front of it. Simor escorts Jane to her door, bids her farewell and returns to the vehicle, which soon begins its journey back to Reeves Hall. My eyes are glued to Jane as she enters the house, dismissing one of her servants, and shuts the door. A minute later, a light appears through one of the upstairs windows—Jane's bedchamber, I surmise. For long minutes, I watch that window. I do not see anything of note except the brief movement of a silhouette. Finally, the light is extinguished.

I sit for some time in quiet contemplation, imagining Jane slipping into bed, her slight form nestled under the covers as she drifts to sleep. *"What will you dream of tonight?"* I wonder. *"Will you dream of me?"*

I huff, vexed with myself. What should I care what the little duchess dreams? The only thing that matters now is to get her to sell the house and leave. But how? I think on the matter some more. Knowing what I do now about her, I do not believe it will do much good to keep plaguing her with offers to sell. But what if I were to find another home for her that she could easily afford with the proceeds from Penhale Manor? A home close to Coleford where surely she must have relations. One that is in a good state of repair and close to the amenities of a village or town. A place that is not isolated as Penhale Manor is, where she and her daughter can live comfortably.

I program in a search on my computer, instructing it on the parameters. Ever since our ship landed on Earth seven years ago, I have had hundreds of thousands of microscopic recording devices placed in strategic locations around this planet, the data feeding into a powerful analytical engine that processes the information and sends it to me in daily bulletins. Each night, from this console, I access this information, whether it be written reports or visual and sound recordings of important events taking place around the globe. With this vital information, I am able to keep track of all the most important political and economic developments, and to make judicious investment decisions to grow our wealth and secure our futures here on this distant planet that is now our home.

Tonight though, my attention is not on the latest happenings in Lord Liverpool's cabinet nor on President Monroe's new federal law regarding the purchase of land in the western frontier of America. Neither is my attention on what the king of Prussia or the Tsar of Russia might be machinating. I am not deciphering messages conveyed between officials in the Ottoman and Persian empires, nor studying the latest conflict between the emperor of China and the encroaching British empire. No, tonight, I am threading through the minutiae of newspaper listings, social chitchat recorded on my many devices and private letters scanned, all in search of mentions of any homes that may be up for sale.

I learn that one squire by the name of Barrington is selling a cottage in the village of Holcombe, not a half mile away from Coleford. I enter the co-ordinates of Holcombe village into my visual database to retrieve pictures of this cottage, but a few flicks through them convinces me it will not do for Jane and her vivacious daughter, Chloe. The rooms look cramped and the grounds outside are very modest in size.

I set to search again. In the nearby town of Frome, I find another cottage for sale through a local newspaper advertisement. Once again, I go to the visual database to retrieve pictures of this cottage. The pictures are pleasing. The cottage is modest, but not too small and quite charming in aspect. I read the particulars in the advertisement. There are four bedrooms, a coach-house to stable horses and a garden. Would Jane be comfortable living in such a place?

I do not question why it has become all important for me to ensure her comfort. I tell myself I am not some ogre wishing ill upon the duchess. If I am to take Penhale Manor from her, at a very generous price I might add, then I would wish to see her well settled elsewhere, that is all. It is a Christian duty to want to ensure the young widow is safely situated, even though I am not much of a Christian.

I print out the advertisement for this cottage scanned from the Frome Times and have the computer render an illustration of the front aspect of the cottage. Once printed, it looks to be a hand illustrated watercolour, not a digitally made image. I have even taken care to instruct the computer to fray the edges of the image, to make it look like it has been sent in a letter.

I take the watercolour illustration and the newspaper cutting, placing them both carefully in a folded sheet of paper which I seal and address to "The Duchess of Coleford, Penhale Manor". Tomorrow first thing, I shall have it delivered anonymously. Of course, she may guess it will have come from me, but that is no matter. All I am doing now is sowing the seeds of what might be, should she sell to me. I will keep my distance, observing her from my console in this basement, and when the time is right, I shall pounce with a one-time, even more generous offer for Penhale Manor.

I very nearly kissed the duchess tonight. Only at the last moment did I exert enough self-control to step back. Next time, I do not know whether I'll have the strength to resist her. That is why there can be no next time. The duchess must leave Penhale. She knows too much already, and she is dangerous to my peace of mind. Once she learns of this cottage in Frome, I hope she'll see sense and agree to a sale. With this, for now, I must be satisfied. I tap the console shut and make my way back upstairs to retire for the night.

CHAPTER 9

JANE

I come awake slowly, my body huddled under the blanket for warmth on this cold April morning. From the angle of the sunlight streaming in through my window, I can tell that morning must be well underway. I have slept beyond my usual time and should bestir myself. I take an additional moment though, to reflect on the happenings of yesterday.

In the cold light of morning, what I saw in that room—the square of red and green light that emitted a curious tingling energy to my fingers—seems like an outlandish dream. Did I imagine it all? No, I decide. I did not imagine it, especially not Brook Reeves's angry reaction to finding me in that room. I remember clearly his threat. *If you know what is good for you, Duchess, you will put whatever you saw in there from your mind. My house is none of your business.* And I remember all too clearly what happened afterwards … but I will not distract myself with thoughts of how Brook Reeves almost kissed me. It's enough I could not get to sleep last night for thinking of it. With an effort, I direct my mind back on the strange occurrences I saw at Reeves Hall.

I can only conclude there is something in that room that he does not want me to know about, something connected to what I saw. But try as I might, I cannot come up with any rational explanation for that strange flashing light. Could it be some sort of scientific experiment Brook Reeves is undertaking? Perhaps he does not want his secret leaked to competitors before he has patented and trademarked whatever invention he has underway. I still cannot fathom what this invention could be. A hand warming contraption for cold winter evenings? That still does not explain to me the green and red flashing light. What flame could produce such an effect?

I sigh and throw off the covers, getting out bed. My daughter's cries from somewhere in the house remind me that I have business of my own to attend to. Quickly, I wash and dress, then go to find Chloe.

Later, our breakfast complete, I sit in my private parlour to go through the accounts. The numbers on my ledger are not reassuring. Replacing the broken windows and roof tiles is going to be a costly undertaking. I suspect the glazier that Evans found in Newquay is charging more than he should for his services, but I am not in any position to turn him down. Those windows must be repaired urgently and the house sealed from incoming rain and rodents.

I cannot escape my disheartening reflections. I have been burdened with a crumbling house in the middle of nowhere, the repairs on which are beyond my ability to afford. Replacing the damaged windows and roof tiles is only the beginning. Next, I shall need to tackle the terrible damp that has spread to parts of the house as a consequence of its neglect. There is still so much to do to bring Penhale Manor to a proper standard for living.

A little scurrying sound behind me makes me swing around in my chair quickly. I do not see anything, but I am quite certain that was yet another mouse making itself at home in my house. We shall have to lay some traps in this room too, I think.

I turn back to my dispiriting accounts. Much of my small reserve of gold guineas is gone. Last week, I had written to Mr Oakley to request an advance on my funds before the next instalment of my allowance is due, but his letter in response, received today, makes clear that this would not be possible unless I were to redeem some of the capital invested, something he would strongly advise against.

He had explained to me before I left Coleford Hall that my annual income of £400 would be paid in quarterly instalments on the first day of January, April, July and October. Of the £100 pounds of my April allowance, only £21 now remains. How am I to eke this amount in the two months to go before July finally comes? Chloe is growing fast, and I have already let out all her frocks. Instead of purchasing a new set of clothes for her as I had intended, I shall have to think of creative ways to make do with what I already have. I suppose I could sacrifice my peach muslin gown, for which I have no use at present seeing as I am in mourning. From that gown, I could fashion two, or perhaps even three small frocks for Chloe. It is fortunate that I am dexterous with the needle—something else I learned in my years as a subservient member of my aunt's household. Truly, there can be no better preparation for the vagaries of the big wide world than to spend time in some lowly position, at someone else's beck and call.

I ponder some more. I could sell the carriage and horses but then quickly discount the idea. Living in such isolation, it is vital we keep a means of transport. There is only one other economy I can think of. We shall have to cut down on our consumption of meat, I decide, limiting it to only once or twice a week. The rest of the time, we shall eat like humble cottagers—porridge, vegetable stew and bread. Perhaps we may supplement this with an egg or two. If others can survive on such a sparse diet, then surely so can we. It will not be forever, I console myself, only for two months until further funds come my way. I am sure we can do it. We shall have to, for I have no wish to be beholden to creditors.

I rise, about to go fetch my peach muslin gown, when there comes a knock at the door. Mary, the new housemaid, enters at my beckon. She bobs a curtsy then hastens towards me with a letter in her hands. "This just came, Your Grace," she mumbles shyly.

I take the missive from her with a word of thanks. As the door shuts behind Mary, I turn it over, curious to see there is no postmark of any sort. Quickly, I break the seal and withdraw two sheets of paper. The larger sheet is a watercolour painting depicting a charming brick cottage. I set it down, puzzled, and take the other piece of paper, a cutting from a newspaper advertisement. On it, I read:

A spacious cottage, Frome, to be SOLD by Private Contract, by Mr Thomas Brixley, House and Public Share Agent, No. 5 Throckmorton Street. Asking price of £2,650. Situated on Vicarage Road, 200 yards from the parish church of St John the Baptist. Comprising on the ground floor an excellent drawing-room and parlour, a good kitchen, wash-house, wine, beer and coal cellars, coach-house and stabling, with a garden behind. Four sleeping rooms and dressing room above stairs. The cottage is most pleasantly situated, combining every domestic advantage. The fixtures to be taken at a fair valuation.

I stare at the newspaper cutting in bewilderment. Why has it been sent to me? And is the accompanying painting a depiction of the cottage that is for sale? It must be. I read the particulars of the advertisement again. The cottage is in Frome. It is a small town I know well, for I visited the shops there often when I lived in Coleford. I am struck by a heartening thought as I ponder the contents of this missive. This cottage could be the solution to my current dilemma, for I could easily afford its asking price and have a generous sum left over, were I to accept Brook Reeves's offer for Penhale Manor.

Brook Reeves. He must be the one to have sent me this. It cannot be anyone else. The scheming Machiavelli! I do not question how in such short a time, he must have gotten hold of this painting and newspaper. The man quite clearly has the means to do many a thing beyond my wherewithal. On the back of that thought is another. He must want Penhale Manor very badly. At this, the contrary part of my nature, a side of myself I am not altogether proud of, rears up with a desire to thwart Brook Reeves in this endeavour.

My mind is in a quandary though. What a relief it would be to hand over the burden of Penhale Manor to someone else and walk away with more than sufficient funds to purchase a charming cottage such as this one advertised in Frome. It is not in my nature, however, to give up in the face of a challenge. And oh, how sweet the victory would be if I were somehow to prevail through these difficult times and succeed here at Penhale Manor.

I rise to my feet, determined to carry on. When next I see Brook Reeves, I shall have words to say. A smile forms on my lips, for I do believe that sparring with the scowling squire of Reeves Hall is fast becoming my newest, most favourite pastime.

CHAPTER 10

BROEK

Sunday morning

I am cursing as I attempt to knot my cravat, which is a daily trial for me. I hiss out a frustrated breath. Great Yol grant me a release from these infernal contraptions that take forever to tie and strangle my throat the entire day long. It takes four attempts before the thing is done. With a relieved sigh, I go join my siblings at the main entrance in readiness to go to church—another troublesome weekly pastime.

Except it has not been quite so tedious of late. I can feel myself grin as I think of my little duchess. Well, of course, she is not mine, yet I have come to feel a proprietary sense towards her. She is my own personal project. Every evening, I watch her window from the privacy of my console. I have learned that she retires to her room at eight o'clock at night. There, she reads by the light of a candle for an hour before snuffing it out. I have found out that she likes to keep the window slightly ajar for ventilation and that for bed, she wears a sleeveless white shift. I know this as I have seen her twice at her window. It has become a prurient pleasure of mine to look out for sightings of her at night. I do not question my reasons for this too closely. Suffice it to say I am studying my subject to gain all possible advantage in my campaign to get her to sell Penhale Manor to me.

I climb into the carriage with Liora, Horis and Simor close behind. As we roll towards the church, I gaze pensively out of the window, little attending to the conversation being had in the carriage. We pass the turning for Penhale Manor along the way, and I cast a glance towards the house. The duchess's carriage is there by the main door, waiting to take her to church. *Good*. This means we shall get there first and that I can ensure there is a place on the pew for her beside me. I wonder, not for the first time, what her thoughts are about the cottage in Frome, and whether she knows that I am the one that sent the particulars to her. I am almost certain she does. The duchess is no fool.

After a quarter of an hour of travelling at a brisk pace, we arrive at the village and stop a few yards from the church. "Well," says Liora. "Here we go. Let us hope Reverend Horton's voice does not put any of us to sleep today."

At this, Simor yawns. "I am half asleep already," he whines. "Could we not one day create a clone that would attend such tiresome things in our place?"

"You are welcome to give it a try," I reply acerbically. "In the meantime, we are all duty bound to attend."

We descend from the carriage and make our way inside the church building. I nod towards acquaintances, keeping my eyes sharp for any sign of people turning away from us or whispering malevolent gossip. All seems well today. We are not greeted with effusiveness, but neither are we made to feel like pariahs. Perhaps word has spread of our dinner party last Thursday. I can imagine Sir Nicholas blustering about the fine dinner and port to be had at Reeves Hall—at least I hope that is what he has been telling the good folk of Penhale and Newquay. I should think our guests, with one honourable exception, would all concur that there was no sign of any pagan practices in our home. As long as my little duchess is not suspicious.

I catch sight of Timothy and Verity Drake, who both smile at us in acknowledgement. I nod back in greeting. They are down-to-earth, sensible folk—well, as sensible as the ignorant natives of Earth can be, again with one honourable exception. That exception now walks through the doors of the church, holding her little girl by the hand. Her eyes search the hall until they meet mine. I make an imperious gesture, beckoning her towards me. I see it in her eyes as she considers whether or not to obey my summons. Then she starts walking in our direction. *Good choice, Duchess.*

They are at a few feet's distance when young Chloe catches sight of me. She snatches her hand out from her mother's and runs to me. "Mr Brook!" she calls.

I lift her into my arms and peer into her face. "Hello, Chloe." My expression impassive, I ask, "Have you grown any more since I last saw you, little one?"

"This much," she replies, indicating an inch with her thumb and forefinger.

"Are you sure?" I enquire. "You still seem rather small to me."

She pouts. "That is because you are so big," she explains.

I hold back a smile. "You may be right," I concur. By now, Jane is at my side, observing her daughter in my arms with a frown. "Duchess," I say to her in greeting.

"Mr Reeves," she responds, trying to inject a touch of hauteur into her tone. "I do apologise for Chloe. She has yet to learn the proper decorum." Addressing her daughter, she adds, "Chloe, come down and let Mr Reeves be."

I angle my head towards the girl in my arms and ask, "Chloe, shall I set you down?"

"No!" she cries, encircling my neck with her little arms and squeezing tight.

I return my gaze to Jane. "It seems Chloe has made her choice," I say, then continue briskly, "Come along, let us sit ourselves down." I do not give the duchess any time to demur, striding towards our pew with Chloe held closely in my arms.

I sit with the little girl in my lap as Jane takes the seat beside me. I hear her greet my sister and brothers, but I am distracted by Chloe, who extends her hand towards the ties of my cravat. "Oh no," I admonish, pushing her hand away. I am not going to have my hard efforts at knotting this monstrous contraption unravelled by one pull of this young girl's hand. Fortunately, I have thought to prepare. "I have something for you in my pocket," I tell Chloe. "Take a look."

With a smile of glee, she brings her small hand to my coat pocket and burrows it inside, bringing out a short time later, a rectangular box painted with colourful pictures of a famous nursery rhyme. The box rattles as she examines it curiously. "What is it?" she asks.

"Inside this box is a surprise for you," I tell her—the surprise being a handful of chocolates. She tries to pry the box open, but it is sealed. "Ah," I say. "That is the trick. To get your surprise, you must find the way to open the box. You must be clever about it and think fast." There are small buttons along one side of the box, and pressing them in the right sequence will unlock it. The buttons each make small, distinct sounds when pressed—though not loud enough to distract the church worshippers. The sequence that will unlock the box is the melody of that nursery rhyme illustrated on the front. I am sure this resourceful little girl who takes after her mother will work it out, though I am hopeful the task will keep Chloe occupied through the greater part of the service.

She sets to work at it while Jane watches us warily and murmurs, "It is very kind of you to entertain Chloe, Mr Reeves, but quite unnecessary. Do please return her to me whenever you wish."

"She is fine where she is, Duchess. Let her be," I say gruffly.

We are quiet for a few moments, then Jane says in a conversational voice, "I received an interesting missive in the post a few days ago."

I raise an inquiring brow. She continues, "It was a cutting from a newspaper with an advertisement for a cottage that is for sale in Frome. Curiously, there was also a small painting of the cottage included."

"Curious indeed," I say. "And was the cottage to your liking?"

Her regard is stony. "Mr Reeves, you have wasted your efforts. I am not selling Penhale Manor."

"I am sure I do not know what you mean."

"I am very sure you know precisely what I mean, sir," she replies pertly, as all rise to their feet for the service, and our discourse comes to an end.

I listen as patiently as I can to the reverend's sermon, but halfway through the proceedings, I lean close to Jane's ear and whisper, "I hear Frome is a delightful market town. And is it not near your home in Coleford?"

She turns towards me and busies herself with tucking a stray lock of hair behind her daughter's ear. "It is a delightful town which I know very well," she says quietly, "but Coleford is not my home anymore, Mr Reeves; it is Penhale Manor."

Not for long, Duchess, not for long. I resume listening to the sermon with half an ear. An interval later, I take out my handkerchief and under guise of mopping my brow—for it is quite warm in church today—I remark *sotto voce*, "There is only a hollow victory to be had in pursuing a dubious objective merely to score a point over someone else."

I hear her shocked intake of breath. Angrily, she faces me again, pretending once more to rearrange her daughter's coiffure. I cannot help but notice the brilliance of her brown eyes when her ire is roused. The creamy complexion of her cheeks too has been infused with a fetching shade of rose pink. Her lips are parted, their plush softness a dewy cherry-red. She looks edible, and I think to myself that perhaps, I should poke her anger more often.

"You ascribe far too much importance to yourself, Mr Reeves, if you believe that is what I am doing," Jane hisses under her breath. She settles back in her seat, but not content, returns pretending this time to examine the box in her daughter's hands. "In any case," she whispers, "one would not call making a good home for myself and Chloe a dubious objective."

I am saved from a reply by Chloe complaining, "Ma, stop talking. I want to hear the box." I raise a sardonic brow at Jane, who gives a little huff of displeasure then settles back in her seat, refusing to address me again until we reach the end of the service. As it finally reaches its conclusion, she bids me return her daughter to her. Chloe by now has the box opened and is merrily munching on the chocolates inside it.

"Say thank you to Mr Reeves," Jane commands with a steely look at her daughter.

"Thank you, Mr Reeves," parrots Chloe, her mouth full of chocolate.

"You are welcome, Chloe," I respond gravely.

Jane nods her head to me in dismissal, trying on a haughty expression once more. *It has little effect on me, Duchess, except make me want to bait you more.* Wanting to have the last word, I lean forward and say, "Perhaps the real reason why you don't wish to leave is because you will miss our arguments. But do think—a tidy cottage in a delightful town close to your old home, and at a very affordable price. I would not dismiss it so quickly if I were you, Duchess. Good day." I walk quickly away, not giving her a chance to reply. As I make my way out of the church, I allow myself a little smile.

CHAPTER 11

JANE

I had hoped to put Brook Reeves in his place last Sunday, but I am not sure my efforts were entirely successful. His jibe about my wanting to score a point over him hit deep, as the truth inevitably does. Not least because the decision to stay on at Penhale Manor is proving to be very costly.

The glazier has finished his work and all windows on the house have been repaired, which is a great relief. However, I have also had to pay his steep bill. Only £14 remains in my purse, of which much must go towards the servants' pay and maintenance of the horses. If I am to stay on at Penhale Manor and not sell to Brook Reeves, I must endure the tribulations of having to make trenchant economies.

There are seven weeks to go until I receive my next funds in July. In that time, we must somehow survive on £2 a week. If we live simply, it may be doable, though I am riddled with doubt about it. I myself am going without meat, keeping our meagre supplies for Chloe, though even then, I cannot afford to feed her meat every day. Yesterday's dinner was a thick vegetable and barley stew, together with slices of bread and butter. It was not a rich meal, but it filled my belly. I cannot complain. Chloe, however, was not so easily satisfied. "I want a meat pie," she demanded.

"You had meat pie yesterday, and we'll have some again in a few days. Not tonight," I replied.

"Don't want this," she groused, pushing away the soup.

"If you do not eat it," I warned, "you will go hungry."

"Don't want it," my daughter insisted with a strangely familiar stubbornness.

In the end, I managed to get her to eat the bread and a slice of cheese I had been keeping for next day's breakfast. I put her to bed later that evening, guilt gnawing at me. What sort of mother was I to deprive my child of the hearty meal she deserved? In vain, I tried to reason with myself. There was enough food on the table to fill her belly with had she not fussily rejected the soup. My daughter would not be expiring from starvation. It was a cold comfort.

The following Sunday, Chloe and I make our way to church once more in the carriage. Despite my dismal situation, as we near the village, I begin to feel a nervous excitement in my being. I do not need to guess why. It is that man, Brook Reeves. He may be my nemesis, for I cannot let him win this little battle we are engaged in, but it is also him that has eroded the numbness of my grief. There is something about our encounters that invigorates me, filling me with renewed life.

I still think of Giles, of course, but with a lessening of pain at his loss. Try as I might to avoid it, his features are beginning to grow hazy in my mind. All I have to remind me of him is a miniature portrait which I wear around my neck and a charcoal sketch of him that I made. I could not bring with me to Penhale the life-size portrait of Giles that hangs in the main gallery at Coleford Hall, for it is part of the entailed estate. One day, I hope Chloe and I will visit there again so she may see a good likeness of her father.

There is also something else, of which I feel a trifle ashamed, that has helped ease my grief over Giles. It is resentment at him for not having made the provisions to take care of his family in the event of his death. Oh, I know that I am being unfair to him. I am sure he thought that we would have a son or two in the fullness of time and that the estate would remain within his branch of the family. And yet, my notion of him as the white knight that came to this young maiden's rescue has sadly been tarnished. What good is it to rescue the maiden only to throw her into penury once more? Poor Giles. Little does he know, wherever in heaven he now resides, that these thoughts cross my mind. I am not proud of them, but there it is, an undeniable fact.

The carriage stops, and we descend. Keeping a firm hand on Chloe so she does not evade me this time, we walk into the church vestibule. Without my volition, I search the room, my eyes not resting until they land on Brook Reeves. It does not at all help my feud with this man that I find him so immensely handsome. There is, of course, his large, well-shaped figure. More than once, as I have slaved over my needlework, I have conjured in my mind a vision of him that first time I saw him, his shirt undone at the collar, exposing the crisp dark hair on his broad chest. It was a display of masculinity I am unused to. Giles was fair, and his lean body was smooth as a babe's. The sight of a dishevelled Brook Reeves had set my pulse pounding in a mixture of excitement and fear.

My feet now take me towards him. I should, if I am to maintain a haughty distance, find somewhere else to sit, far from all the Reeves family. My feet, though, have other plans. They take me to him, without even his having to beckon me as he did the last time. As I approach, I am struck again by the attractiveness of his countenance. Eyes of a rich brown stare fixedly at me under a set of straight black brows. A bold nose looks down at the world, telling it to mind its own business. Cheeks and jaw look to have been carved by a master sculptor, such is the perfection of their symmetry. And beneath the well-formed and full lips are a set of even white teeth.

Yes, the rogue is too handsome for his own good, I think as I approach him. Though it is not solely his handsomeness that attracts me to him. It is the way he looks at me. There is nothing about my appearance that should make a man stare. I am a mousy slip of a thing, far too accustomed to not being noticed, and so his notice of me is notable. It is a rare experience to be truly seen, one I have not enjoyed since Giles. Of course, his stare may not be one of admiration. I would hazard a guess that it is not. There is no softening of his expression. In actual fact, his face is set into something of a scowl. Yet I do not mind it. Though he may not admire me with his look, he pays me the respect of an esteemed adversary—one that he would never make the mistake of underestimating. I like that very much. Too much perhaps, for it is partly his scowling attention during our argumentative encounters that spurs me to prolong this battle rather than give in with good grace.

Soon, I reach his vicinity, and that is when I am hit with the other great reason for my attraction: his heavenly scent. It is like nothing I have scented before. I do not know who the maker is of his cologne, though not all that I inhale is come from a bottle. There is a wickedly male muskiness that emanates solely from him. Good Lord! Is it any wonder that I am revelling in our encounters, no matter how prickly they are? Lord forgive me, but I am mere flesh and blood, and before me you have lain the greatest of temptations. It is that which spurs me to say, a trifle coquettishly, "Mr Reeves, we meet again."

"Duchess," he responds in a low, deep voice. Then his eyes flick down to Chloe, who is grasping at the cloth of his trousers with her small fist, vying for his attention. "And what have we here?" he enquires a moment before picking her up in his arms.

"It's Chloe," my daughter chides, reminding him of her name.

"So it is. Hello, Chloe." Her small hands stroke the roughness of his cheeks, and Lord have mercy, I am now jealous of my own daughter. "Did you bring a surprise?" she demands.

He lifts a brow. "Should I have?"

"Yes, yes!" she nods eagerly.

His brow creases as if in deep thought. "Then perhaps, I may have remembered to bring something along with me. But you will only have it if you promise to sit very quiet and still."

Chloe is not sold on the bargain just yet. "What is it?" she wants to know.

"Something you will like very much, but you shall only get it if you sit nicely for your mama and me." He points to the pew and reluctantly, she goes to sit in the middle between myself and Brook. I am relieved that he is not pandering to her wish to be fussed the whole time through the service. My daughter must learn to sit like everyone else.

She perches now between us, but her curiosity is such that she cannot help but ask, "Is it a sweet?"

"It is a surprise, Chloe, and therefore I cannot say."

Chloe makes a little grimace of disappointment. "I want it to be a sweet," she whines. Unabashedly and much to my mortification, she adds, "We did not get meat pie for dinner."

"Oh? Then maybe you had a fish or a game pie," responds Brook, playing along.

Chloe shakes her head mournfully. "Only horrid soup and bread, that is all we eat these days," she moans, and at this moment, I wish the ground could swallow me whole in my shame.

"Chloe, that is enough," I say more sharply than I intend.

Brook's gaze rakes over my wildly flushed face, and his scowl deepens. I am saved by the bell—or rather by the organ—as the service begins, and we all rise to our feet. Throughout the next hour, I studiously avoid looking in his direction at all. Chloe is thankfully quiet, fidgeting at times but settling down at a whispered reminder from Brook of the surprise that awaits her if she sits still. I am surprised that she manages it so well.

The lure of something sweet is far stronger than I realised. Or more likely, it is to do with the deprivation she has experienced of late. Pain clutches tightly at my heart.

In this moment, I would gladly sell up. I would do it in a thrice if it could mean I had the funds to feed my daughter well. Whyever have I clung stubbornly to this accursed house? Why have I let my pride stand in the way of the sensible thing to do? I am gripped by shame, as well as by resentment. It is all Brook Reeves's fault. If he had not provoked my contrary nature, I would never have embarked on this madness.

The service finally comes to an end. I wait, staring down at my feet, as Chloe claims her prize from Brook, a paper bag with lemon drops, which she takes from him with a gleeful look. "What do you say, Chloe?" I remind tersely.

Her mouth already full with the sweets, she mumbles a thank you. Then, with a brisk *good day*, I am leading her away, not stopping to greet any acquaintances, preoccupied only with making the fastest possible escape. We reach the carriage and get inside, and after curtly instructing Evans to make haste, we blessedly begin our journey home.

I lean my head back, letting Chloe prattle on, her speech thick with the sweets in her mouth. I close my eyes and take deep breaths in and out, trying to stop the heaving sobs that want to escape from me. I cannot cry in front of Chloe. Poor child would be alarmed to see her mama in tears. Soon, she too would be sobbing along with me. I try to calm the raging pain borne of shame in my breast. I need hold on only long enough to leave Chloe in Betsy's capable hands and make it to the privacy of my bedchamber. Then, I can allow my grief to finally rip through me.

It is the longest fifteen minutes before we are finally at Penhale Manor. I descend quickly, taking Chloe with me and go to find Betsy. A few mumbled instructions and I am free to make my escape. I rush up the stairs, not quite running but nearly, and hurry to my room. I shut the door behind me and turn the lock. Then my feet slide from under me as I fall to the floor and bury my face in my hands. And then I cry.

I cry as I did not when news of Giles's accident was brought to me. I cry as I have never done before. The agony of the past three months, as well as every affliction that has beset me since I was orphaned at age fourteen, all flow out of me in deep, wailing sobs. Each time I think I have reached the end of it, more is drawn from within me. Such pain have I been holding on to but never knew. I had to keep it well hidden, well under control if I were to survive. And now that the floodgates have opened, all I can do is let it out.

Finally, I quieten. I lie with my head against the door, eyes closed in weary defeat. It is quite some time before I rise to my feet and go wash my face. In the mirror, the redness of my eyes betrays me. There is nothing for it though. I must check on Chloe and see to our dinner. And of course, an endless pile of needlework awaits.

I unlock the door and make my way out on heavy footsteps. I stop by the nursery and find Chloe napping, the excitement of the day having caught up with her. With a smile at Betsy, who is busy pressing clothes with a hot iron, I go down to the kitchen. There, I find Mary busily chopping up the vegetables for yet another stew. She stops as I enter and points to the table on the opposite side of the room. "These came just now from Reeves Hall," she says.

I follow her glance and see four neatly trussed pheasants, plucked of their feathers, laid out on the table. Without warning, tears form in my eyes again. My daughter wanted a meat pie, and Brook Reeves sent over the meat so she could have it. I have no more shame to feel. The tears, which I manage to hold back, are tears of thankfulness and relief. "I have prepared the dough," continues Mary, "so I can make a pie for each bird."

"Yes, thank you, Mary," I say, my throat thick.

I leave the kitchen and go to my parlour. In the basket sits a mountain of clothes to be mended, but first, I take myself to the desk where I begin to write a short note.

Mr Reeves, esquire,

Reeves Hall

Dear Sir,

I write to thank you for your kind gift. Chloe will have her meat pie tonight, and for that, we are both grateful.

Yours sincerely,

Jane Cavendish, Dowager Duchess of Coleford

P.S. There is a matter I wish to discuss. Would you be able to call on me at your convenience?

I seal the note and take it to Evans, bidding him to deliver it to Reeves Hall. It does not take long for a reply to arrive. Brook's note is terse.

Jane,

I shall call on you tomorrow morning. Enjoy the meat pie.

BR

CHAPTER 12

BROEK

I watch Jane's window from my lair, hoping to catch a glimpse of her, but tonight, I am not rewarded with any sighting. The light goes on in her bedchamber, then soon thereafter is snuffed out, in a change to her usual routine.

I frown, wondering what is going on at Penhale Manor. The note she sent me stated there was some matter she wished to discuss. It can only mean one thing. She has changed her mind and decided to sell. If she is dining on soup and bread, then her situation is more parlous than I had thought. That knowledge is enough to ignite my rage once more. Damn the female! Had she but accepted my offer first time, none of this drastic economising would have been necessary.

I retire to bed in an ill temper and wake with no discernible improvement in my mood. At breakfast, I am sullen and morose. My family, thankfully, knows better than to engage me in conversation when I am under such a dark spell. As soon as I am done with the meal, I bark a message on my communicating device—hidden within a signet ring on my finger—asking for my horse to be saddled.

"Going somewhere?" enquires Liora.

I do not respond, merely stand and make my way out of the room. Grabbing hold of my tailcoat, I slip my arms into it then sit on the bench by the door to pull on my boots, grimacing with the effort. Great Yol but I despise these garbs! Once I am ready, I stride quickly out of the front door, to find Galok waiting at the foot of the steps with my horse. "Thank you," I say brusquely, already lifting my foot to the stirrups. Within seconds, I am galloping away.

I reach Penhale Manor a short time later, dismounting and throwing the reins to a servant that comes out from the stable at the sound of my horse's hooves on the cobbled stones. I take the steps up to the house two at a time and ring the bell. When the door opens, I boom, "I am here to see the duchess."

The maid bobs a curtsy, inviting me inside then leading me to the parlour. I wait there, walking about, too distracted to sit. It is not long before the door opens and a pale-faced Jane enters the room. "Mr Reeves," she says impassively.

"Duchess," I grit out.

She points to a set of chairs by the fireplace, and we both take our seats. I decide to get straight to the point. "So, you wish to sell Penhale Manor," I state decisively.

At this she stiffens. "What makes you so certain that I wish to sell, Mr Reeves?" she demands.

"Is that not the matter for which you have summoned me?" I counter.

She hesitates, then nods, dropping her eyes to gaze at her joined hands. There is a moment's silence between us. Then I tell her, "My offer still stands. In fact, I am willing to raise it to £3,600."

Her gaze flies to me in pained confusion. "There is no need to do so," she cries. "I do not want your charity, sir."

"It is not charity," I respond smoothly. "I am a fair man, Duchess, and wish to take into account the many improvements you have made to the house since my last offer. I believe the additional £100 is an honest reflection of the expense and effort that has been expended."

"It is still very generous, Mr Reeves, but I thank you, sir," she murmurs.

"Then, if you are in agreement, I will have my solicitor draw up the contract of sale." I pause before I go on, "It may take a week, perhaps two, for the contract to be made ready. In the intervening time, I should like to propose that we seal our bargain with a sum of £100, which I shall make sure to send forthwith."

She wrinkles her brow at this. "Is it quite necessary? I assure you, once I have given my word, that I will not back out from the agreement."

"And I assure you that neither will I, yet I would prefer that we supplement our word of honour with this small advance on the final amount." I see her hesitate and harden my tone. "Do not be prideful, Jane."

A fire returns to her eyes, as I had hoped. "I can hardly be accused of being prideful," she bristles, "when circumstance makes me accept an offer I would otherwise decline."

"It was pride that made you decline it in the first place," I assert, rising to my feet. "Now, cease with the arguing. The deal is done. Good day, Duchess." I do not wait for a response but stride out of the room to take my leave.

On the ride back to Reeves Hall, I am hardly more cheery than before, though I ought to be well satisfied. Have I not accomplished all I set out to do? Penhale Manor is mine, and the duchess will soon move to far more appropriate lodgings where she can live comfortably with her daughter. Furthermore, before the day is out, she will also be in funds enough to have a decent supper. A good morning's work this has been.

Yet still, the pall that has been cast over my mood does not dissipate. I had enjoyed sparring with my duchess, and now that it is over, this victory, if one could call it such, feels very hollow indeed.

CHAPTER 13

JANE

Three weeks later

The day has come for our departure. Six weeks I have spent at Penhale Manor, yet it has felt like more with all that has occurred since I arrived. I had come here in hopes of making a good home for me and Chloe. This hope was fractured upon my first sight of the house, and though I fought on valiantly to keep it alive, in the end, I could not prevail.

My pride has been dented, but my purse is full, and I will shortly be the proud owner of a charming cottage in Frome, just as soon as contracts can be exchanged. On my instructions, Mr Oakley visited the cottage to ensure it was in sound condition, then put an offer for it at a little less than the asking price. The offer was accepted, and now with the sale of Penhale Manor complete, all that is left is for us to depart for Somerset once more.

Our trunks are packed and stowed in the carriage. Betsy and Chloe are already settled in, all ready to go. I linger inside the house a while longer, walking from room to room to make sure nothing has been forgotten. I am not too disheartened to bid it farewell. I suppose we have not been here long enough to make it feel truly like our home. The damp crumbling walls, the mice and the cobwebs have not helped to endear this house to me.

There is one aspect to living here, though, that I shall miss. It is my encounters with Brook Reeves, esquire, of Reeves Hall. I do not see him often, for he is a busy man. Occasionally, he has called to enquire after Chloe and me, always bringing some gift with him—oranges from his glass house, delicate chocolates, cut flowers from his garden. He does not stay long for these visits, merely makes his enquiries, proffers his gift and then bids me good day, though not before making some remark to raise my ire. I can almost believe he takes pleasure in doing so. Then, he departs before I can hit back with a good word of my own, leaving me to stew over what I shall say to him the next time we meet.

The chance to do so comes round every Sunday at church, when I sit beside him, Chloe wedged between us. Then, at the right moment, I whisper my prepared riposte. I almost think he attends church only to hear it, because he never fails to reply in a way that only provokes me further. And so on it goes, this diverting game we play, though now it must stop.

On his last visit, just yesterday, I thanked him for the bouquet of flowers he brought for me. He merely shrugged and replied, "Some colour is needed to counteract the dullness of that black you wear every day."

"Sir!" I cried. "You must know that I am in mourning."

To this he made a harrumphing sound in his throat and gifted me with one of his scowls. Gruffly, he wished me luck on my journey the following day and said his final goodbyes. On his way out, of course, he could not resist having the last word. "Take my advice, Duchess, and spare the people of Frome the dismal sight of your widow's weeds. That husband who left you in these straits does not deserve a shrine to his memory." And then he left, not giving me a chance to voice a rejoinder.

There will not ever be a chance to speak to that infuriating man again. I have seen the last of him. In these final quiet moments before I leave, I can acknowledge that I shall miss my time with him. I am changed since coming to Penhale, and that is partly due to him. I came here a grieving widow. I am still that widow, but my grief has eased. With a sigh, I cast one last look at my erstwhile home, then walk out with a determined step and close the door behind me.

In the carriage, I gaze absently out of the window, thinking of Brook Reeves. If only, for once, it could be me to have the last word. What would I say to him? *Take my advice, Mr Reeves, and spare the people of Penhale the dismal sight of your scowl.* I think some more then add another pithy line. *Whoever that lady is who left you out of charity with the rest of the world, she does not deserve a shrine to her memory.* I smile to myself, thinking of his countenance if ever I were to say such words to him. Of course, I would not wait for a reply. I would flounce out victoriously. The image is so vivid in my mind, that as we approach the gates of Reeves Hall, I cannot help but tap the coach door and bid Evans to stop.

CHAPTER 14

HORIS

"There, that should take care of it," I tell Gav'ox as I close the final suture on his arm. Earlier today, he had slipped carelessly on the floor while drinking from a bottle of home-brewed krilk, a popular drink on Uvon made with a proprietary blend of spices and syrup. Gav'ox has spent years trying to recreate his own version of krilk with the spices we have here on Earth. He claims this latest brew is as close to the real thing as it is possible to be.

I cannot vouch for his claim, for I have not yet had a chance to sample it. It certainly seems to be a potent brew if it made Gav'ox lose his balance, smash the bottle to the floor and tumble over the shards. I have removed at least five small pieces of glass from his arm, but the worst damage was caused by a shard that cut a deep slash above his elbow. This is what I have just finished stitching up.

I usually treat my patients from the medical bay in the main house, but I was out walking my dog, an energetic and friendly border collie, when the call came from Gav'ox, and it was quicker to make my way to him than to have someone transport him to the house. Gav'ox had been on duty at the gate lodge when this incident happened, and really should not have been drinking anything potent at all. Broek will not be happy when he hears of this—not that Broek is ever happy, to my knowledge. Long gone is the smiling and joyous brother I knew on Uvon.

As Gav'ox eases his shirt back on, I tell him plain and simple, "Broek will not like to hear that you were drinking krilk while on duty at the lodge."

He shrugs, acting unconcerned. "There is no law against it, and Horis, at no point was I intoxicated. I stepped on a slippery surface and fell. That is all there is to it."

"He will find out, you know."

"And I will tell him what I told you. It was an accident."

I nod and begin putting away my instruments in the small medical bag I always carry with me. Outside the lodge door, I hear a loud bark. Shaffi must be growing impatient, waiting for me. A moment later comes the sound of the bell ringing. Someone is at the lodge gates. Gav'ox goes to check the visual on his console. "Damn!" he mutters. "It is that inquisitive female from Penhale Manor, the duchess. I thought she would be long gone by now." He lumbers his massive frame out of the door, and I hear him call out, "Yes?"

Her voice reaches me, sounding steely. "I am come to call on Mr Brook Reeves. Please let the carriage through."

I hear the gruff response from Gav'ox. "I am sorry, Your Grace, but I have strict orders from Mr Reeves not to let anyone inside without an invitation."

"Quite clearly I am not anyone," she says with a hint of impatience. "Now open up."

I am already at the lodge door, drawing it open to the barks of my excitable dog. "Down, Shaffi," I command. She does so with a little whine, but already, the duchess has seen me.

"Mr Harry Reeves," she calls. "How fortuitous. Would you please speak with your gatekeeper and instruct him to open the gates."

I walk towards her with a smile. "Your Grace, how good to see you," I begin, my mind racing as to how I am going to keep her out. Broek was crystal clear on the matter. Nobody enters

Reeves Hall without permission, especially not the duchess. "I understand you are leaving for Somerset," I say to her now. "We shall be sad to see you go."

"Yes," she replies. "We are on our way, but I wanted to stop by and say a personal farewell. Would you be so kind as to let me in?"

I scratch my head in a quandary then hit on a bright idea. "I am afraid, Your Grace, that Brook is out at present. I will naturally let him know that you called." Of course, that is not quite the truth. Brook is in the basement, busy with his work.

She lets out a frustrated breath. "Oh, that is a shame! I very much wanted to speak to him before I left."

I wonder briefly what she can want to say to my surly brother but hold my counsel. "I am very sorry, Your Grace," I say gently. "Is there anything I myself might help you with?"

Before she can answer, the carriage door opens, and her little girl jumps out with the help of her nursemaid. "Doggie!" she cries, looking at Shaffi who barks enthusiastically. The little girl, Chloe, runs up to us, crying, "I want to see doggie."

I smile despite myself as she reaches out a little hand through the iron grille and attempts to pat my dog. Shaffi seems equally delighted, licking at her hand and jumping excitedly. "Chloe, no!" calls the duchess, pulling her daughter's hand away.

"It is quite alright," I say reassuringly. "Shaffi is very gentle and won't harm her." I make a quick decision. "In fact, how about I bring Shaffi out and you can meet each other properly?" I go to the small side gate and let myself out, holding firmly on to Shaffi's collar. "Chloe," I say. "Come meet Shaffi."

The little girl approaches and puts her hand out to stroke the black topcoat of my dog. "Shaffi?" queries the duchess. "That is an unusual name."

"It means *companion* in my language," I reply, then quickly correct myself. "That is, in one of the dialects spoken in Brazil."

It is the back story we concocted to explain our sudden appearance in English society. According to this story, we are descended from an ancestor, a man by name of Phineas Reeves, who hailed from an obscure landed family in Cornwall. He travelled to South America some three generations ago and there, made his fortune. We figured that our being raised abroad would explain the hint of a foreign accent still in our speech, despite the many hours we spent practising English.

The duchess kneels beside Shaffi and scratches the top of her head. "What a pretty thing you are," she coos admiringly.

This appreciation of my dog makes the duchess go up a notch in my estimation, although truth be told, I like her already a great deal. It is a shame she must leave so we can take over Penhale Manor, though I have been assured she has found a lovely cottage to buy with the proceeds from the sale.

Shaffi sniffs the ground, barking loudly. "What is it?" asks Chloe, a trifle nervously.

"She has sniffed something, a rabbit maybe," I reply. An instant later, Shaffi shakes off my hand and bolts across to the other side of the road, chasing whatever creature she has just spied. I sigh and reproach myself for not having held firmly enough on to her collar.

Everything then happens very quickly. Chloe cries, "Shaffi!" and darts across the road after my dog. The duchess calls out in alarm, trying to catch her daughter, but the little dervish is too quick. And at the same time, the mail coach, which usually passes by at this time, comes hurtling down the road at speed, heading straight for the little girl.

"Chloe, no!" shrieks her mother, racing after her. The coach rushes by, clipping the child's side and sending her flying into the air. A moment later, the speeding vehicle has disappeared, and I see little Chloe lying still on the ground. "No!" cries the duchess again, rushing towards her daughter, myself at her heels.

We reach her at the same time. The duchess touches her daughter's face, calling out her name repeatedly. "Wake up, Chloe. Wake up!"

I feel for a pulse. It is weak, but there. I raise Chloe's chin to free her airway, then look about me. It is not safe here on the road. I must move the girl and quickly, though I fear damaging her spine. I look across at Gav'ox, who is staring at us in horror. "We need something flat and hard to move her," I call out to him. He nods and disappears inside the lodge.

The duchess looks to me now with tearful eyes. "Help her. Please," she pleads.

"I shall try," I say, then add, "She is alive," as a way of reassurance. While I wait for Gav'ox to return, I check Chloe's head and body for injuries. I feel swelling to the back of her skull, presumably where she hit the ground after her fall. There is a bleeding gash at the side of her body where the coach must have clipped her, but the cut, thankfully, is not too deep. The most worrisome injury is her head and the impact it must have received as it hit the ground. We urgently need to get Chloe to my medical bay and put her on the life support equipment there.

It seems a lifetime before Gav'ox returns bearing a thin wooden board. I do not have the capability to wonder where he obtained it from. Gently, I nudge the duchess. "We must get Chloe on this board," I tell her, "but very carefully. I will hold Chloe's head to keep it steady while Gav'ox slides the board under her body. Help us by steadying her legs."

She nods in understanding, and I send a quick prayer of thanks to Yol that the duchess is not a woman prone to hysterics. I place my hands to each side of Chloe's head, then look to Gav'ox. With agonising slowness, he pushes the board under the prone girl's body, while her mother and I stabilise her head and legs. "Gently," I warn a time or two. Finally, it is done. I take off my cravat and use it to tie Chloe securely to the board. Seeing my actions, the duchess retrieves a shawl from the carriage and uses it around Chloe's legs.

I look now to the carriage, where the maid stands wringing her hands while the coachman calms the horses. "Come over," I beckon, and the young maid is quick to do my bidding. *Good.* "Your name?"

"B-Betsy," she mumbles.

"Betsy," I say. "I would like you to get inside the carriage and hold Chloe steady on the board as we carry her in. Can you do that?" She nods. "Keep her very steady," I repeat.

"Yes, sir." Betsy quickly climbs into the carriage, then with Gav'ox assisting me, and the duchess hovering nervously by our side, we lift Chloe on the board and take her to the vehicle.

It is a tricky business, pushing the board inside while keeping it as steady as we can. Thankfully, the carriage is wide and spacious. As Betsy holds one end of the board, I climb into the carriage holding the other end. Once I am inside, I make sure Chloe is laid flat between me and Betsy. The duchess scrambles into the carriage after us and places a gentle hand to her daughter's face. I check the little girl's pulse again and look up at her mother. "She is still with us," I say. Though there is no time to lose.

Outside, Shaffi's barks hail her return. Through the still open door, I glance at Gav'ox, who has taken hold of my dog's collar, and state decisively, "I am taking her to the medical bay." He does not argue, but goes to open the gates wide. I shut the carriage door and tap the communicating device on my finger to call Krilea, uncaring of the other occupants with me. When she responds, I say in our language, "I need you in the medical bay now. Prepare life support." If I have any thought about breaching the privacy of Reeves Hall and disobeying Broek's orders, it is very fleeting. Saving Chloe is all that matters now.

CHAPTER 15

JANE

It feels as if I have entered some strange nightmare world. Nothing seems quite right, chief of all the fact that Chloe lies unmoving on the makeshift wooden cot. Beside me, Harry Reeves speaks some words in a foreign language, and a disembodied voice speaks to him in reply. I look around me but cannot see where this voice is coming from.

I would turn tail and run from this strangeness if it were not for one fact. Harry Reeves has promised to help Chloe, and oddly, I trust him to do so. There is an air of competence about him, as well as kindness. I glance across at Betsy. Her eyes are wide with wonder and fear, but she too stays firmly in her seat.

The carriage rolls through the open gates and along the winding avenue that takes us to the main house. It is the first time I see it in daylight. In my befuddled state, I note that it is large and grand, and immaculately maintained.

Inside the house, we are taken to the strangest room I have ever seen, but I do not have time to ponder it. There is a young woman, a servant, who speaks to Harry in a foreign tongue. Carefully, we move Chloe from the board to a white leather-padded cot. Then Harry turns to me, his voice tight with urgency. "Duchess, things may seem odd to you, but I do not have time to explain. Please trust me on one thing. I will do my best to help Chloe. Now I must ask you to keep your distance and let us do our work to save her."

I stare at him, undecided. But truly, what choice do I have except to trust this strange man in this strangest of families? I nod and go sit on a chair in the corner of the room, though I do not let Chloe out of my sight. Beside me, Betsy clutches her hands together and chants a prayer under her breath, stopping every so often to gape at her surroundings. Soon, I follow her lead and say my own prayers. *Dear Lord, deliver us from this purgatory. Do not take my precious Chloe yet from me. Save her, oh Lord. Save her.*

Before my bewildered gaze, there unfolds the most peculiar of happenings. The cot on which Chloe is lying begins to move, as if by magic, sliding into a cavity in the wall from which there comes a buzzing sound. On the wall, a large white screen is suddenly filled with various images. I see the silhouette of a person and realise that it is Chloe, or some sort of representation of her. There are more sounds and a voice speaking in an unfamiliar tongue, but I cannot discern where it is coming from. Preposterous as it may seem, the voice is coming from the wall beneath the screen. Harry places a mask over his mouth and washes his hands in a bowl over which water gushes through a gleaming type of tap. He then pulls on a pair of very thin gloves. The girl, whose name I learn is Krilea, follows suit. *What is this place?*

The cot on which Chloe lies has come back out of the wall cavity it entered. Now Harry goes to her, inserting a thin tube into her mouth made of some strange transparent material. It is attached to a wider tube leading to a small cavity in the wall. I cry out in protest, "What are you doing to her?"

He speaks calmly through the mask he is wearing, "This will help Chloe breathe." Then, he touches his finger to markings on the wall and suddenly, a whooshing sound is heard. It seems he is telling the truth, for I can see the rise and fall of Chloe's chest as she breathes.

From a hidden drawer compartment, I see him then take a vial of some clear-coloured liquid and attach it to something that looks like a fine syringe. I stiffen in horror as he injects this liquid into Chloe's arm. What can he be doing? As if reading my mind, he answers me, "This is a medicinal draught that will help reduce the swelling in Chloe's head." Can something administered to the arm affect another part of the body? How is that possible? My mind cannot fathom all that I see.

Finally, he and Krilea turn to Chloe's other wounds. They cut her dress with sharp scissors and clean off the mud and blood with a wet cloth. Keeping his hands steady, Harry then treats the gash along Chloe's hip, using a fine needle and thread to close it up. When he is done, he places a white bandage over the wound. My poor Chloe sleeps through all these tribulations, but she is alive—for I can see her chest move with each breath. *"Oh Lord, keep sight of my precious girl,"* I murmur into my joined hands.

The door to the room opens and in walks Brook Reeves, a customary scowl on his face. He interrogates Harry sharply in a foreign tongue as he approaches Chloe on the cot. A frown knits his brow as he looks down at her. More questions are fired at Harry; more responses are received; none of it I understand. I see Brook touch a gentle hand to Chloe's shoulder. Finally, he turns to me, his expression stony. He walks to where I am sitting and stands, towering over me. "Duchess," he says. "Horis has done all he can for now. Chloe will be given a draught to help her sleep until the swelling in her head reduces. All we can do then is wait."

"Will she recover?" I ask him in a wavering voice.

"Yes, I believe so. Horis will look after her."

I am slowly emerging from the baffled stupor I have been in this past hour. I have many questions now, but I start with this one: "Horis?"

"My brother, Harry," he explains. "His real name is Horis."

"Who are you?" I demand to know. "And what is all this?" I point towards the various contraptions around Chloe.

He sighs. "All you need to know are two things, Jane. First, Chloe is in good hands. Second, you were never supposed to have seen the things you saw today, for they are none of your business. We tried our best to keep you out."

"And now that I have seen all this?" I prompt.

His mouth becomes a thin line. "And now that you have seen, you cannot be allowed to betray our secrets."

"What do you mean? How?" I breathe, but I already know the answer.

His voice is a death knell as he pronounces, "You cannot leave Reeves Hall again. Here you will remain."

CHAPTER 16

JANE

I sit beside Chloe, studying her sleeping face for any change. I hold her small hand in mine, in wonder at how fragile she is and yet also marvelling at her resilience, for she is still alive, still fighting on despite the enormity of her injuries.

Seemingly endless hours have passed since Brook Reeves informed me that I was to be a prisoner here. He left soon after telling me that I was not to leave Reeves Hall again for fear of betraying their secrets. Since then, I have stayed here, keeping a vigil over a sleeping Chloe. Betsy has also left the room. A footman came to fetch her some time ago when our trunks were brought in, so she could unpack our belongings. I do not know nor care what rooms we have been given. I do not care about much at this time, except that Chloe wakes.

A servant came, I do not remember how long ago, inviting me to go for my luncheon. I declined. Some milk and biscuits were brought in shortly after. That is all I have consumed since I broke my fast hours ago at Penhale Manor. I do not even know the time, for there is no window in this room. How it is ventilated or lit are a mystery to me. No candles or lamps are in sight. I must assume though, that it is now late afternoon or early evening.

Harry—or Horis as I should call him now—comes by at regular intervals to check on Chloe; so too does his helper, the young woman named Krilea. He is here now to look over his patient. I have come to understand he is something of a doctor, though like none I have ever met before. Horis smiles reassuringly and informs me, "Chloe is progressing well."

"How can you tell?" I ask.

He points to the screen on the wall, which is filled with strange symbols that I cannot decipher. "This machine monitors Chloe's vital signs," he explains. "I can read from the screen that the swelling in Chloe's head has reduced by twenty-two percent. Her heart is beating healthily, and she is breathing well. These are all good signs."

"How can a machine do all these things? Is it a black art, some sort of magic that you practise?" I ask, unsettled by his words.

He laughs. "Nothing of the sort. There is no magic here, Your Grace, merely highly advanced scientific knowledge."

I ask the question again, hoping for a proper answer this time. "Who are you, and why is it you have such advanced scientific knowledge?"

He looks away as he replies, "I am not at liberty to say."

"Your brother said I was not to leave Reeves Hall again. Do you agree with that?" My tone is sharp and demanding.

In answer, he takes a chair and brings it over to my side, then sits, leaning forward on his elbows in thought. Finally, he looks over to me with a kindly expression and says, "Your Grace, we mean you no harm. We are doing all we can to save Chloe. But you now know things about us that we have kept secret for very good reasons. Just think what would happen if word were to spread about the way we live. Do you think we would be allowed to carry on as we are?"

"I—I suppose not."

He nods in agreement. "All we want is to be left in peace to live according to our ways. The world around us is not capable of understanding who we really are. Already some folk here suspect us of witchcraft. You yourself did so just now."

I hunch my shoulders defensively. "What else am I to think?" I cry in frustration. "I do not understand who you are or why you live so differently to the rest of us. Can you not explain?"

He sighs. "All I can say, Your Grace, is that we are men and women just like you, not demons or witches or anything supernatural. We come from a land far away, a civilisation that is highly scientific and advanced in its knowledge."

"Where? What land? In Brazil?"

He laughs again, genuinely amused. "No, Your Grace, not Brazil. It is somewhere much further away, of which you can have no knowledge."

I ponder his words. They still make little sense to me. How can there be a land that is so highly civilised and yet remains unknown? I narrow my eyes suspiciously at Horis. "If your civilisation is so highly advanced, as you say, then why has it not sent representatives to England to enlighten us with its great knowledge?"

He looks uneasy, rubbing a hand nervously over his cheek. He is not telling me the whole truth. I am certain of it. "Your Grace," he begins again. "Our homeland is further away than you can imagine, and our people, seeing the level of ignorance and backwardness here, decided it was best to keep their distance."

"You think us backward and ignorant?" I protest, indignant at the unfairness of such a charge.

His eyes go to Chloe and the machines around her, then come back to rest on me. "Look at Chloe and think, Your Grace," he says earnestly. "If you will pardon my saying so, your daughter would not have survived her accident had she been taken to a local surgeon, who in all likelihood would have bled her with leeches. It is our superior knowledge that has helped to keep Chloe alive."

"It is God that keeps her alive," I correct him pointedly.

He nods in acknowledgement. "God keeps her alive, yes, and our scientific knowledge too, which one could say is God-given."

I am about to argue with this, angered still at his choice of words, but my eyes catch the steady rise and fall of Chloe's breaths, and I cannot argue with the truth. I take a deep breath of my own and try to remain calm. My mind scrambles to keep up with all the fantastical things that Horis has just told me. There is one detail, out of the many, that particularly does not make sense. "If your people decided to keep their distance from us," I demand accusingly, "then why is it that your family is here?"

He looks surprised at my quick-wittedness. "Well you see," he begins then stops. He tries again. "We were… It is hard to explain."

I raise a questioning brow at him. Quietly, he mumbles, "We were banished."

"Banished? Why?"

He rises to his feet hurriedly. "I have said too much. It is best I go," he mutters. An instant later, he is gone.

I am left to consider all the information I have been given. My head hurts with the effort to make sense of these things that seem beyond my understanding. I pinch the skin of my hand. Maybe it will wake me from this nightmare dream. It does not. I am still in this strange, windowless room, and Chloe lies on a cot, tubes in her body attaching her to a machine that makes whooshing noises. *Dear God, please help us!*

Hours pass. My head drops in fatigue, but as soon as it does, I raise it again, determined to keep watch over my daughter. There is a knock at the door. A servant enters, informing me dinner is about to be served. He wishes to escort me to my room so that I may get changed. I refuse. With a bow, he leaves the room again.

More time passes. My stomach gurgles in hunger, but I am steadfast. I will not desert Chloe in this strange place.

The door swings open sharply. Brook strides in. He takes one look at me, swaying with fatigue by my daughter's side, and glowers. "Time to get some food and sleep, Duchess," he grits ferociously.

"I am not leaving Chloe," I tell him in a steadfast voice.

He stares at me, brows knitted in his customary frown. "Then I shall have to… persuade you." Next moment, he has me bent over his shoulder, gripping me with a strong hand.

I kick and cry, "Set me down!"

He ignores my cries, and his powerful arms subdue my straining body with little effort. "Let me go!" I cry again. Then as I see him cross the threshold, I call out in alarm, "Stop! I cannot leave Chloe."

"Horis will sit with her," he responds calmly. He walks on, then ascends a tall set of steps. I do not relent with my protests, but they fall on deaf ears, his grip on me tight and strong. We come to a door, which he opens with a quick flick of his wrist. I do not see much from my upended view—a polished floor, colourful rugs, the base of something that might be a bed.

"Go quick and bring up a tray of food for your mistress," Brook commands in a brisk voice.

"Yes, sir," I hear Betsy reply, and her footsteps as she flies out of the room.

With a grunt, Brook deposits me on the bed. Immediately, I sit up, determined to escape. "Do not even think of it," he roars, pushing me none too gently back down. "Must you always be so difficult?" he exclaims in disgust.

I try to respond but find myself trembling. "I—I…" Speech too has become impossible. My body shakes uncontrollably.

His scowl deepens. "Great Yol," he growls, then strides towards a connecting door. "Stay where you are or else!" he throws over his shoulder as he disappears into the next room.

I have no choice but to obey, in the state I find myself in. I lie on the bed, my hands still trembling, my head dizzy from fatigue, hunger and worry. It does not take long before Brook returns. In his hand is a tumbler half full with an amber liquid. He places it beside him on a short chest of drawers, then sits on the edge of the bed, helping me to an upright position. He steadies me with a firm arm around my shoulder and once more, I am enveloped in his scent. It does not set my pulse racing this time, but rather slows it down, the familiarity of it bringing comfort.

He guides the tumbler to my lips. I keep them resolutely sealed, which only brings a sardonic curl to his own lips. "It is good old-fashioned brandy, Jane," he barks. "Now drink up." I do as he says. One cannot waste good brandy, after all. I feel it burn my throat as I take several small sips. I do not manage to drink the entire contents of the tumbler, but once he sees I have had enough, he sets it aside.

My hands, fortunately, have stopped their trembling, yet I am still unbearably weak. My head rests against the solid width of Brook's shoulder. I take a deep breath and try to speak. "Chloe," I say.

"Horis is with her," he says quietly, his voice a deep rumble at my back. "She will not wake for many hours as we are keeping her sedated until the swelling in her head subsides."

"I should be with her," I breathe.

"You are no good to her in this state," he snaps. A little more gently, he continues, "Eat, Jane, then rest. Horis and I will watch Chloe. If there is any change in her condition, I will let you know."

I close my eyes then, conceding defeat. I do not know whether I dream it, but I feel his hand stroke over my hair, a gently delicate touch. Time stills. The spell is broken only by the opening of the door as Betsy returns, bearing a tray of steaming food. Brook releases me and stands to leave. "Stay here," he grunts warningly, "and do not get any ideas about leaving this room. I will have someone stand guard outside in case you are foolish enough to try." With these parting words, he walks out of the room.

Betsy brings the tray over to me, and I begin to eat listlessly, listening to her chatter with half an ear. "It is ever so strange here, Your Grace. I have never seen a kitchen like the one below. Why, there is not even a fire! When I asked Velnas—that's the cook—how we were to heat your food, he put the plate into a glass cupboard, touched his finger to it and it lit up! Then the cupboard door opened, all by itself, and your food was steaming hot. Like magic!"

"The work of the devil, most likely," I declare sourly.

"Oh no, Your Grace, it is not that at all," exclaims Betsy. "I asked Velnas, you see, and he said it is science." She nods sagely.

I let her prattle on as hunger takes over and I finish every last morsel of the food I have been given. Once I am done, Betsy takes the tray from me and sets it outside the door. "Is there a privy nearby?" I ask, feeling a sudden need to relieve myself.

Her face lights up. "You will hardly believe it, Your Grace. There is a privy inside the washroom right behind that door." She points to the connecting door through which Brook had fetched the brandy earlier.

"There is a washroom and privy there?" I ask dumbly.

"Yes!" she nods excitedly. "And beyond the washroom is the master's bedchamber." She adds conspiratorially, "I hear the master was none too happy to have you put in the room beside his, but there was nowhere else. All the other bedchambers are taken."

I wonder if Betsy is right, or whether I have been placed in the room beside Brook's so he can keep me captive. The thought makes me shiver, although for some reason it is not entirely unwelcome. With a servant guarding my door and Brook in the next room, there can be very little opportunity for escape—not that I wish to do so now. Thoughts of escape must wait until Chloe is recovered. I rise from the bed and go to the washroom door, opening it carefully to peer inside.

Like all the rooms in this house, it is well-lit, almost by magic, though I am sure Horis would say it was science. The washroom is large and covered in gleaming white tiles. I search for the privy and catch sight of a shiny dark contraption, like the commode I used the night of the dinner party. I approach it cautiously and lift the lid. Yes, I am right. It is the same design as the one downstairs.

With a sigh of relief, I sit on it and do my business. Once I am done, I search for something to wipe with and find a pile of very fine cloths stacked in a small tray. I use them gratefully but cannot see a bin to place the soiled cloths in. After a moment's hesitation, I throw them into the cavity inside the commode. I am about to rise when I remember the curious jet of water that splashed me the night of the dinner party. I angle my head to look at the panel behind me. There, I see two round markings, one coloured blue and the other green. These had been covered up in the retiring room downstairs, evidently to prevent their discovery. It was only when I had run my finger over the panel that I had felt the hollow space hidden under the cloth.

I study the two round markings, thinking fast. That water spray, I decide, must be some mechanism to clean a person's nether regions, but which button should I press? I decide to try the blue one. Immediately, I feel a jet of warm water rise up to the exposed parts of my body. It is not an unpleasant sensation. A short while later, the water stops, and I dab myself dry with another cloth.

What, I wonder, is the green button for? Is it worth trying? Of course, I am never one to shy away from a mystery, so I reach over and press it. In an instant, there is a loud gurgling sound below me, and as I rise quickly in alarm, I see the bowl of the commode flushed with a freshly-scented green liquid. *Oh, I see. How ingenious.*

I pat the skirt of my dress down and search for the jug of water to wash my hands with. However, there is none to be found. I open the washroom door and call out, "Betsy, please bring a jug of water."

"Oh no, Your Grace," she replies as she hastens towards me. "There is no need for a jug. That is the other magical thing. The water comes out on its own. Let me show you." She enters the room and waves her hands under a tap that is fixed to the wall above a tiled basin. As if by magic, water begins to pour from it. She beams at me, her joy evident. "And it is the same with the bathtub, Your Grace. At the press of a button, hot water comes out of the tap. Imagine that! No more having to carry it up in buckets." I can see she is dazzled by such scientific innovations. And why not. I cannot imagine it is easy work to carry water buckets up and down the stairs each day.

As I go to wash my hands, she asks eagerly, "Will you take a bath now, Your Grace? That way you will see how it magically fills with hot water."

I do not have the heart to disappoint her. Besides, a wash in the bath would be welcome. "Yes," I say.

No sooner have I agreed than she is rushing towards the large, oval-shaped tub and pressing a button, not dissimilar to the one on the commode, though this one is red. Instantly, great gushes of steaming water pour out of the spout and into the tub.

Betsy turns to me in triumph. I make the proper admiring sounds as she adds a cup of scented salts to the bath. Then, she is helping me out of my dress and underclothes. A moment later, I step into the tub and submerge my body in the fragrantly hot water.

I cannot help a sigh of pleasure. This, I must concur, is a superlative innovation. For long minutes, I luxuriate in the bath. Betsy assists me to wash my hair with the soap and rinse it clean. When I am done, she holds out the largest, softest towel I have ever beheld and wraps it around my wet body. Back in the bedchamber, she lays out my white shift for me and brushes out my hair. It has been a very long time since I have had the services of a lady's maid, not since I lived at Coleford Hall. I had forgotten how pleasant it is to be so pampered.

I smile gratefully at Betsy as I get under the bedcovers. I look around the room curiously, wondering what I must do to extinguish the light. Betsy anticipates my question. With a great air of exultation, she confides, "Your Grace, it is magical. You simply have to say what you want and it is done." She pauses meaningfully, then says in a clear voice, "Lights out."

Immediately, the light in the room dims to impenetrable darkness. I feel a nervous shiver. A moment later, Betsy's voice says loudly, "Lights on," and the light returns. She grins, obviously proud of her newfound knowledge. "You can also tell it how dark or how light you want it to be," she says, then demonstrates. "Lights low." Instantly, the room dims to a light glow. She tries another instruction. "Lights on very bright." A moment later, I am dazzled by the brightest of white light.

I decide to take matters into my own hands. "Lights low," I say, and the white light is thankfully replaced by a low glow.

"Thank you, Betsy," I say, dismissing her. She bobs a curtsy and hurries out of the room. Outside my door, I hear her speak in a friendly tone to the man standing guard. He responds in a low voice, but I cannot make out the words. Shortly after, silence falls.

I lie back in the bed. The mattress is springy and the sheets like soft silk. Everything at Reeves Hall is of the highest order of luxury, it seems, but there is a price to be paid for this sumptuous splendour, I think bitterly. That price is freedom.

My thoughts fly to Chloe. I wonder how she fares in that windowless room downstairs, and when it is she will wake. I feel an urge to go to her. I am about to throw off the covers and do just that, when Brook's voice speaks in my ear, as if he is in the room with me: "Jane, I thought you might like to know that Chloe is doing well and the swelling on her head is easing."

I look to my left and right. "Where are you?" I ask in fright.

"I am with Chloe in the medical bay," he answers immediately. "I will show you—*onscreen*." A moment later, a screen I had not noticed on the opposite wall comes to life with pictures—moving pictures—of Brook sitting in the chair beside Chloe. Looking straight at me, he says, "She is sleeping soundly."

"How—how is this happening?" I whisper, but he hears me anyway.

"There is a recording device in this room," he replies. "It transmits images and the sound of my voice to the screen in your room."

"Like magic," I murmur very low.

"Not magic, Jane, but science," he answers me briskly.

A horrifying thought occurs to me. "If you can hear me, then are you seeing me too?" I ask, burrowing under the covers so only my face is visible.

He snorts. "No, Jane, your modesty is quite safe. To activate the visual recording, you have to instruct the computer with the word *onscreen*."

"And to stop the visual recording?"

He smiles, the first smile I have ever seen from him. "Then you merely have to say *offscreen*."

My curiosity gets the better of me. I am buried under the bedcovers, so there is nothing of an immodest nature to see. Quickly, I say, "*Onscreen*."

Now, Brook is smiling wide. It quite takes my breath away. "Duchess, you look like you might drown under the weight of those blankets." His eyes sharp, he remarks, "Your hair is wet."

"Well, yes," I say. "That happens when one has a bath."

He frowns. "You should not sleep with wet hair, Jane. You will catch a chill that way."

"I have been doing it all my life, Brook," I respond, using his given name for the very first time. Or is it his name? "Is your name truly Brook?" I ask.

"It is close enough. In my language, we say *Broek*."

"Broek." I try the name out on my tongue.

"Jane," he says, all trace of amusement gone from his face. "From here on, you will dry your hair before going to bed."

I raise a sceptical brow. "Broek," I say, putting emphasis on his newly discovered name, "do you expect me to sit by the fire for an hour at night?"

His face takes on its customary scowl. I think I hear him mutter, "Backward people." Then, he speaks up. "In the washroom, there is a dryer. It is an oval glass dome on the wall. Stand below it and lower it over your head, like a cap. As soon as it senses your wet hair, it will start blowing hot air to dry it. When your hair is dry, it will stop on its own. Simply push it back up on the wall."

I sigh. Yet another newfangled contraption. "That sounds interesting," I say politely.

"Dry your hair with it," is all he says in reply.

I do not dignify this with a response. Instead, I look at my sleeping daughter and murmur, "Goodnight, Chloe. Sleep well." Then I add the word, *"Offscreen."*

A moment later, the screen on my wall goes dark, and I settle to sleep. I am beginning to drift into slumber when Broek's voice breaks into my thoughts. "Go dry your hair, Jane."

With an angry huff, I throw off the covers and march to the washroom. There, I spy the oval glass contraption on the wall — I had thought it to be a wall sconce. Angrily, I pull it over my head, only to feel a hot gust of air. *Good Lord!* I stand under it for several minutes, my head beginning to burn with the heat. Then, just as suddenly, it stops. I push the infernal thing away, then check my hair. It is dry to the touch but definitely in need of a brush. I leave the washroom and find my brush on the dressing table, running it through my hair until it is free of tangles. Then, finally, I return to bed and settle under the covers. Some moments later, Broek speaks to me one last time. "Good girl," he says. Then I tuck my head into the pillow and sleep.

CHAPTER 17

JANE

I lie in the plush comfort of the bed, wondering sleepily whether all this is a freakish dream that I have yet to wake from. Memories of yesterday trickle into my conscious mind, but I push them away. It cannot be true. I have imagined it all and soon, I shall waken to the normal course of things.

Seemingly out of nowhere, Broek's voice breaks into my thoughts. "Jane, are you up? Hurry and dress, for we sit to breakfast in less than half an hour."

My heart jolts in alarm. I do not know if I can ever become accustomed to a voice that speaks to me through some devilish contraption in the wall. It is not natural. And also, instantly, I realise that I am not, after all, in the midst of a dream.

"Broek," I breathe in agitation. "You gave me a fright."

There is a pause, then he replies, voice rough and low, "Do not fear me, Duchess. You will come to no harm here."

That is a matter for some debate. "One could argue that it is harmful to lose one's liberty," I mutter.

He ignores the remark. "Get dressed and come down," he instructs me crisply.

"I want to see Chloe," I say.

"Then you had better hurry," he counters smoothly. "Horis is with her now in the medical bay. Go see her then come straight to breakfast. And Jane—" His voice takes on a menacing edge as he continues, "Do not make me have to come fetch you." I shudder in memory at how he carried me out of the medical bay yesterday while I kicked and cried for him to set me down. His meaning is clear. He will do it again unless I bow to his wishes. Why Julius Caesar himself has nothing on this dictator. One, moreover, that is holding me captive in this house. Captive! The very notion of it is preposterous. Surely no one can keep me here against my will.

"If the word *offscreen* can shut off the picture screen," I grumble, thoroughly unamused, "then surely there is a way to shut off the sound of your voice."

"There is, but I would be a fool to tell you," he replies coolly. "I shall see you at breakfast." The silence that follows tells me I have been just as coolly dismissed.

Fully awake now, I throw back the covers and rise from the bed. I enter the washroom and make use of the odd commode, then remember to wave my hand under the tap for water to come out. I will concede, privately only to myself, that of all the peculiar contraptions in this house, this one is a useful creation. The voice in the wall, not so.

I hurry back into the room, anxious now to be with Chloe. Betsy has already set my underclothes and gown on a chair in readiness for me, so it is a quick matter for me to dress. Once ready, I go to the door and turn the knob, almost expecting to find it locked. Am I not a prisoner here? But no, it opens, smooth and sleek, with nary a whisper of a squeak. Much good this silent approach does me, for on the other side of the door stands none other than my guard. At least, I believe this person is there to guard me. I am unused to females working in such a capacity, but this one is unlike most females I know. She is a veritable Amazon, standing almost a foot taller, and far broader than me. And from her great height, she gazes at me with contemptuous loathing.

"Good morning," I venture. "Miss?"

"Call me Catana," she says curtly. Then she swivels on her heels and strides along the corridor, expecting me no doubt to follow in her train. This I do, for I am keen to get to my daughter. In terse silence, we negotiate the steps down to the ground floor and turn the corner of the corridor until we reach the white door of the medical bay. There, she shifts to one side of it, crosses her arms to her ample breast and glares at me expectantly. I do not know quite what I have done to earn this woman's ire, but I have better things to occupy my mind than to wonder about it. I reach a hand to open the medical bay door and enter forthwith.

Inside, the room is bright and white, as I remember it. My eyes fly to the cot where Chloe lies, a still, slumbering form. I go to her, my throat tight with apprehension. Loud in my ears is the whoosh of the contraption that, so I understand, flows air into her lungs to help her to breathe. Her mouth is obscured by a mask to which is attached a long tube. Her sweetly long lashes cast a shadow over her pale face. My poor, poor girl. I sink into the chair beside Chloe and take her hand. It feels cool to my touch.

"She has made excellent improvement overnight," Horis assures me from where he stands by the screen on the wall, reading the strange symbols on it. He turns to smile at me. "If she continues to show such progress, then we should be able to reduce the dosage of her sleeping draught in another day."

"Will she wake then?" I ask, hope rising in my breast.

"I believe so, though it may take some time. The process of healing cannot be rushed." I nod my understanding though wish fervently that it could indeed be rushed. I will not rest easy until my girl opens her eyes and speaks her first words to me. With a slight bow, Horis takes his leave, and I am left alone with Chloe. I sit and watch her, murmuring a prayer under my breath.

Without any notice, the door opens, and that Amazon of a guard, Catana, rakes me with her unfriendly gaze. "It is time to go to the dining room," she says without preamble. Krilea is there too, a reassuring smile on her face as she goes to check on Chloe. I am tempted to protest the summons, but wiser counsel prevails. I nod and rise to my feet, giving Chloe's hand a final gentle squeeze. Then I am following Catana, having to walk so rapidly to keep up with her pace that I am almost breaking into a run. Well really. Where have grace and manners disappeared to?

A trifle breathless, I arrive in the large dining room, which I remember from my previous visit to Reeves Hall. Several people sit around the table, of which I recognise all four of the Reeves siblings. Their chatter ceases at my appearance in their midst. All eyes follow me as I go to find my seat. There is only one empty space, the same seat I took the last time I was here, beside Broek at the head of the table. With grave courtesy, he rises to his feet and pulls out the chair for me. I thank him quietly as I sit.

Conversation resumes around me, though I am little in the mood to take part in any of it myself. I do not forget that I am here as an uninvited guest. A footman serves me coffee and fresh rolls of crusty bread thereupon Broek dishes up some scrambled eggs for me and passes the butter. What gentlemanly manners! One could almost forget the minor fact of my being held here as his captive. But of course, I do not forget. And being the contrary character that I am, I cannot fail to bring the matter up.

"If I am to remain at Reeves Hall," I say while casually buttering my bread, "then how is my disappearance to be explained. I am expected to arrive in Frome any day now to take possession of my new cottage, and should I not arrive, questions will no doubt be asked."

"I have thought of this," he replies, not in the least disconcerted. "You will write to your solicitor and inform him that you have had second thoughts about purchasing the cottage and that you will be remaining at Penhale Manor as my tenant after I so very generously offered you the property at a most reasonable rent."

"I will write no such thing," I reply with great resolution.

"Oh, I think you will," he affirms calmly. "It is a much better choice than the alternative proposition."

I regard him suspiciously while my mind races to consider alternatives, with little success. He sees my confusion and almost smiles, the great oaf! Finally, he deigns to explain himself. "If you don't write the letter, news shall reach society at large that the Duchess of Coleford's carriage suffered a devastating accident, overturning on the road and falling down a great ditch, thereby mortally wounding all of its occupants. Do not doubt, Duchess, that I have the means at my disposal to create convincing evidence of your demise, and I can do it without harming a single hair on your tiny body."

I take umbrage at this last remark, for it is much easier to attend to such trivial things than the more serious matter of my demise, real or otherwise. "I may be small, sir, but tiny is taking it too far," I respond with great dignity.

He huffs, unimpressed, and reaches over to a dish a little further down the table, from which he serves me a flat, pancake-like food that is evidently not any pancake that I know of, given that it is of a purplish colour. I stare down at it on my plate. "Would you be so good as to tell me what this is?" I ask finally.

Broek's sister answers from where she sits across the table from me, "These are Uvonian pancakes, Your Grace, a great delicacy in the land we come from."

Uvonian? Might that, or perhaps Uvon, be the name of their home country? I tuck the information away in my mind for later consideration, then take my first, very cautious bite of this purple food. I am agreeably surprised. It is light, with a delicately moist crumb, and slightly but not cloyingly sweet.

Encouraged, I take some more. Observing me, Laura Reeves laughs, "I take it our gastronomy meets with Your Grace's approval."

"Thank you, it is unusual but pleasantly palatable," I say, then seeing the friendliness of her manner, I feel bound to ask, "Are you easy with the notion, Miss Reeves, that I am to be held captive in this house?" I cannot quite conceal the bitterness of my tone.

She gives me a nonchalant shrug, but it is Broek that answers on her behalf. "Duchess," he says, "We do not wish you any ill, but the life of every single person sitting at this table, except for yourself, would be put in grave danger should the manner of how we live ever come to public knowledge. And so to answer your question, she and all of us are very easy with the notion of holding you captive here."

I bristle. "That is to assume that I would talk about what I have seen at Reeves Hall. I do assure you that I can and will maintain my silence on the matter. You have my word of honour on it."

He shakes his head gravely. "No doubt you are right, but Duchess, we cannot put your word to the test. The consequences would be devastating, should it be proved false."

I turn my gaze to the other occupants of the room and see several faces nod in agreement. Horis smiles shyly in my direction then assures me, quite earnestly, "Do not think of this as captivity, Your Grace, but as your new home where I hope we can make you feel very welcome. You will have every luxury here and want for nothing. Chloe will not only have the best care, but once she is recovered, she will have other children to play with too." He points with his chin to a man, sitting at the other end of the table. He looks vaguely familiar, but I cannot place where I have seen him before. "Wolkan, our chief of security, has twin daughters the same age as Chloe. They will be good company for her." Oh he is wily, this shy, gentle Reeves brother, thinking to appeal to my motherly nature. I am almost but not quite convinced. Captivity is captivity, no matter how gently couched it might be.

My gaze lands on Simon, the youngest of the Reeves brothers. He it was that showed me great kindness on the evening of the dinner party. I study him now and see him look down at his plate in discomfiture. Of all the people here, he it seems, is not so easy with the notion of holding me captive. I take note of that information for another day.

My eyes are pulled back towards Broek, a silent presence at my side, who is observing me closely. He raises a sardonic brow, telling me in so many words that I had best do as he says. I look down at my food, my appetite gone, and examine my limited choices, coming to a fast decision. "Very well," I murmur. "I shall write a letter to my solicitor."

CHAPTER 18

JANE

The day passes slowly. I write a letter to Mr Oakley, as instructed, then resume my vigil by Chloe's side. The thought of being a captive here holds no fear for me in comparison with the dread that my daughter may never wake. What use is freedom if my heart is broken?

I sit and watch Chloe's sleeping face, wondering if I shall ever see her mischievous smile again. Over and over, I berate myself. Why had I not held on to her hand when she had gotten out of the carriage? The road to Penhale is not a busy one, but it is a road nonetheless, with horses and carriages travelling at great speed. If only I could be allowed to venture back in time so that I could change the tragic course of events. A time travelling machine! Now that would be a marvellous and worthy scientific invention—far better than a contraption that allows people to talk to me through a wall.

"Jane," Broek's voice says, coming through the infernal wall and nearly making me jump out of my skin.

"Broek," I gripe. "Must you always give me such a fright?"

"You shall have to accustom yourself to it, Duchess. It is the way we communicate with each other here."

"It is unnatural to speak to someone without seeing them in the flesh," I retort.

"It will become natural to you in due course," he responds equably. "Now, Duchess, I have not disturbed your peace merely to converse. I wish you to know I am leaving on business for a few days and that you may walk freely around the house. Should you wish to go outside for some air, inform Wolkan—

Horis will show you how to call him on the communicator. But Duchess…" He pauses and his voice when he resumes is such that I can be in no doubt that his face is wearing a dark scowl. "Do not even think of trying to walk out of the confines of Reeves Hall or try to send a message to anyone outside. You will not be allowed to do so."

"You cannot keep me here forever," I point out reasonably.

I hear his weary sigh. "I am not in the business of dealing in forevers," he says eventually. "Let us just say, for the foreseeable future, you are to remain here as my guest."

"As your prisoner," I correct.

"Have it your way, Duchess. Now, I must go." And then he is gone. That is another thing I dislike about conversations through a machine in the wall. There is no courteous bow of farewell, merely a sudden and deafening silence.

I spend the day in the medical bay, leaving only to take my luncheon and dinner when Krilea comes in to sit with Chloe in my stead. I hear the hustle and bustle of a lively household on my occasional forays out to the retiring room. It is clear that several persons live in this house, more so than I had originally thought.

I question Horis about this the next time he comes in. "Yes," he agrees, "there are many of us here. In addition to my brothers and sister, thirty-six loyal servants accompanied us to England." I take note of this new information, adding it to what I have learned already. The Reeves siblings, for an unspecified reason, have been banished from their country, and with them on their exodus came a large group of loyal servants. I can only surmise that their family must have been an important one back on Uvon, or whatever is the name of their far-off, mysterious country. This is a worryingly large number of people whose interest lies in stopping me from leaving Reeves Hall. Do all of them want me to stay captive? Or is it just Broek? It seems I shall have my work cut out to make my escape, when Chloe is well enough for me to attempt it. When, not if. She must get well. And we must leave. Those are the two incontrovertible imperatives.

"The west wing of the house is for the sole use of myself, my brothers and my sister, and now you, Your Grace," Horis continues. "The east part of the house, where we are now, has separate quarters for family retainers. Wolkan, whom you have met, resides here with his wife and children, others too. Several of them have married since coming to England, and with their growing families, require more living space than can be found in the house. That is one reason why Broek was keen to acquire Penhale Manor."

I nod, beginning to make more sense of this great puzzle, though there are still very significant gaps. "And you were all banished from Uvon," I say casually. "What crimes did you commit to be so punished?"

He looks taken aback at my perspicacity. "I see I shall have to watch my words," he says ruefully. "However," he adds with finality, "I believe Broek should be the one to explain." He stands to leave but casts a last glance at Chloe before doing so. "She is doing as well as I could have hoped at this stage," he tells me. "We need to be patient, but I do believe she will recover." With one final smile, he exits the room.

Later that evening, he returns to take over the vigil from me, instructing me to retire to bed for the night. "I will stay with her, then Krilea," he promises. Reluctantly, I give Chloe a kiss goodnight, then go up to my bedchamber where Betsy attends to me. I settle into bed, sinking my body into the softest of sheets. There can be no doubting that I am being well treated here at Reeves Hall.

I reflect back on dinner with Horis, Liora and Simor—for I have learned their true names. It had been a quiet yet pleasant affair. I had felt Broek's absence keenly, despite his usual silence at mealtimes. The man's presence is powerful. He has the rare ability to both comfort and rile me at the same time. To their credit, his siblings made an effort to include me in their discourse. There is an easy affection between them, and to me they showed great courtesy.

I sigh as I pull the covers over me. Everything seems to have gone topsy-turvy. This is no ordinary captivity I am experiencing. I am more an honoured guest than a prisoner. The truth remains, however, that I am not permitted to set foot outside the grounds of Reeves Hall. And my Chloe lies immobile in a white, windowless room while her body is attached to strange contraptions. *Please Lord, let her wake.* Wanting absolute darkness so I can lose myself in the numbness of sleep, I instruct, "Lights out." Soon, the room falls dark, and I tumble into a deep slumber.

NEXT DAY, I am quietly reading a book by Chloe's side when my prayer is finally answered. "Ma," she croaks. I nearly drop the book in my haste to go to her. I stand and lean towards her, so that I am in the line of her vision, stroking very gently the hair back from her face.

"Sugar plum," I say, calling her by an affectionate name her father used for her and that I have taken to use too since Giles's passing.

Her eyes blink, trying to take in the strange surroundings and then fixing on the only familiar thing—me. "It hurts," she moans softly.

"I know, my darling," I say soothingly. "You fell and hurt your head, but we shall give you something soon to help take that pain away."

I press the button on the wall and speak into it, summoning Horis, the way he showed me. He is not long to arrive. With a kindly smile, he examines Chloe, speaking to her in reassuring tones. Once he is done, he turns to me and states, "It is good news, Your Grace. My examination reveals there is no lasting damage, and your daughter should make a complete recovery."

I take a deep breath of relief and let it out, though I cannot yet rest easy. "She is in pain," I say.

"Yes, her head is still sore. Now that I have ascertained her brain function is sound, I may give her a draught for the pain. It will send her to sleep again though, so please do not be concerned if she falls unconscious again."

I nod my understanding, then kiss Chloe's cheek. "Sugar plum, Horis is going to give you something to help take the hurt away. Rest, my love, and you shall soon feel better. Shall I sing you a lullaby or read you a story?"

"Story," she murmurs weakly.

"Very well," I say, then begin to recount Puss in Boots. By the time I am finished, she is asleep once more.

CHAPTER 19

JANE

Over the next few days, I settle into my new life here at Reeves Hall, my time spent mostly in the medical bay with Chloe, with the exception of luncheon and dinner. I have also been for short walks in the parkland when I have been in need of fresh air and exercise. Always during these walks, I have been followed by a guard at a distance, though thankfully I have not seen that glaring Amazon again.

Of Broek, there has been no sign. Horis is reticent when I ask, telling me simply that his brother is gone to London on business. I do not like to admit, even to myself, that I miss his glowering presence.

Sunday comes, and I am reminded yet again of my captivity, for I am left behind at Reeves Hall while Horis, Liora and Simor go to church. "You should count yourself lucky," says Simor cheerfully as he bids me goodbye. "I wish I did not have to sit an interminable hour listening to Reverend Horton's rambling."

Although I am always one to count my blessings, I am afraid I cannot agree with Simor there. Faith in the good Lord is what has sustained me through each hardship of my life. Rather than joining everyone at church as would be right and proper, I have to content myself with reading some psalms and kneeling in prayer in the privacy of my room.

The following day, Horis deems Chloe improved enough to leave the medical bay. She has been given a room, with Betsy for company, which lies opposite to mine. I marvel at how quickly she is healing from her ordeal. The bandages on her head and side have been removed, only a darkened scab remaining as evidence of her accident. Later in the day, she receives a visit from Melda and Truphi, Wolkan's twin daughters, and it is a balm to my heart to hear her joyful laugh once more as she plays with the two little girls.

Tuesday, there is still no sign of Broek, but a letter awaits me when I go down to breakfast. I am glad I am still allowed to receive correspondence. But perhaps it has already been read, and deemed safe? I break the seal and read a missive from Mr Oakley. He notes my decision to remain at Penhale Manor and informs me that the proceeds from its sale have been invested in the funds, which should increase my annual income to £550. He goes on to write that this ought to provide sufficient monies for the rent that I am to pay Mr Reeves. Little does he know! Nevertheless, it is reassuring to be reminded that, should I ever find a way out of this place, Chloe and I shall have the funds to live comfortably.

I hand the letter over to Liora, who waits on expectantly, and she reads it before returning it to me. Horis clears his throat. "Erm, Your Grace, there is another matter I wanted to broach," he says timidly. "Now that you are a permanent member of our household, it is incumbent that you have a full medical check, as is mandatory for everyone here."

I raise my brow in confusion. Why would I need this if I am in the full bloom of health? I say as much to him and he chuckles, "It is the way with us. Once every six months, each one of us undergoes a check to ensure that all is well with regards to our health. The diagnostics equipment in the medical bay can identify disease before it manifests itself as symptoms in the body. Our approach is to prevent rather than treat ill health."

"I see," I reply cautiously. "Very well then."

"Good," he smiles. "How about I see you in the medical bay in an hour?"

And that is how I come to be lying on the white cot, dressed only in a loosely fitting, thin gown that I was given to change into when I arrived. "Please stay as still as possible, Your Grace," Horis instructs. "Shortly, the bed is going to move inside this tube where there is equipment that will take images of the inside of your body. It is painless, though you shall hear some buzzing noises for a time." He shows me a button to the side of the cot. "Press this at any time if you feel too distressed to continue," he says, which I do not find reassuring at all.

Nonetheless, I determine to face this unknown procedure with steely composure. That is not to say I am able to prevent my heart from leaping when I sense the cot begin to move and I find myself enclosed in this tomb-like space. Soon after, I am assaulted by red light and noise, though there is, thankfully, no pain. I close my eyes and submit to my fate, reciting a prayer for sustenance. I do not know how long I am inside this nightmare of a tomb, but finally, my ordeal is over.

The cot moves back out into its usual position in the medical bay. There, I find Horis busy at the big screen on the wall, examining various images and symbols. "So, Horis, am I at death's door?" I ask, trying to make a feeble joke of the matter.

He turns to me with a laugh. "Nothing of the sort. You are in excellent health, Your Grace." Well, I could have told him this. In fact, I am very sure I did. He comes towards me now holding a small implement made of glass, with a pointy metal end.

"What is that?" I ask warily.

"You will only feel a pinch, I promise," he says in reply. "I am merely taking a small sample of your blood."

"I remember distinctly your disdain for our doctors, and their practice of bleeding patients," I respond tartly. I do not like the idea of being pinched and bled—and frankly, I am glad never before to have needed the services of a doctor, not even when I delivered Chloe, for then I was attended by a very capable midwife.

"And well I might be disdainful!" exclaims Horis. "Rest assured, Your Grace, that what I am about to do has nothing in common with the backward practices of your quacks. They propose to bleed their patients to rid the body of impure fluids. What nonsense! No, what I shall do is to take a very small amount of your blood so that I may examine it for signs of any ill health."

"Then get it done quickly," I tell him, unable to mask the nervous impatience in my voice. I am not of a saintly nature, I am afraid, nor have I ever made a claim to be. He reaches for my arm, and I feel a little more than a pinch, but then thankfully, the matter is done.

He goes away again, no doubt to have a good inquisition of my blood. I let my eyelids droop as I endeavour to return to even breaths and allow my poor heart to stop hammering in my chest.

Then, he is back once more, adjusting the cot to a sitting position. I raise a brow. "Well?" I enquire.

He comes to sit at my side and says, "There is a minor infection—nothing to worry about—but I shall give you a draught for it now. I can also administer the pregnancy prevention shot at the same time, if you wish. It is standard practice to do so, unless you are intending to procreate again in the near future."

I stare at him as if he has grown two heads. Did I hear him correctly? He sees my look and blushes; well he might for the impertinence of the question. "I did not mean to offend," he goes on to say. "We, over here and in our homeland, have a different perspective on morality when it comes to, erm, to sexual activity. It is accepted—nay it is even expected—that all persons who have reached adulthood are active sexually. You see, we do not need the sanctity of marriage to engage in what we see as a natural act."

"But that is immoral!" I splutter.

"Not in our eyes," he responds gently. "However, we do exercise caution when it comes to procreation. We believe it is in the best interest of children and our society as a whole for couples to be in a formal union before they procreate. As you are not in such a union at present, Your Grace, I would suggest administering the shot. It is painless, I promise, and will not harm you in any way. It will simply stop you from conceiving a child over the next six months."

"I have no intention of conceiving, with or without your shot," I state icily.

"Then will you allow me to give it to you now?"

I shrug, pretending an insouciance I do not feel. "It is no matter whether you do or not," I proclaim loftily, "for I shall not be engaging in any immoral act. Of that you may be assured."

He nods in understanding then fetches the medicine he is to administer. I glance at the vial in his hand suspiciously. "Only a pinch," I say.

"Only a pinch," he affirms. Quickly, he gets it done, and for once, he is telling the truth, for I feel only a mild discomfort. In the realm of my mind though, the discomfiture is great indeed. What sort of a people are these Uvonians if their morals are so lax as to applaud sexual congress without marriage? I had thought that a scientifically advanced society would also be advanced in other ways, but not so, it seems. I cannot help another unsettling thought. If all adult Uvonians are expected to engage in sexual congress, then is Broek doing so, and in that case, with whom? Could it be with that female guard, Catana? That would in some way explain her hostility to my presence here. I feel a constriction somewhere in the region of my chest.

The thought of Broek consorting with this Catana is not a happy one, though I am not sure why this should matter so to me. I am attracted to him, yes, but I am not so weak as to have developed feelings for the man. Perish the thought!

As soon as I am able, I change back into my gown—in the privacy of an anteroom, of course, and not within Horis's presence—then go to find Chloe. After making enquiries, I discover her in what looks to be a play room, for it is filled with toys. Under Betsy's supervision, she is playing happily with her two new friends.

On seeing me, she beams. "Ma, come see." She beckons me over to a contraption in the centre of the room. It is circular in shape and sits on four sturdy wooden legs. The centre of it is covered in a thick sort of shiny fabric. All around its edges are plush cushions scattered on the floor. With surprising strength, Chloe pushes herself on her arms and climbs atop this contraption. The next instant, she is bouncing up and down like an acrobat, the strange fabric laid on it exerting some sort of propelling force, sending my daughter flying high and shrieking with joy.

"Chloe!" I rush over to her, my heart pounding wildly. She could injure herself. A hand on my arm stays me.

"It is quite safe," says a woman whom I recognise as Udra, the mother of the twin girls. She smiles. "Truly, your daughter will come to no harm."

I smile back uncertainly and watch Chloe. After a time, I find my worry begin to ease. I do not quite see the wisdom of creating such a contraption for children, but there can be no doubt that Chloe is enjoying herself enormously and not coming to any harm with it.

I spend some time conversing with Udra and watching over Chloe. Soon, however, a light growl in my belly reminds me that it is nearly time for luncheon. I excuse myself and head towards my bedchamber to refresh myself. There are several turns to take in the corridor, for this house is large and something of a labyrinth. I navigate a wrong turn, then correct my course. Eventually, with a little puff of victory, I manage to reach the west wing, where my bedchamber is located. I turn the knob and enter the room, needing to avail myself of the commode in the washroom. On fleet steps, I go there, pushing open the door in my haste, then come to an abrupt stop.

The washroom is hazy with steam, the source of which I quickly discover is the rain shower—another newfangled contraption located behind a door made entirely of glass. Under that shower, a person is bathing. A very tall and broad person, whose bare buttocks are clearly visible through the glass. I stare and stare some more. *Broek*. It is him, back from his travels. And he is bathing in my washroom. I had known that it connected to his bedchamber, but I had not gone so far as to think this meant it was his washroom too. I see now my mistake.

I ought to leave. The man will not thank me for this intrusion, and really, it is not at all seemly for me to be here. Yet I am like stone, unable to move even an inch. Presently, the water stops raining on him, and he opens the glass door, brushing wet clumps of hair from his brow as he steps out. Still, I do not move. I cannot. The sight before me is simply too arresting. I have not ever beheld such a magnificent exposition of masculine beauty—strong limbs and an exquisitely carved chest, all dusted with fine dark hair that sticks wetly to his golden skin. And at the juncture of his thighs. Oh my gracious Lord! Amid a dark nest of hair there hangs a long and thick shaft, the size of which has my eyes bulge. It swings a little from side to side with the motion of his body.

Then Broek sees me and stops. He makes no move to cover himself. Instead, he stands, hands on hips, and lets me look my fill as rivulets of water drip down his formidable body. I know

I ought to make my excuses and flee, but still, I cannot. I am no stranger to the sight of an unclothed man. After all, I have been married. Yet this…. this is powerful masculinity as I have never seen before, and I cannot look away. It is only when I see his male organ thicken and strain upwards that I come to my senses. "Forgive me," I whisper, and quickly retrace my steps out of the washroom.

On shaky feet, I stagger towards my bed and fall onto it. Burying my face in my hands, I take deep breaths to calm my excitement. I expect the door to fly open any moment with an irate Broek coming to chastise me for my wicked trespass. I hear the closing of a door beyond mine and realise he has entered his bedchamber to dress. I wait, thinking he will soon come to call. But he does not.

It is some minutes later that I hear his voice on that wretched wall contraption. "The washroom is free, Duchess, should you wish to use it. I shall see you at luncheon." Then he is gone.

CHAPTER 20

BROEK

I am already sitting at the head of the table when Jane enters the dining room. Quickly, I get to my feet and pull out the chair for her beside me. As I do, I scrutinise her pinkening cheeks. There can be no doubting what my little duchess is thinking about. Earlier in the washroom, I could have retrieved a towel and covered my nakedness, but I did not wish to, not when I caught the look of desire on her face. Instead I let her look and look her fill, though I could not stop the thickening of my cock.

Eyes cast down, Jane concentrates on her food, while I watch her silently, letting the sound of Liora and Simor's friendly bickering fill the quiet around us. By the time the second course is served, a side of poached salmon in a lightly creamed sauce with an array of steamed greens, I see her make a conscious decision to get over her embarrassment. My duchess shall not spend her meal, meek as a mouse, head bowed in shame. She looks up defiantly at me and says, with calm courtesy, "Your trip prospered, I hope."

In answer, I hark back to the other matter. "You do know, Jane, that there is a small indicator light on the door to inform you if the washroom is occupied."

"As a matter of fact, I did not know," she mutters. "I shall be sure to look for it. And so, to your trip. Was it a success?"

"It achieved its objectives," I shrug.

"And what were these?"

At first, I do not respond, considering whether I should allow her to pry into my affairs. There is no harm in it, I conclude, seeing as she is not going anywhere nor about to speak to any outsiders. There is also a strange urge within me to be frank with her. I am not in the habit of sharing details of my life with other people, but in much the same way as I have bared my body to Jane, I feel a compulsion to tell her something of myself.

In a gruff voice, I say, "I had business to attend to. A ship of ours has returned from its voyage to India with supplies of tea and calico. Though I have family retainers working at the docks for me, I like to be there when one of our ships arrives, to inspect the goods and ensure they are properly stored in our warehouse. Then of course, there is the business of negotiating the sale of these goods as well as to see to our other investments. I made a visit to the stock exchange to trade bonds and securities." I give her a pointed look and add, "Unlike the landed gentry of this country, who may sit back in their great houses and collect rents from their tenants, we of the merchant class must work to earn our money."

She responds tartly, "I hardly feel as if I belong to the landed gentry at all. My own father was a churchman, more in the business of saving souls than collecting rents—which might explain why he left me with very little in the way of material means when he departed this earth. And while it is true that my marriage to the late duke elevated me to that landed class for a time, my situation now cannot be said to be anything but that of an impoverished widow, dependent on funds invested in that very same stock exchange of which you made mention."

"In any case," she continues, "I see that you have done well out of it. I do not know with what wealth you arrived in England, but it is clear that you have prospered and that much of it is due to your efforts."

"Praise, Jane?" I mock.

"I tell it how I see it, that is all."

"Then you see it very well," interjects Horis. "I myself do not have a head for business as Broek does and could never manage our affairs half as successfully as he."

"Your talents, which are many, lie elsewhere," I reply with a snarl. "Do not belittle the importance of what you do here, Horis."

Jane watches this exchange with lively intelligence. I decide it is time to change the topic of conversation. Quietly I say, "I was glad to hear of Chloe's recovery."

Her eyes glitter with emotion as she replies, "I was never so glad as when she woke and spoke her first words to me. For this I must thank the good Lord, but also Horis. I am truly grateful." At the other end of the table, Horis nods his head shyly in acknowledgement. I gaze at him with gratitude in my heart too. If it had not been for his quick response, I do not think little Chloe would be alive with us today.

Then, I cannot help needling Jane. "I suppose now that Chloe is well," I remark, "you will put all your efforts into finding a way to escape Reeves Hall. Do not waste your time, Duchess, for your efforts will be fruitless."

She flashes me an angry glance. "What else is there to do with my time than to divine ways to end my captivity? It is not as if I have anything better to do."

"Suit yourself," I grunt, "but do not say I did not warn you. There is no possibility of leaving here without my consent, which I shall not give. Resign yourself to staying at Reeves Hall, Duchess. In terms of comfort, it is a far cry above Penhale Manor or even the rustic cottage you intended to live in. Some would consider themselves most fortunate to have found themselves in this situation."

"And yet," she says coldly, "the most precious of commodities—trust—is missing in this supposedly enviable situation. I am not trusted even to attend church service on a Sunday, for which I shall not count myself as fortunate."

I raise a brow in enquiry. "You wish to go to church?" The thought had not crossed my mind, I must admit.

"Evidently!"

"I would consider taking you there," I say, pondering the matter, "but for one thing. Everyone in the village believes you gone. We cannot have them see that you are still here."

She grasps at this fact. "What harm can there be in that? After all, Mr Oakley believes me to be residing at Penhale Manor. My appearance at church will only confirm the truth of this."

I cross my arms to my chest and scowl at her eagerness to be gone from Reeves Hall, which I am finding highly annoying. "Mr Oakley may believe what he likes, for he is far away," I growl. "However, the residents of Penhale will soon know that you are not in residence at Penhale Manor and conclude the truth—that you are here. Do consider, Duchess, what this will mean for your reputation as a woman of virtue to be seen living, unmarried, in my household."

"Well that's just it!" exclaims Liora, excitement lighting her face. "Broek, you must marry the duchess. It will solve so many of the evils of this situation."

"Marriage?" Jane cries in horror.

I study her sardonically while Liora continues to expound her idea. "Well of course! Why did we not think of this sooner? Just think, if you are married, then nobody will question your living at Reeves Hall and you shall be able to attend church, though goodness knows why you would wish to." She turns to me. "And marriage to a duchess will increase your respectability, Broek. Nobody would ever dare gossip openly about us or about witchcraft when you are allied to a titled lady of the realm. Besides which, it will be in the duchess's own interests to avoid gossip once she is married to you, so she will hardly want to tell people about the way we live here."

"I think that is an excellent idea," pronounces Horis.

"One of your better suggestions, Liora, definitely," agrees Simor.

I'll allow, the idea is not without its merits. I am in fact warming to it rapidly, but Jane, it seems, is not of the same mind.

She splutters, "Well pardon me if I disagree," and rises to her feet while I throw her a mocking gaze to mask my dismay at her lack of enthusiasm. "If you will excuse me," she says, "I shall go see to my daughter." And with great dignity, she makes her exit from the room.

CHAPTER 21

JANE

I occupy myself the rest of the day making sure to keep well away from any member of the Reeves family. How dare they suggest that I should marry Broek? It is a hare-brained idea. How could I ever besmirch the memory of my love match with Giles by marrying not just for convenience but to obtain a modicum of freedom from my captivity?

I cannot in all conscience do it. And regardless, I do not believe it would release me from the prison chains I am in. I would have to continue to live here, at Reeves Hall, under Broek's dictatorial rule. No, my future lies in making a good home for myself and Chloe, and living out a respectable life as a widow. I am not sure, in any case, that Broek would wish to marry me. He did not at all look enthused at the prospect. His reaction fills me with dismay, although of course, I have no desire to marry him either.

It would behove me, and others, to cast the idea from our minds. There shall be no marriage between Broek Reeves and me.

And yet, we are becoming friends—more than friends. A wicked voice in my head crows that as Broek's wife, I would get to see more of his gloriously naked form, to touch him, inhale his manly fragrance, and to feel the great size of his male appendage inside me. At this last thought, I have to fan myself, such is the heat flowing to my cheeks.

I am not sure why this idea excites me so. I did not mind very much the act of sexual congress between a man and his wife. At times it was pleasant, though more often it was something of a chore. I gladly gave myself to Giles, taking satisfaction in seeing his pleasure. I did not relish the mess it made of the sheets afterwards, nor the need to wash that sticky and sometimes pungent residue of the act from my body. And yet I cannot deny, the thought of Broek filling me with his girth—and length—is thrilling.

I shake the thought away. It will not be. I must keep to my course and formulate a plan. Somehow, I will convince Broek that he can trust me, so that he lets me go.

I approach dinner with some trepidation, but there is no further mention of marriage. Broek continues to watch me closely, a closed expression on his face. I cannot fathom what he is thinking. Is he seriously considering marrying me? As soon as I am able, I make my excuses and retire to my room, first looking in on Chloe and reading her a bedtime story.

I go into the washroom and start a bath, not needing the services of Betsy to complete such a simple task. Certainly, it is the greatest of convenience to be able to fill the tub with hot water, merely at the touch of a button. I applaud the inventor, whoever he may be. I brush my teeth with tooth powder and rinse my mouth out, then undress. A moment later, I gently sink my body into the steaming water and sigh in contentment. Now this… this is something that would make me think twice about leaving Reeves Hall. Of course, I fully intend to end my captivity, but it is also true that I shall then miss this wonderful luxury. I must take advantage of it as much as I can before the day of my departure arrives. I close my eyes and let my mind wander in a happy reverie.

"Jane," booms Broek's voice through the washroom wall. I sit up in fright, splashing water over the edge of the tub in my haste. I do not at the best of times like the sudden assault of a voice speaking at me through the wall, but in the echoing confines of the washroom, the reverberation of it is most disconcerting.

"Broek," I declare angrily. "How many times have I told you not to startle me so."

"And I have told you it is something you must accustom yourself to."

"I had thought at the very least that you would not think to intrude on me in the privacy of the washroom," I say primly.

"I had thought the same too," comes his quick rejoinder.

I feel my anger rise. "That was a mistake, honestly made," I retort.

"And yet the mistake lasted an awfully long time, Duchess." He almost purrs this last.

That he is right does not make things any better. It would be best to end the conversation here and now. "Go away, Broek," I say curtly, resting my head back against the tub. "I am busy and not in any mood to converse."

There is no reply, and I begin to believe that he has indeed gone, without the courtesy of a farewell. Then I hear his voice again. "Do not fear that I shall force you into marriage, Duchess. I prefer my women willing."

I do not know why this vexes me when I have no intention at all of marrying the grumpy lout. "It is a preposterous idea," I tell him, trying to sound indifferent, "and I am glad we are in agreement on the matter."

"I did not say that it is a bad or preposterous notion," he contradicts, "only that I would not force you into it."

The exposed skin on my arms prickles. I lower myself further into the heat of the bath water, though it does not stop the tingles forming in my body. Does Broek actually wish to marry me? I whisper the question in a voice trembling with excitement.

He makes a grunting sound. "Wishing is too strong a word, Duchess. On consideration, I can see some merits to a marriage and would not be opposed to it."

"There will be no marriage," I say with finality. Am I trying to convince myself as well as him?

"As you wish, Duchess," he says coolly. "And for your information, there will be no visits to church. No one outside these walls is to know that you are living here."

"We shall see about that," I hiss quietly.

"Enjoy your bath, Duchess." Then he is gone, and I get out of the tub. There is no more pleasure to be had in it tonight.

I AM LYING in bed, sleep the furthest thing from my mind. There is too much to think about, and matters are not helped by an awareness, in every inch of my body, that Broek Reeves lies in his bed on the other side of the wall from me. I wonder if he is asleep. The hour is late, after all.

In any event, I decide to do it. Horis has shown me how. In a clear voice, I say, "Connect Broek." An instant later, a small click indicates that I am connected to the contraption on the wall of his room. "What is this talk I hear about witchcraft?" I demand.

"It is what happens when ignorant people see something they do not understand," he answers in a measured voice, not sounding in the least surprised at my intrusion.

"Who has been saying these things?"

He lets out a long breath. "I do not know exactly where the rumours originated. Some weeks ago, I happened to be in Newquay on a business errand when I came upon Timothy Drake. He invited me for a drink at the local tavern. When I spoke to the tavern keeper to order an ale, the man refused to meet my eyes and acted in quite a rude manner." He pauses, then continues, "I did not think anything of it, except Drake noticed, of course, and looked damned uncomfortable about it. It made me begin to suspect that something was the matter, so I questioned him. At first, he refused to say anything, then it all came out. He told me rumours were rife about our family being part of a pagan cult that practises a form of witchcraft. He disclaimed any belief in this gossip himself, but thought that it was fuelled by the strangeness of our ways, although he could see this was most likely explained by us having lived abroad for so many years."

"Vile ignorance," I mutter in disgust.

"Indeed. It is the reason why we decided, against my better judgement, to hold a dinner party to present our family as 'ordinary' to the world outside."

"Why against your better judgement?"

He sighs. "Duchess, I do not like to allow outsiders into this house. There is too much risk that they will discover things that will raise questions about us. Your little foray into the parlour being a case in point."

I shift in the bed to a more comfortable position. "Tell me, Broek," I ask, "why were you banished from Uvon?"

He grunts, "I see someone has a loose tongue. Was it Horis?"

I do not answer, waiting for his reply.

He is quiet for several instants, and I fear that he will not tell me. Then he begins to speak in a deeply resonant voice, as if to himself. "Mother and Tarla—the two females I loved and trusted most. They are the reason for our banishment."

He stops, and I prompt, "What did they do?" At the same time, I am wondering who this Tarla might be.

"You must understand, Jane," he says quietly, "that I come from a powerful and privileged family. We do not have an aristocracy on Uvon with titles like you do here, yet it was understood that in the hierarchy of our society, we stood high above the rest."

I hesitate to breathe, lest I interrupt the flow of his narrative. I wait while he collects his thoughts, saying nothing. Eventually, he resumes his story. "Mother was the matriarch of our formidable family, for you see on Uvon, males and females have an equal footing. Father was like her shadow, playing the role of consort, but she was the one with the power and the ambition. In Uvon, we do not have a monarchy or a parliament. Instead, we are ruled directly by a governing body that consists of six delegates elected for a term of ten years, with no possibility of re-election. Mother was one of these six delegates. It should have been enough to have reached that highest level of power, but it was not. When she reached her ninth year on the governing body, she was not ready to relinquish her position. She was still thirsty for more. Power is an intoxicating thing, Duchess, once one has had a taste of it. For some, it becomes a craving."

I hear the bitterness in his voice. Quite clearly, his mother's thirst for power had catastrophic consequences for the family. "I have little experience of wielding any power over others," I muse out loud, "nor of its intoxicating effect. I wonder what it would be like, to be one of a select few to rule an entire nation. I cannot quite imagine it."

He laughs harshly. "You have had more experience of fighting against the evils of others who would wish to dictate to you what you ought to do, is that not so?"

"Yes," I agree. "In my life I have been far too used to subservience, not the other way around." I give a little huff of disgust. Then I turn my attention back to Broek's story. "What happened in her ninth year?"

"Tarla," he says flatly.

"Who was she?"

"The most beautiful woman I have ever known," he says wistfully. "It was not just the perfection of her face that made her beautiful. It was her wit, her vivacity, her passion for living. No sooner had I met her than I was lost." At his words, I try very hard not to feel envy for this unknown woman, but I am not quite up to the task. It is a fact that I am no more than ordinary looking. I have already experienced a miracle once in my life—that of a handsome duke falling in love with me. It is in the realm of unlikelihood that another such miracle should occur. Not that I want another duke to love me, but to have a man see me in all my ordinariness and feel passion would be something tremendous indeed.

Broek continues his tale. "We were together for two years and had planned to join in a union—that is what we call marriage in Uvon. Tarla was already a celebrity in her own right. Her songs and poems were known all over the land. Everybody loved Tarla. Her name was on everyone's lips. And through me, she met Mother. That was when she decided she wanted to seek election to the governing body. There was a vacancy, you see, as one of the incumbents had died suddenly, and Tarla wanted to take his place."

I am beginning to see where this story might be heading. "I suppose she was successful in that election," I say.

"Yes, she was," he confirms. "I had at my disposal the scientific knowledge to help her win. You see, Jane, I am the inventor of tiny recording devices, no bigger than a grain of sand, that can be launched in their millions all over the land. The information they gathered was invaluable. We were able to anticipate changes in voters' opinions and react instantly with the right messages to swing them to our camp. As a result, Tarla won a resounding victory."

"What you describe," I ponder, "is an all-seeing eye. It is almost like playing God."

He laughs, but there is no amusement in his voice. "As usual, Jane, you have the right of it. You may imagine therefore the intoxicating effect of wielding that sort of God-like power, and the guilt that follows." I begin now to understand that the grimness of Broek's disposition might in part be due to a sense of culpability for the role he played in this sorry tale.

"Tell me the rest," I beg him.

"There is not much more to tell. Tarla planted the seed of the idea. What if there could be two super-delegates who controlled the governing body? Mother and Tarla, ruling jointly. Unknown to me, they plotted, thinking to facilitate their ascent through the use of my nanoprobes—that is the name of my invention."

"Something went wrong with their plans, did it not?" I question.

"I am not sure how the information was leaked, but Tarla was first to learn of it and she quickly turned the tables on Mother, accusing her of plotting a treasonous act with the help of her son—thereby implicating me in the plot."

I sit up in the bed, awash with rage. "How dare she!" I cry.

"It was to save herself, Jane," he says dryly. "Like a rat fleeing a sinking ship, she knew she had to put a clear distance between herself and my family. She denounced Mother and me the day before we were due to celebrate our union."

"Oh, the black-hearted, wicked woman," I say on a gasp. "May the loathsome creature burn in eternal hell!" I continue, unable to contain my righteous anger.

Broek allows me to rage against the despicable woman without interruption. Finally, he says, much too mildly given the shocking nature of the matter, "It is all in the past now and best forgotten, but that is why I was banished."

I am about to disagree. Such a betrayal cannot be forgotten, ever. But another question comes to mind. "Why did not your mother come with you to England?" I enquire.

His voice is cold and final as he replies, "The penalty for treason is death."

"And your father?" I whisper, though I think I know the answer.

"He elected to die at her side."

"Broek," I murmur, too moved to utter the usual platitudes.

He must hear the distress in my voice, for he grits harshly, "Save your sympathy, Duchess. They are long gone." He adds, a little more softly, "Fortunately, there was no evidence to incriminate me, and my life was spared, though it was decided we all should be banished forever from Uvon, to set an example. Ten years ago, we left our home and have never looked back."

I digest this information. Finally, pieces of this puzzle are beginning to slot into place. I have one more question this night. "And your innovation, the nanoprobes, what of it?"

His laugh is bitter. "I could not leave it for others to misuse as Mother and Tarla planned to. I destroyed all evidence of them in Uvon and brought the knowledge for how to manufacture them with me. Over the course of the journey here, I created several thousand more nanoprobes, but I have never let anyone but myself have control of them—not even my brothers and sister. I used the probes on our arrival here and continue to do so as a way of gathering the knowledge to allow us to live in safety and comfort."

"So *you* are now the one with the God-like power," I murmur.

He grunts, "If you wish to see it that way. However, I only use the power to protect the people under my care."

I stretch my arms overhead and yawn, weariness descending upon me. Sleepily, I remind him, "You said power is intoxicating and leads a person to crave more."

"I have far too vivid an example of the pitfalls to ever crave it or find it intoxicating, Jane," he responds dryly. "I use the knowledge I obtain purely in the service of my people."

I turn to my side and burrow under the blanket. "One day, Broek, you will need to destroy the nanoprobes here too. Nobody, not even you, should have the power you describe."

"One day, maybe," he concurs, "but not yet."

My breaths deepen as I feel myself drift into slumber. I am nearly in the land of Nod when I hear him ask softly, "Today in the washroom. Did you like what you saw?"

I mumble indistinctly, "You already know the answer."

There is a smile in his voice as he says, "Goodnight, Jane." I do not respond, for I am already fast asleep.

CHAPTER 22

BROEK

I am at my console doing the usual scan of the hundreds of analysis reports from the data collected by my nanoprobes. This is something I do every morning and night, unless I am away on a business trip. I have become adept at quickly digesting information and logging away in my mind anything that could be of importance towards our shipping interests, our investments in stocks and in the security of our lives here at Reeves Hall. I am mindful also of any information that could be useful towards my mission.

There is something different about today though. As my probes' all-seeing eyes show me details of prominent people's lives, Lord Liverpool sitting at the bedside of his dying wife, a member of the cabinet having an illicit interlude with a much younger man—all details which I would usually log for future reference should I need any leverage over these individuals—I am reminded of Jane's words. *One day, Broek, you will need to destroy the nanoprobes here too. Nobody, not even you, should have the power you describe.*

What matter to me if a highly ranked politician of this country has an affair with a much younger man? Could there ever be a time where I would need to use this knowledge in the advancement of my family's interests? It is a possibility but a very minor one. We have wealth aplenty and a thriving mercantile business. Moreover, we live quietly and have no wish to walk among the members of the *haut ton*. And yet divesting myself of this tool that allows me to reach across the world into so many prominent people's lives is not an easy action. It would entail a loss of the power that sustains my sense of security in this alien land.

Power. Great Yol, am I turning into Mother, craving the rush of it? Try as I might, I cannot hate the memory of her, for I understand more than most the path she trod. Tarla, on the other hand, I can and continue to despise. Underhandedness and betrayal are harder to forgive than a reckless craving to continue exerting power. I have no doubt in my mind that had it not been for Tarla, Mother would have finished her term on the governing body and retired gracefully, most likely to dip her toes into other ventures. It was the evil whisperings in her ear that turned her astray, and I have to bear my share of the blame for creating the tools that were part of her downfall—the nanoprobes.

One day, Broek, you will need to destroy the nanoprobes here too. One day, yes. That day has not come yet, but it is drawing ever closer. I rub my eyes tiredly and stretch. I slept little last night after my twilight conversation with Jane. She drew out of me memories which I have long kept locked away, and once they were out, they plagued me relentlessly. I do not speak of the past. My brothers and sister know better than to bring the matter up. Yet at the prompting of this small whisp of a woman with a mighty will, I spilled my secrets. What is it about Jane that makes me so compelled to share such things with her?

That is not all this female has done. All night long, my cock was hard at the memory of her eyes on me, and the ardent desire I had seen in them. She did not deny it either. The duchess wants me, and Great Yol, I want her too. I palm my thickening cock, willing it to stand down. Only one woman can sate my need, yet she refuses to marry me. Damn her!

I am about to turn off the console and leave when an alert shows up on my screen. Someone is at the door hidden behind the wine racks, trying to gain entry. I touch a button to get a visual and am pleased to see Jane, her brow furrowed in concentration as she palpates the door, looking for a way to open it. She has evidently discovered the mechanism for pushing aside the wine rack and seen what it conceals. I always knew she was dangerously inquisitive.

Quickly, I get to my feet and head out into the corridor, towards that door. With all that she knows about us now, there is little harm in her seeing our below-ground operation. It is not as if I will be allowing her to leave Reeves Hall, at least not in any foreseeable future, and besides, I have an overwhelming urge to see her in the flesh. I get to the door and touch the button for it to swiftly slide open. Crossing my arms on my chest, I stand in the doorway. "Nosing about are we, Duchess?" I enquire with a sardonic raise of my brow.

Jane's eyes are wide with surprise. She grapples for a suitable response. "I—well, I was told I was free to explore this house."

I quirk my lips, trying not to smile. "So you were."

She tilts her head sideways, wanting to see what lies behind me. "What is this place?" she asks.

I step aside to let her in. "Why don't you come in and see?" I say.

She steps over the threshold and follows me, looking around curiously. "How interesting," she murmurs, almost to herself. "This is some sort of subterranean part of the house." We pass by various closed doors and she wonders out loud, "What is behind these doors?"

I point to the first one. "Behind this door is the source of the energy that made your fingers tingle when you touched that wall panel during our dinner party. It is also what provides the fuel to heat this house. You did not think the water that comes out of the spout is hot by magic, did you?"

Her mouth is a wide O. "May we go inside?" asks the inquisitive minx.

I shake my head. "Only qualified individuals are allowed in there." We walk on, and I point to another door. "Through here is the facility for providing us with clean water and disposing of all our waste. And no, you may not go inside." She makes a little moue of disappointment but wisely holds her counsel. Finally, we reach my control room. I let the security device scan my face while Jane watches in avid curiosity. A moment later, the door slides open, revealing my personal domain.

She follows me inside, her gaze taking in the multiple screens of my console that are currently displaying only a blank white background. She knows enough by now to realise that they can transmit moving images, as evidenced by her next words, "Did you see me on this screen just now when I was trying to open that door?"

"I did, Duchess. That is why I came straight over to let you in."

She nods, and I can tell by the crease of her brow that her mind is working rapidly, trying to put together all the information she has acquired and to reach the inevitable conclusion. "This is where you get to play God, is it not?"

"Yes," I rasp. I clear my throat and go on, "This is where I receive the information collected by the nanoprobes."

"Show me," she commands briskly.

I give her a wry look. "What is it you wish to see?"

She thinks for a moment then enquires, "Do you have the means to send the nanoprobes anywhere in this world?"

"Yes."

"Then may I see my uncle's house please?"

I take a seat in front of the console and tap out a few instructions. A moment later, the screen lights up to display visual images of the house where her uncle and aunt reside.

Jane gasps beside me and leans closer to the screen. "There it is," she says in wonder.

"There are several open windows," I say. "If you wish, I can instruct the probes to fly inside and transmit to us from within. Which room shall we enter?"

"Oh," she says, her eyes round with awe. "We can do that?"

"We can."

She points with her finger to a room on the first floor to the right of the house. "Let us go there," she declares.

I instruct the probes accordingly. An instant later, the visual moves closer to the house and begins to transmit images and sound from inside. In one corner of the room sits an older female at her desk. "Your aunt?" I ask.

She nods in reply, her eyes fixed on the female. "Get closer," she says imperiously. "I wish to see what she is doing."

With a quirk of my lips, I do as she says, moving the probes to hover just over the lady's shoulder. We watch as she carefully breaks the seal on a letter that is addressed to a *Mr Robert Price, esquire*. Beside me, Jane is muttering in disgust, "I knew it! She is reading my uncle's correspondence." I adjust the probes so that we may read the contents of the letter. It is a formal missive from a Mr Smithson at Drummonds Bank in Charing Cross, London.

Dear Mr Price,

I write in relation to the monies of your niece, Miss Jane Price (now Dowager Duchess of Coleford), held with Drummonds Bank, the sum of which currently stands at £5,790. As you are no doubt aware, the terms of the late John Price's will named your good self as executor and guardian of Miss Price in the event of the gentleman's decease. As per your instructions, the quarterly interest from these funds was disbursed to you in your role as guardian.

Such disbursements were terminated upon her marriage, and we were subsequently instructed by the Duke of Coleford to re-invest the interest into the funds on his wife's behalf, so as to provide for her, should the need arise in the future.

I understand that the Duke sadly passed on 16th February of this year. May I take this opportunity to convey my deepest condolences both to yourself and the Dowager Duchess on behalf of Drummonds Bank. I would be grateful, sir, if you could inform me of the Dowager Duchess's new directions so that I may write to her and request further instructions as to what she wishes done with her funds.

I remain your respectful servant,

Henry Smithson

I feel Jane stiffen beside me while she peruses the contents of the letter. Her chest heaves as she takes deep gulps of air. "I had no knowledge of this," she breathes in agitation. "All those years living at my uncle's house, I was made to understand that I had been left penniless, that they had taken me in from the goodness of their hearts as charity." She turns to me, her voice thick with the onset of tears, "I was made to live as a drudge in their home, barely better than a servant, while they stole what was mine. And then Giles, dear Giles, had the bank invest the money for my future. He was thinking of me. He loved me."

I watch in helpless horror as she bursts into loud sobs. I am not equipped to deal with such a thing as a lady's tears, let alone her sobs. At first, I gaze at her, unsure of what to do, but very soon, instinct has me part my legs and draw her into my embrace. Seated as I am, she is at the perfect height for me. She comes to me willingly, leaning forward and burying her face into the cloth of my coat as she cries her tears.

I hold her to me gently, patting her back to give comfort and let her cry it out. Eventually, she stops her sobs but remains in the shelter of my embrace. I find that I have buried my nose in the soft fragrance of her hair. I close my eyes and inhale her sweetness.

After a time, I hear her mumble into my coat, "God forgive me, but I had begun to think uncharitably of poor Giles. How could he have left me in such difficult straits? The truth is, all along he had ensured those funds were kept for me."

I say nothing but lift my head to look at the screen once more. There, I see Jane's aunt writing out a reply to the banker, ostensibly in her husband's name.

Dear Mr Smithson,

I thank you for your kind condolences and have conveyed them to my niece. With the entail on the late Duke's estate, all his properties have now passed to the new duke, and since the Dower House is also presently let out, I have in great charity taken in my niece and her young daughter to live with me in my home. With this change in circumstance, I would be grateful if you would resume the disbursements of the quarterly interest on the funds to my local bank in Frome, from which Jane shall draw whatever monies she requires.

Yours sincerely,

Robert Price, Esquire

As the lady rummages in a drawer for wax and a seal, I say quietly, "Jane, you may wish to see what your aunt has written."

She turns in my embrace to face the screen, though I keep my arms draped around her waist, anchoring her to me. She wipes her eyes with the back of her hand and quickly reads the missive. It is not long before the expected eruption occurs.

"Why the wicked witch!" she cries. "I cannot credit it. Even she would not sink so low."

"My faith in mankind is such that I can very well believe it," I bite back acidly.

Her voice takes on the steely determination that I so admire. "We cannot let her get away with this."

"She will not," I say grimly. "If you write to this Mr Smithson, I can have the letter reach him by the end of this day."

She turns back and fixes me with a quizzical glance. "How? The mail coach will take at least three days to reach London."

I hold her gaze and tell her, "Scientific innovations, Jane. Believe me when I say, your letter will reach Mr Smithson today."

She nods, too emotional at present to show much curiosity about it. "I will do it straight away," she says. It is then she notices my arms, still wrapped around her. She stills a moment, then says quickly, "Thank you, Broek."

I nod and let my arms drop. Together, we leave my control room and negotiate our way back to the basement door, which I shut securely behind us.

CHAPTER 23

JANE

It is late evening, and Betsy has just finished brushing out my hair. I say goodnight and dismiss her, then climb into the large bed, the luxury of which I am rapidly getting accustomed to. I ponder my next actions. It is too soon for sleep, and moreover, there has been much on my mind today.

I wrote my letter to Mr Smithson, telling him in the strongest terms that henceforth, he was to address all correspondence pertaining to my funds directly to me at Penhale Manor and never to involve my uncle in such matters again. I also instructed him to reinvest the interest back into my funds. I shall have no need of it at present, though it is greatly reassuring to know that once I am finally released from my captivity here, I shall have a generous income to live on with Chloe. We will not be rich, but we will be comfortable.

I glance at the book that lies on the table beside my bed. I ought to read, as I generally do before I sleep. Then I gaze ahead to the large screen on the wall before me. Remembering first to raise the covers to my neck, I say my command, "Connect Broek. *Onscreen.*"

A moment later, I hear the click of our connection and his voice instructing, *"Onscreen."* My screen comes alive, showing me Broek, also in his bed. But there, the similarity ends, for while I am covered to my neck, he sits with his back to the bed board, the sheet loosely draped in his lap. His chest is bare. In fact, I am beginning to suspect that he is not wearing any clothes at all, for I cannot see the edge of any drawers peeking from where the sheet lies atop him.

My breathing halts as I stare. Such a broad chest. So manly with all that dark hair. Firm brown nipples, peeking through the hair. Muscular arms, their skin a golden glow. Oh my gracious Lord!

Finally, my breath returns in a great big gasp. "Broek, you are not dressed," I chide.

"Should I be?"

"Well, of course," I declare with great certainty.

"It is not as if you have not seen it before, Jane, and this is how I sleep at night. Would you prefer I shut off the screen?"

Quickly, I cry, "No! Do not." Then, more softly, "You are right. A man's chest is nothing new to me. I was simply taken aback, that is all." I take a deep breath and start again. "Broek, I have been thinking."

He purses his lips. "What now?"

I sigh. "Broek, now that I have found out about my aunt's doings, I do not believe I could ever live in proximity to her. A cottage in Frome would not do for me and Chloe at all."

His lips curve almost into a smile. "Then it is a good thing you did not purchase that cottage," he replies smoothly.

"Yes, quite. But now that I am in comfortable funds, I must think where Chloe and I are to live."

He regards me steadily through the screen. "There is no need to tax your mind over the matter. You are to live here."

"Broek," I say, assuming my most reasonable tone, "I cannot stay here, and well you must know it." I hold up a hand to stop his speech as I continue, "I do understand, truly I do, why you are fearful and mistrusting. If my word is not good enough for you to trust that I will reveal nothing of what I know, then maybe we can come to some other arrangement."

He crosses his arms to his chest and scowls. "What other arrangement?"

I lean my elbows forward on my raised knees and say confidingly, "In order to win trust, one must first give trust. So, this is what I propose. I shall give you something, some compromising material, that you may hold as leverage over me. Perhaps it could be an incriminating letter that would destroy my reputation if ever it were made public. With that evidence in your hands, you would ensure my silence." I smile winningly, impressed with my great idea.

"No," he says flatly.

"You will not even consider it?"

"No," he repeats.

I begin to plead. "Broek, my dear friend, for that is what you have become. I cannot live like this in perpetuity, unable ever to leave these walls. It would drive me to madness. I cannot allow Chloe to grow to adulthood like this. What future would there be for my precious girl? Please, Broek, I beg you to listen and see sense."

His scowl deepens, but he does not at first respond. I can see that he is considering my words, that he feels the weight of them. Hope springs in my breast. He will see sense. He must. "There is one way out of this dilemma," he grits finally and fixes me with his dark eyes. "You must marry me."

I blow out a very frustrated breath. "How would marrying you solve anything? I would still be forced to stay here."

His expression hardens. "Here is hardly a penance, Jane. You would have all the advantages any lady in society gains through marriage—the protection of a husband, a comfortable home, good public standing. Once we are wed, you will be allowed to go to church and mingle in society, if that is what you wish. And Jane, you will also gain something else."

"What would that be?" I query.

Very deliberately, he pulls the sheet away from his lap and shows me. My suspicions were correct. He is not wearing any clothes at all, and bared to me now is his massive male appendage, fully erect. I stare in fascination while my heart races. In a husky growl, he states, "You will have a man fuck you to satisfaction every night, and I will finally get to bed you."

My mind is fuzzy. The words will not come. Eventually, I manage to whisper, "Satisfaction?"

"Have you ever felt satisfaction during sexual intercourse, Duchess?" he asks softly.

"I—I do not know what you mean."

"Then I will show you," he promises. "Drop that sheet from around your neck, Jane."

I hesitate. "It would not be proper," I mutter.

"We have gone well beyond proper already, Duchess. Forget about the outside world. No one but us is here. Drop the sheet."

With nerveless fingers, I do as he says. Beneath, I am wearing a white cotton shift. "Now take off your shift," he instructs. "Reveal yourself to me as I have to you." His fierce gaze holds mine as he spits out, "Do it, Jane. And do not feel an ounce of shame."

I fumble with the garment and pull it over my head with hands that shake, then drop it on the bed. A shiver runs through my body, even though the room is perfectly warm. I am bare to Broek's gaze. Hesitantly, I look across at him. He stares at me intently. "I wish I could touch you," he says huskily.

"W—where would you touch me?"

"Oh Duchess, there would not be an inch of your skin that would not feel the touch of my fingers, my lips, my tongue." He groans and palms his jutting shaft. "I would start with your perfect little breasts. Touch your hands to them."

Slowly, I bring my hands up to cup my modest bosom. "Like this?"

He breathes heavily. "Squeeze them. Feel their softness give under the press of your fingers, like plump little cushions." I do as he says, a thrum of excitement building within me at my wantonness. "Mmm," he grunts deep in his throat. "If I were with you, Jane, I would pinch one peak between my fingers, and the other, I would put in my mouth and pinch with my teeth."

Involuntarily, I feel my fingers pinch the tips of my breasts. He purrs in approval. "Oh yes, my beauty, like that. Do it again." So, I do. "Good girl," he rasps in praise. Eyes burning with ardour, he asks, "Do you know what I would do next?"

"W—what?"

"I would suckle that luscious peak like a babe at your breast."

"Oh!" I cry, both shocked and aroused. As he says these wicked things to me, I notice he is touching himself in quick jerking motions along his thick shaft.

"And when I have suckled my fill of one breast, I will devour the other," he growls. "Would you like that, Jane?"

"Yes, I think so," I say on a breath.

"Let me see how much you would like it." At the confusion in my eyes, he explains, "Part your legs for me, Jane, and show me your cunt."

I do not know what devil is driving me, but I do as he says. Slowly, I draw my legs apart, exposing that very intimate part of me to his gaze.

"Touch yourself there," he instructs gruffly. My eyes not leaving his, I slide a hand down my belly and through the soft tuft of hair on my mound. He growls deep in his throat. "Mmm. Keep going, Jane. Touch that moist flesh."

My hand slides lower still until it dips into the soft flesh hidden beneath. "Are you wet there, Jane?" he asks roughly. I nod, feeling shy. "Bring up your hand, show me how wet," he barks. I can only obey that commanding voice. I slide my finger along the moist flesh then bring it up in the air for him to see. It glistens in the soft light of the room. "Oh yes, my sensuous girl," he declares with a gleam in his eyes. "I think you will like it very much when I suckle your breast." I feel a little quiver run through me at the salacious nature of his words.

"Touch your cunt again," he rasps. I bring my fingers back to the moist flesh at the juncture of my thighs. "Just above the entrance to your cunt, Jane, there is a small protruding nub of flesh that is pleasurable to touch. Find it." I start circling my fingers searchingly, finding my slick opening, then moving upwards. A small protruding nub? I cannot find such a thing, I think to myself, as I move my hand impatiently over the area. "Slow," booms Broek's voice. I slow my questing fingers, reaching back to the opening of my cunt then following a path upwards with gentle taps. "Oh," I gasp.

He purrs in satisfaction. "You have found it, clever girl. Keep touching yourself in that spot. Feel how it pleasures you." I do as he says, pleasantly surprised at just how pleasurable it is to touch my fingers there.

Broek continues with his licentious talk. "After I ravish each perfect peach of a breast, do you know what next I shall devour?" I shake my head. He frowns at me in disapproval. "Of course you do." His eyes trail down to my fingers, stroking over the sensuous nub.

"You would put your mouth there?" I ask uncertainly.

"Oh, yes, Jane. I would kiss and lick and suck you there. Would you like that?"

My fingers quicken their motion, unconsciously echoing the jerking movement of his hand on his swollen shaft. "Would you, Jane?" he demands again.

"Yes. Oh, yes, Broek. I think I should like that very much."

"Keep stroking yourself there," he rasps. "Close your eyes and pretend it is me devouring you with my tongue." I close my eyes and imagine him caressing me there. My own flesh is swollen and throbs with each stroke of my hand. It feels so wonderfully good. A feverish sensation is building within me, swelling with the motion of my fingers, getting stronger and stronger. "I cannot wait to taste you," Broek continues. "First chance I get, Jane, I will bury my face in your cunt and feast on you." He groans. "Great Yol, but I know you will taste like heaven. Keep stroking, sweet girl. Keep going and do not stop until you reach your pinnacle of pleasure."

I can feel it, feel myself reaching up for that pinnacle. I hear his grunts of encouragement, interspersed with tender praise. "Broek," I whimper.

"Yes, sweet girl. You are nearly there. Keep going. You can do it."

Something is happening. I feel my body throb and convulse. I know instinctively that I have reached that pinnacle. I am gripped by a sharp burst of ecstasy. And then it is over, like a wave that has risen high then crashed to the shore, though I continue to feel the reverberations. I still my hand and pant breathlessly.

"Good girl," croons Broek, and I am filled with pride at his praise.

I breathe deeply and try to slow my racing heart. Then I open my eyes and seek Broek with my gaze. I notice there is a pearly streak of fluid painted across his belly. "You reached your pleasure too," I murmur.

"How could I not, watching you, sweet Jane?" Once more, I am filled with pride at the knowledge that ordinary little me has managed to bring this magnificent man to pleasure. Perhaps later, I may feel shame for this wanton behaviour, but not now. He sits forward on his bed and looks at me intently. In a low voice, he growls, "Feel what we did just now, Jane, and imagine how much sweeter it will be when I am with you in the flesh. Marry me, Duchess, and every night, you shall have this pleasure."

"I—I." I cannot answer.

His voice is gruff. "Go to sleep, Jane, and think on it. *Offscreen*." And then he is gone.

Wearily, I murmur, "*Offscreen*," to stop transmitting to his chamber, then I reach across the bed for my shift and pull it back on. I settle under the covers once more then command, "Lights out." Darkness descends, and though I have much to reflect on, I feel myself sink into exhausted—and contented—sleep.

CHAPTER 24

JANE

Morning comes, and with it a faint throb down below as my body recalls what it did the night before. As consciousness returns, I cannot stop my hand from wandering there and searching out that joyful nub. I stroke it gently, feeling it respond to my touch with a little echo of delight, but the sensation is muted. The excitement I felt last night is gone, and I do not need to think why. It is Broek that makes me feel that wild wantonness. And Broek wishes to marry me.

My resistance to such a notion has taken a blow. Marriage will grant me the freedom presently denied to me to go out and about should I so please. I have always lived a quiet life, first with Giles at Coleford Hall, then alone at Penhale Manor. Even so, I could visit the shops, exchange pleasantries with village folk and go out for vigorous walks. That last I am able to do at present, for the grounds of Reeves Hall are extensive, but it would be a welcome boon to be able to do the other things too.

Marriage would give me a secure and comfortable home here, as well as provide Chloe with a father who would care for her wellbeing. I have not missed the growing affection between Chloe and Broek. She is happy here. With the fortitude of children, she has adapted remarkably well to the change in our circumstance and learned the use of all the contraptions around her. Some days ago, I heard her call out imperiously, "Connect Horis," then have a lively conversation with the man about a bump to her knee. She has almost forgotten that once we used to light our home with candles and that water would have to be brought up to our rooms in a jug. All these curious innovations do not feel strange to her, but natural.

Then of course, there is that other matter. That to do with what we did last night, and what Broek promises to do to me every night. I cannot deny that I am enthralled by the notion.

And yet I am not quite ready to agree to his proposal. I did not lie last night. I have come to care about Broek and think of him as a dear friend. While I believe Broek has come to care for me and know that he will never harm my person, I do not yet think that he loves me nor I him. It cannot be love we feel—how can it be, when we are always arguing? My love for Giles was never like this. No, it is impossible. We cannot marry.

There again, perhaps I ought not to think of romance but be pragmatic. After all, I have already been fortunate to find a great love and should hardly expect to find another in this life. No, love I will not expect, but affection and respect I require, as well as another vital quality—trust. I cannot marry a person who does not trust me wholeheartedly, and yet he will not trust me with his family's secrets until I do marry him. Which comes first, the chicken or the egg? I rail in frustration and throw off the covers. Best to be getting on with the business of the day.

At breakfast, Broek is his usual quiet and stern presence. Yet do I detect a softening in his glance? I study his countenance again, paying special attention to the expression in his eyes. He notices this and lifts a brow. "Have I grown a second head?" he enquires softly.

"No indeed," I reply with a smile. "I was merely wondering whether that scowl you wear is a mask to conceal a very soft heart."

"Then cease wondering. You of all people should know, Jane, that my heart is anything but soft."

Liora joins in our conversation. "We call him Grumps," she tells me, eyes twinkling in merriment.

I consider this. "Some might think it a fitting name, but I shall not use it."

"But do you not agree that he has a grumpy disposition?" This time it is Simor who enquires.

The question makes me pause. Broek is often serious, yes, but during my stay at Reeves Hall, I have seen his many good qualities. Moreover, he has reasons to be grave. "I do not think it a fair assessment," I reply thoughtfully. "Broek has the cares of the world upon his shoulders and holds a great responsibility for the welfare of this family. What you see as grumpiness is merely a manifestation of all these cares."

My words seem to have pierced Broek's equanimity, for he stands and throws down his napkin. "While you continue this fruitless debate," he says harshly, "I have work to get done." He strides out of the room, followed by our three sets of eyes.

"Now you have bungled it," exclaims Simor. "My brother will not thank you for painting him in such light."

"Though it is true what you say," reflects Horis. "Broek does carry all these cares and has done so ever since we left Uvon."

"Yes, but he should not," grumbles Liora. "We do not need him to act as our protector, for we are all well capable of taking care of ourselves."

This does not sit well with me. I must remonstrate. "Tell me, who is it that works tirelessly to manage and grow your family's wealth? Correct me if I am wrong, but was it not Broek who went to London to oversee your shipping business and make investments in the stock exchange?"

They stare at me. "You seem mightily protective of my brother," Liora declares suspiciously.

"Broek has explained to me the circumstances that caused you to leave Uvon, and I have grown to think of him as a friend." No more than that, I tell myself.

Now it is as if I am the one to have grown two heads. After a moment of surprise, Simor snorts, "A friend who keeps you captive."

That is unfortunately true. Quietly, I say, "I am working to earn his trust. He must know, and so should you all, that I would never disclose your family's secrets to the world." I rise to my feet. "Now please excuse me."

I walk out of the dining room with a heavy feeling in my heart. Much as I have started to care for the Reeves clan, the truth remains that I am their captive, and they do not trust me.

I am half-way down the corridor before Simor catches up with me. "Your Grace," he calls, causing me to halt my steps and turn to face him. His face is unusually grim. He goes to speak then stops, looking behind him. "Come with me," he decides, leading me further down the corridor then opening the door to a small room furnished with an overflowing book case along one wall and a wide desk, its back to the window. On it sits another of those large screens similar to the one Broek had in his basement room. "This is my study," he explains. "We may speak privately here."

I follow him inside and stand in the middle of the room as he shuts the door behind him. Once that is done, I enquire, "What is it you wish to speak of?"

Abruptly, he asks, "Did you mean it when you said earlier that you would never disclose my family's secrets?"

I have to look up to see into his eyes, for like all his brothers, he is tall. His features are so like Broek's, but a softer and younger version. I hope he can read the sincerity in my expression as I reply, "Yes, of course."

"How do I know you would keep your word?"

I shrug impatiently. "You cannot know it. You must take it on trust."

"Why should we trust you, Jane?" he asks softly, dispensing with the formality of my title.

I pause, considering the question. Why on earth should they trust me, a stranger that has intruded into their midst? I sigh heavily. Trust is a curious thing, difficult to gauge. Finally, I say sadly, "Your family has been betrayed enough, by your Mother, by that wicked Tarla. You do not need yet another betrayal. I am forever in your debt for saving Chloe, and I understand what could be the consequences of any loose talk about your family. I am not a gossip, Simor. I know how to keep things to myself, and I would not want it on my conscience to be the one that brought you down."

He examines me thoughtfully. "If Broek spoke to you of Tarla, then he must trust you more than you think," he ponders.

"Not enough to release me," I respond.

He is quiet, thinking the matter through. Finally, he says, "I cannot go against my brother. If it were up to me, you would be free to go, and not only because I trust your word, but because I also think our fear is overblown. I do not believe a loose word or two from you would bring the world crashing around our ears. We have lived thus far with the curiosity and gossip around our family. We have been able to withstand it."

"I do not want my life and my daughter's life to be a prison," I plead.

"No, I do not think you do." He lets out a frustrated breath and says, "I cannot help you, Jane, but I know of one person here who would like nothing better than to see the back of you. You may have met Catana. She works with Wolkan to guard our security."

"The glowering Amazon?"

He smiles. "That is one way to describe Catana. She is quite possessive of Broek."

Possessive? I wonder if she has reason to be. I tamp down on the jealousy surfacing in my breast and try to think rationally. Catana is a guard, so she would be well placed to help me escape. Her dislike of me is the very thing that could buy us our freedom, Chloe and me, Betsy too. What about Evans, my coachman? I have not seen him since the day of Chloe's accident. I pose the question. "Where is my coachman, Simor? His name is Evans, and he drove us through the gates in my carriage."

Simor replies, "Broek paid him off generously and gave him references, then took him to London on his last trip there. He had not seen anything much to gossip about, for he never entered the house."

"Oh," I say dispiritedly. I had hoped to have the means of transportation for my escape.

"I am sorry," continues Simor. "I cannot help you further." A shutter goes down on his expression, and I know this discussion is over.

I mumble, "Thank you, Simor. I will bid you good day." With a weak smile, I let myself out of the room, then go seek out my daughter.

THROUGHOUT THE DAY my mind considers all that I have learned. If I stay at Reeves Hall, I know that I will eventually succumb to Broek. The attraction between us is much too powerful. It is imperative therefore that I escape before I lose all will to do so, and Catana is my only hope. In truth, I do not want to leave him, but I must.

I have a troubling thought. Would Broek feel abandoned and betrayed by my escape? Probably, but surely he deserves it for being so unreasonable. After all, it is him that is keeping me captive. He must know that I refuse to live without my freedom. What else is there for me to do but to attempt an escape?

A voice in my head replies, *"You could marry him."* Yes, that could be one solution, but I do not want to marry a man out of duress. It would make a mockery of the marriage vows. The more that time passes since my moment of wantonness last night, the more rationally I am beginning to see things. I cannot continue at Reeves Hall, much as I care for Broek, much as I am attracted to his person and much as I am enjoying the privilege of a hot bath in the tub each night. Freedom trumps all these things. And therefore, I must find a way to speak to Catana.

This decision sours my mood at luncheon and dinner, where in a departure to my usual cheery disposition, I am morose and unwilling to speak more than the basic civilities. I feel Broek's scrutiny, as ever, but I keep my head bowed and eat my food, excusing myself at the first opportunity. I cannot afford to develop any tender feelings for the man. He is the one putting me in this impossible situation.

Later in the evening, after I have put Chloe to bed, I go to the washroom and run the water for a bath. If I am to leave this place soon, then I shall enjoy my fill of this particular luxury. I divest myself of my clothing and enter the tub, submerging my body in the welcoming warmth of the scented water. Ah yes, this is good. I can feel my peevishness leach out of me, measure by measure.

"You are angry with me." Broek's voice breaks into my contented haze. "You refused to even look at me at dinner."

I let out a long breath. "I was, but I am not so now," I murmur. "You may thank this marvellous bath for the improvement of my humour."

"I shall bear that in mind whenever you are out of sorts with me again," he responds a trifle huskily.

"Hmm."

"Tell me, Jane, what made you so ill-disposed towards me today?" he enquires, piercing my sense of serenity.

"Is it not obvious?" I respond acidly. "In case you have forgotten, Broek, you are holding me captive here. That is surely sufficient a cause for one's anger."

"*Onscreen,*" he says. A moment later, I see him on a screen I had not realised existed on the opposite wall of the washroom. He is in that subterranean room where he plays God with his probes that spy on the world.

"There is one solution to your captivity, Jane," he rumbles, leaning forward on his elbows and looking fixedly at me through the screen, though I know he cannot see me.

"Yes indeed," I reply quickly. "It is to release me."

"I wish to look into your eyes as we speak of this. Let me see you, Jane."

"Absolutely not!" I exclaim in shocked disapproval.

"Jane, do not play games," he glares, holding on to his patience by a thread. "We are well past this false modesty. Now let me see you so we can talk this out properly."

"Why can we not do so in the way of civilised people, when we are both dressed appropriately?" I enquire sullenly.

"Jane."

"Oh, very well. *Onscreen.*"

I know the exact moment when he catches sight of me. His eyes flare, and I feel a corresponding throb in the lower part of my body. I am underwater, so I do not suppose he can see much more than an outline of my figure. At least, that is what I tell myself.

"Jane." His voice is hoarse. "Have you had any further thoughts about our marriage?"

"I have thought about it carefully, Broek. I regret to tell you my answer is no." His mouth compresses to a thin line, so I hurry to explain, "I am tempted, believe me I am." My own voice grows husky as I admit, "I have grown to care for you, Broek, more so than I would wish." My eyes search his as he sits grimly at his desk. Resolutely, I continue, "But I will not marry under duress a man that does not trust me to set foot outside his home."

He is silent as stone. "Trust me, please, Broek," I plead, "and I will show you that trust is not misplaced."

Still, he does not speak. Feeling my throat constrict, I lower my eyes to my exposed body. My hands fly to cover my bosom and mound in a late show of modesty. *Trust.* It is a reciprocal thing. If he cannot have any faith in me, then I cannot feel easy baring myself to him. He must see the gesture, for his next words are cold and implacable. "Then we are at an impasse, Duchess. *Offscreen.*" And just as coldly, I am dismissed.

CHAPTER 25

JANE

The ensuing week passes slowly, a cool distance forming between Broek and me. During meals, he is stiff and formal, though he continues to scrutinise me closely. He no longer speaks to me at night through the contraption in the wall. Contrarily, I miss the intrusion. On occasion, I have been tempted to summon him myself for a talk, but I have resisted. It is better that I should not, for with each day, my determination grows. I must escape this captivity.

I am beginning to accustom myself to this environment, the things I had found strange and alarming becoming commonplace. Not only am I now used to voices coming through the wall, but also to members of this household communicating with each other through a tiny contraption hidden within the ring they wear on their finger. I have grown very fond of those purplish Uvonian pancakes that are served each morning, and as to my nightly bath—well, that is something I shall miss greatly when I am gone.

I occupy a curious position in this household. I am treated now, no longer as a temporary guest, but as a permanent member. The people here are at ease around me—with the exception of Broek—and I am shown warmth, dare I say also affection by the other members of the Reeves clan. On Chloe, they positively dote. And yet come Sunday, I am left at home while they all go to church, and each time I wish to set foot outside I must do so first with a guard at my heels. The summoning of a guard so that I may walk outside is my daily salutary reminder that I am a prisoner here.

During each walk, I examine my surroundings carefully and try to formulate a plan of escape. It will be just me and my daughter leaving Reeves Hall, for when I obliquely mentioned the prospect of leaving to Betsy, she made it plainly evident that she wishes to stay. "Me and Velnas be courting," she told me just two days ago. "And Your Grace, things are ever so much better here. I could not go back to the way we lived before." On further consideration, perhaps that is for the best. Although I shall miss Betsy's services, she is prone to chatter, and I could not trust that she would keep silent on what goes on at Reeves Hall.

In preparation for our departure, I have already packed necessities in a small knapsack, together with my purse containing the remainder of the one hundred guineas that Broek paid me on the day we agreed to the sale of Penhale Manor. The rest of my belongings will need to remain at Reeves Hall, for now. I will find a way to get my trunks back at a later date, once I am safe from captivity.

Tonight, I lie in bed, conscious as ever of Broek's presence in the next room. In order to stop my mind from thinking about him naked in his bed, I try to consider practicalities. If I were to escape Reeves Hall, where would I go? And how? If somehow I could get Catana to let us out through the back gate, we would need a horse. I cannot see how we could slip away in the carriage without being noticed, but a horse—that is more of a feasibility. Travelling on horseback in a north-eastern direction would eventually get me to Bodmin, but it is a long journey to attempt with Chloe. In the opposite direction is the village of Penhale, but I discount it. There is very little there apart from a few shops and cottages, and no inn to seek shelter at while I commandeer a carriage for a further journey. No, we shall have to ride a few miles further to the town of Newquay. By my estimation, it is an hour's ride away from Reeves Hall. Once there, I will find accommodation at an inn and make enquiries about a small cottage to rent. Yes, that is what I will do.

Now, all I need is to speak to Catana and convince her to help me. That may not be an easy task. I yawn and resist once more the urge to call Broek on the wall contraption. I do not like this coldness that has crept between us. Over and over in my mind, I hear his words that last time we spoke. *Then we are at an impasse, Duchess.* Yes, Broek, I think to myself. We are at an impasse, and that is why I must break it by leaving Reeves Hall. Once I am safely away from here, who is to say what could happen next. This need not be the end of whatever it is that has developed between us, but a new beginning.

Next morning, I am disappointed to find Broek gone on yet another business trip. I eat my breakfast quietly, missing his scowling presence next to me, and wonder how long it will be before he returns. His absence casts a pall once more over my humour. I do not like him gone, and less do I like it when we are at cross purposes with each other. I decide to go for a walk earlier than my usual time in the afternoon, just so that I may raise my spirits. "Connect Wolkan," I speak to the contraption in the wall of my chamber, and once I am connected to him, I tell him of my wish to go for a walk.

He hesitates a while, as if I have disconcerted him with my request. I had not realised that I had become a creature of habit, going for my constitutional promenade at the same time each day. "Hmm," he murmurs, as he thinks the matter through. "I suppose I could ask Catana to mind you." My heart leaps. Catana. Finally. Then, with greater certainty, he goes, "Yes, Catana. I will have her wait for you at the main door in five minutes, Your Grace."

"Thank you, Wolkan," I say.

At the appointed time, I am at the door where I meet that glowering Amazon again. So, there has been no change in her disposition towards me. I do not care to speculate why I am so disliked. It is too painful to think of Broek with this tall and busty female doing intimate things such as he did with me, and more perhaps. Instead of dwelling on so discomposing a thought, I decide to attend to the positive aspect of her dislike—that it will make her more likely to champion my departure from here.

She does not address me, merely marches out of the door, expecting me no doubt to follow. Her strides are long, and it is with a puffing breath that I draw up next to her. "Good day, Catana," I begin cordially.

She does not respond. I decide to get straight to the matter in hand, for there is no ignoring such obvious incivility. "My presence here offends you," I say. To this she makes a snorting sound and continues pacing forward at a punishing speed. I see I shall be having to conduct this interview while fighting for my breath. I do not let this impediment deter me. "Certainly, you wish me gone from here," I continue bravely.

"Ha!" is the only response I get.

"Then our two objectives align," I say on a wheeze. "Perhaps you could see your way to assisting me in leaving Reeves Hall."

She stops so abruptly that I very nearly collide with her mountainous form. "Assisting you is the very last thing I wish to do," she snarls.

I am gasping for breath but do not waste the opportunity. "And asking for your assistance is the very last thing I wish to do," I manage in between pants, "but one must make a virtue out of necessity." Her gaze is hostile, so I hurry on with my plan, "All I need is for the back gate to be unlocked and to be provided with a horse for my journey. I shall take care of the rest."

She continues to glare at me. Then with a scornful toss of her head, she turns away and begins marching forth once more. I follow as we make a circle around the house until we return to our original starting point. I am by now almost out of breath, but I am proud that I have, despite my far smaller form, managed to keep pace with Catana. She stops by the front door of the house and eyes me balefully. "The answer is no," she says shortly. She sees me into the house and leaves without a backward look.

I stay a moment in the front hall, regaining my breath as disappointment floods through me. Catana was my only hope for escaping this place. Now, I cannot think what to do. Dispiritedly, I go seek my daughter. Her joyful laughter will be a balm for my weary soul.

BROEK IS ABSENT the following morning and the subsequent one. I go about my days in a cloud of despondency, a stark contrast to the seemingly cheery disposition of those around me. Of course, it does not go unnoticed. Tonight, Horis catches me up after I excuse myself from the dinner table.

"Jane," he says with a frown, now in the habit of calling me by my given name. "Is something the matter?"

I do wish these people would stop pretending all was normal and well with my presence in their home. "The matter?" I enquire, "you mean apart from the fact that I am being held here against my will?"

He winces at this. "I had thought you reconciled to staying with us," he now says. "Have we not treated you well? Or is there someone that has said or done something to vex you?"

I am beginning to lose patience with the entire Reeves clan, even kindly Horis. This may explain why I am somewhat less than civil in my reply. "What vexes me, Horis, is the fact that you and everyone else here has no compunction in holding me captive, thinking that spoiling me with the generosity of your welcome will somehow obscure the realities of my situation. Do not, pray, ask facile questions of me." I turn away from his horrified countenance and march up to my room where the only salve for my foul mood is to run a hot bath.

Next day, there is still no sign of Broek. My ire now turns on him. Why must he absent himself for so long? Does he not know that in curious contradiction to his surliness and the fact of his being my gaoler, I find joy and solace in his presence? I want him here. I want to feel the intensity of his gaze on me. I want to battle words with him. Lord in heaven, but I miss the dictatorial man, even though I may have to leave him. What this says about the strength of my feelings, I do not wish to ponder, though a voice in my head whispers insistently, "Marry him. Marry him." It takes much strength of will, which I am fortunate to have in abundance, to ignore this whispering.

As I undress that evening in readiness for my nightly bath, I see a folded sheet of paper pushed under the door of my chamber. I hasten to pick it up and read this terse note.

Be at the back gate tomorrow, 3 o'clock.

There is no signature, but it can only be from Catana. She has agreed to help me. Excitement and fear thrum through me. Tomorrow at last, I shall be free. My mind sets rapidly to thinking. Chloe is in the habit of taking a nap after luncheon and waking at around three. I shall perforce have to take Betsy into my confidence so she can have my daughter ready in time. Then there is the matter of making my exit from the house unnoticed. The servant's door at the back, I decide. It is by the kitchen. Perhaps Betsy can distract Velnas while Chloe and I slip out. Yes, that could work.

Even the bath tonight cannot ease the tension from my body. When night comes, I toss and turn in the bed, unable to find the repose of sleep. A thought tugs painfully at my heart. I shall not see Broek before I leave. Will I ever see him again? I must. I must. This cannot be the end of things between us.

Next morning after breakfast, I seek out Betsy and quietly explain my plan. Her eyes widen in surprise and concern. "Your Grace, are you sure of this?" she asks in a small voice.

"Yes, Betsy," I respond firmly. "It is what I must do. Will you help me?"

She nods. "Yes."

I smile at her gratefully and return to my chamber where I check the knapsack again for good measure. I place inside it a slice of bread and cheese wrapped in a napkin, in case Chloe becomes hungry during our journey. From the wardrobe, I take out my black cloak and gloves, laying them on the bed in readiness for later. My stomach flutters with nerves, and yet it is only eleven o'clock in the morning. There are still four hours and a luncheon to go before I can take my leave from here. I pace the room in anxiety. In desperation, I pick up the book at my bedside table and make my way out of the room to the front parlour, which is usually quiet at this time. I sit myself down in an armchair, take a deep breath and force myself to read.

I do not know how long it is before I hear the sound of the door opening. I look up from my book, and my heart stops. *Broek*. I cannot prevent a wide smile taking hold of my countenance. He is here, at last. His lips too curve into an answering smile. Book forgotten, I am on my feet, hurrying towards him as he approaches me. "You are back," I say breathlessly, looking up into his searching eyes. His glorious scent envelops me.

Gently, he places a hand on either side of my face and examines me. "I am back," he says in a hoarse voice. I bask under the heated intensity of his gaze.

The moment is over quickly. His hands fall from my face, and he steps back, taking out a letter from his coat pocket. "This came for you," he says simply.

I take it from him and break the seal, reading it quickly. It is from Mr Smithson at Drummonds Bank. He writes to acknowledge receipt of my letter and to confirm that the interest on my lump sum will be re-invested into the funds on my behalf, as instructed. He sounds a note of apology too, for having written to my uncle, and takes note of the directions at Penhale Manor where he must henceforth send his communications. Of course, I will not be there, but once I have secured a more permanent home, I can write to him again with my new directions. The important thing is that his correspondence will no longer be sent to my aunt's house.

I pass the letter to Broek, who reads it impassively. "Good," he says, returning it to me.

"Yes," I smile gratefully. "The matter seems to be resolved satisfactorily." I pause. "Although, truth be told, Broek, my sense of justice makes me wish there was some way to punish my aunt and uncle for what they did."

"Rest assured they have been punished," declares Broek decisively. At my look of confusion, he explains, "I went to see them not two days ago. Your uncle was not best pleased with his wife over the matter, though he cannot have been in ignorance of it all the years that you lived in their home."

I stare in awe at him and breathe, "You went to see them?"

"Did I not just tell you so?"

"What happened? Tell me!"

He is curt in his reply. "Suffice it to say that they have agreed to repay you every penny owed."

"What did you do? How did you make them agree?" I wonder breathlessly.

He shrugs uncomfortably. "I have my ways, Jane. Have you not accused me before of playing God with my nanoprobes?"

"So, you discovered something, some knowledge to hold over their heads?"

He nods in the affirmative.

I cannot help a chuckle. "Then, all I can say is that on this occasion, it is a good thing that you hold such power." I step towards him and place both my hands on the solid wall of his chest. "Thank you, Broek."

His hands fly to mine quickly, trapping them to his chest. "You do not need to thank me," he says gruffly. "I only did what was right."

"And yet I do thank you." My eyes stare into his as he lowers his head slowly to mine. I know he is about to kiss me, and I cannot find any strength in me to resist him. The first touch of his lips is soft, inviting. Up close I breathe him in and tremble with a powerful surge of desire. His lips draw mine to him again, this time a little less gently. Over and over we kiss, tugging relentlessly at each other's lips until I part mine on a gasp. Then I feel the sweet invasion of his tongue. Never before have I been kissed liked this. It is wicked. It is madness. And yet I feel myself meld into his intimate embrace, wanting more. His hands release mine so he can anchor me to him as he devours me with his mouth, and I let myself be devoured. Oh what ecstasy this is.

My tongue goes out to meet his, and I taste him. So potent. And now that we are attached, mouth to mouth, tongue to tongue, we cannot let go. A spark has been lit under our fire, and we ignite. My hands grip the back of his neck, nails digging into skin as I tear into him in my hunger. Small I may be, but in my need of him, I am a lioness. I pounce, and I do not let go. This kiss is endless, growing in power as I feel every inch of my body throb. I do not let go of his lips as he lifts me and strides to the couch. He deposits me atop him while he continues to ravage my mouth with his kisses.

And now that my body is spread over his and his arms are holding me close, I feel the hardness of his male shaft pushing relentlessly against me. Ah. Without conscious thought I grind my hips to his length, feeling a wonderful pressure on the small joyful nub at my mound. And as my tongue delights in the taste of him, as I hear his muffled groans, I press my body fiercely to his, seeking that culmination of pleasure. But I want more than simply to push and stroke and grind. Instinctively I know what it is I need, what it is I have craved these many days and nights. Against his mouth I breathe the words, "Fill me."

He groans again, a deep and needful sound. Then his hands drop from around me to make quick work of releasing his manly shaft. Next instant, he has my dress and petticoat bunched up, and then there is nothing between us. "Take me," he cries hoarsely. I do not know whether it is him that positions his shaft to my entrance or whether it is my grasping hands that bring him to me. All I know is a deep, aching need to have him inside me.

His large girth pushes slowly through the gates of my body, and inch by inch, he fills me. I hear him grunt, though I know not whether it is in agony or ecstasy. "Take all of me, Jane," he pleads, wild desperation in his eyes. And so I do. I cry out loud as I impale myself on him. He is thick, so thick, and though I am slick down below, it is a tight fit. Inexorably, he continues to push deeper and deeper into me. I look into his feverish eyes as finally, it is done, and I hold the entire length of him inside me. For an instant, we exchange a wondrous stare, marvelling at this magnificent joining of our beings.

And then all at once, we take action. Broek pulls my face to his and takes my lips in a punishing kiss. Then his hands are at my rump, pressing me to him as he begins to pump his shaft up into me. Then it is I who grasps his face in my hands. It is I who devours his mouth with mine. And it is I who pounds my body to his, our joint moans loud as we both of us seek that divine pinnacle of untold pleasure. On and on he fills me. On and on I crush my body to his. On and on we kiss and moan and groan. We are bestial in our need. It is beyond rational thought.

"Broek!" I cry as I feel myself nearing the precipice.

"Come, Jane!" he roars. He thrusts even harder up into me.

"Ah! Ah! Ah!" I moan as I am gripped by a wave of tumultuous contractions. It is just like that last time, except it is far stronger. I feel Broek's shaft swell impossibly large as he cries, finding his own release and pulsing his spend into me.

I collapse like a rag doll over Broek, my face buried in the crook of his neck while I breathe him in. For a long time, we lie still, our bodies joined intimately. Inevitably though, sanity begins to return as I realise what it is I have just done. Broek tenses under me, sensing the change in my state of mind. His arms grip me tight as he snarls, "Do not dare to feel shame for this, Jane."

"But I should. I have been wicked."

"No," he bites out. "Never that. I will not have you ever regret this." His shaft, still buried inside me, thrusts up with each last word he speaks, as a reminder—or a rebuke. Then he kisses me again, and I am powerless to resist the temptation of his caress. What we did was wrong, I know it. Yet he is also right. I cannot regret the joy we experienced together, even as I know that I shall be leaving Reeves Hall today. See him again I might after this, or I might not. I am glad we were able to have this moment, before I left. I will forever remember the ecstasy of joining my body to his.

At last he ends the kiss with a sweet nibble to my lower lip. With god-like power, he senses the softening of my resistance. Against my lips, he growls, "You are a goddess, Duchess."

"And there I was thinking you were a god," I say in teasing reply.

He huffs out a short laugh. "You make me feel like one, sweet Jane."

I sigh against his mouth and give him one last kiss. "We had best tidy ourselves, lest we be disturbed," I say wistfully.

He grunts in answer but gently lifts my body away from his and sits me down on the couch. With little regard for his modesty, he goes to a side table, his shaft hanging loose from his undone trousers, and comes back with a linen cloth. Leaving me no scope for any timidity, he brings the cloth to my wet mound and wipes me clean in a brisk, industrious manner. When he is done, I stand and re-arrange the folds of my dress while he tucks himself back into his trousers. My hands go to my hair, which is in wild disarray.

"I had best retire to my chamber and tidy myself before luncheon," I say with a hint of shyness.

He nods. "I have some work to do, so I will see you then." He draws me gently to his large body and claims my lips in a parting kiss. Of course, being Broek, he cannot resist having the last word. "You would be wise to say yes to my offer of marriage, Jane, now that you know what satisfaction I can bring you when we fuck." Then he is gone before I have the chance to reply.

No, I think sadly. There will be no marriage, at least not until I am free.

LUNCHEON IS AN awkward affair as I field Broek's intense and knowing gaze while his siblings cast us puzzled glances. Adding to my discomfort is the knowledge that soon, I shall be gone. My heart feels like it is shattering into a myriad pieces, but I know what I must do.

The meal over, Broek takes his leave once more to catch up on work in his subterranean lair. As we rise from the dining table, he bids me farewell, then with a show of possession, tucks my body to his and kisses me firmly on the lips. Oh Broek, I think in desolation. *If only you knew that I do not mean to stay here another day.* His family watches on with interest, but thankfully say nothing. In any case, I do not linger in their vicinity, but take myself up to my chamber. Before I leave, there is one more thing I must do.

Quickly, I remove a sheet of paper from the dresser drawer, together with ink and a quill. I sit at my dressing table to write my letter. It takes a few efforts to get the wording right. I write to explain why it is I must leave. I also write what is in my heart—or something of it. I try to make Broek understand. When I am done, I re-read the missive one last time before I fold and seal it, then write Broek's name at the front.

With only a few minutes to spare, I take the letter through the washroom and to Broek's chamber. It is the first time I have ever seen this room. I linger a moment to take in the large bed with burgundy-coloured sheets, the shirt draped carelessly over a chair, the various nicknacks. There is a faint aroma of his cologne and of him. I take a deep steadying breath, then place my letter on his dresser. Without thinking, I steal the discarded shirt, bringing it to my nose, and go quickly back to my chamber, stuffing the shirt into my rucksack. Then, it is time to leave.

I go across the hall to Chloe's room. I find her dressed and ready. Putting on a wide smile, I say, "We are going on a big adventure today, but we need to be very quiet. Will you do that for me?"

She nods thoughtfully. "What 'dventure?" she asks curiously.

"It is a surprise. Now come."

With Betsy leading the way, we walk to the servants' staircase and make our way down towards the kitchen, which is located beside the back door. I nod at Betsy, and she goes forward while we wait in silence. I hear her begin an animated conversation with Velnas. After a time, I deem it safe to proceed. With Chloe's hand held tightly in mine, we move on soft feet to the door and let ourselves out. I cast a furtive glance about me, but there is nobody there. "Quick, this way," I tell Chloe. "Nice and quiet." I hurry her down the path towards the back gate. It is several yards away, and with each fraught step I am fearful of discovery. But all goes well.

We reach the gate, and I see that it is slightly ajar. With shaking hands, I push it open and take my first step into freedom. I make sure to shut the gate behind me so as not to draw attention to it. Then I look around me. Where is it? My heart sinks in disappointment. Could it be Catana has failed to provide me with a horse? If so, how are we to make the long journey by foot? Just as I am beginning to despair, I hear a muffled whinny to my right. I follow the sound, and there, in the shelter of a wide oak tree, I see a brown mare—my very own mare, Daisy. I say a silent thanks to Catana.

With a relieved smile, I go to her, stroking her coat and murmuring softly. There is no time to be lost. I turn to Chloe. "This is my surprise," I tell her, imbuing my voice with the proper enthusiasm. "We are going on a ride with Daisy."

She laughs excitedly. "Daisy!" she cries.

"Come Chloe," I say firmly. I lift her small body and deposit her on the saddle. "Stay still and hold on here," I instruct. Now comes the challenging part. There is a large wooden stump, conveniently placed there, for which I whisper another word of thanks to Catana. With great care, I step on the stump and put one foot on the stirrup. Then with all the strength I have in me, I pull myself up onto the saddle, arranging my legs in the side position and smoothing my cloak down. All the while, my lovely Daisy stands docilely.

I take hold of the reins, deciding to wind them around Chloe's body and mine, as a makeshift way of securing my daughter to me. "Are you ready?" I ask her.

"Yes!" she cries.

I kick the stirrup gently, and then we are off, breathing our first taste of freedom in over a month.

CHAPTER 26

BROEK

My meeting with Liora, Horis and Simor seems to take an eternity. Of course, at the start there was some teasing about the duchess, but I quickly put a stop to that. "She is marrying me and that is all there is to say. Now let us talk business." After what happened between us today, there can no longer be any doubt that the duchess wants me, almost if not as much as I want her. I will make her my wife at the soonest opportunity, I vow to myself. But there is business to attend to first.

I listen as Liora updates us on the improvement works at Penhale Manor, which are proceeding apace. During the years of our journey in space from Uvon to Earth, we had all prepared for our eventual life here in different ways. Horis, who had already enrolled for medical studies before leaving our old home, continued his studies on board the ship. Liora, on the other hand, chose to specialise in construction and engineering. She has been responsible for much of the improvements we made at Reeves Hall and for the underground sections that we built. Now, she has turned her attention to Penhale Manor. It will soon be fit and ready for occupation. I had initially thought to make it a home for Horis and his bride, whoever she may be, though I have not spoken of it to him. Now, I am glad I have not, for I wonder if Penhale Manor should not be a new home for me and Jane after our marriage.

Then it is Simor's turn to speak. He tells us of the research he has conducted on the viability of a proposed new railway from Stockton to Darlington and the drawings made by an engineer named George Stephenson of a steam-powered locomotive, which my nanoprobes were able to capture and transmit to us.

Liora wrinkles her nose at mention of this. "It is all so primitive," she complains.

"And the use of coal to power these engines is surely not a good idea," adds Horis, looking mildly horrified. "Just think of the damage that will be caused by the emission of carbon into the atmosphere."

"It is a risk, yes," agrees Simor, "but coal is plentiful here and it is the only fuel at present that can be used to propel this nation into the industrial development that we wish to see."

I look to Simor questioningly. "What think you of this Stephenson's designs? Will they work?"

He grimaces slightly. "There are still some issues to be resolved. He is right to make use of coupling rods to link together the driving wheels. This will reduce the chance of the wheels slipping on the iron rails. However, there are weaknesses to the design of the centre-flue boiler. It will provide a poor heating surface, and moreover, be quite hazardous."

"Should we invest in the project?" I ask.

"Yes," responds Simor, "I believe, despite its weaknesses, it will be a stepping stone in the right direction."

We discuss the matter some more before turning to Horis for an update on his area of purview. He is in charge of two important disciplines: medicine and the growth of our specialised greenhouse crops. Without either of these things, our quality of life would be much poorer, but Horis does not always see his work in the important light that we do.

"How goes it with the new hybrid seedlings you have been experimenting with?" I ask him now.

"They are showing promise," he says, "but it is early days yet. I shall know more how it goes in a week or two."

I nod and enquire about other matters. We discuss these at length, then just as we are concluding the discussion, Horis, looking a trifle uncomfortable, speaks to us of Gav'ox. "I believe he is sinking into addiction to intoxicating substances," he says. "Lately, all he talks of is Uvon and the life we left behind, then tries to drown his sorrows in drink. There are treatments I could try to help him overcome the addiction, but the impetus must first come from him."

"I do not like to say it," adds Simor, "but the other day I saw him slumped in a drunken stupor when guarding the back gate."

I give an aggrieved sigh then declare, "We cannot have lapses in our security. I will speak to Wolkan about taking him off active duty until further notice. Are we all agreed?"

My siblings nod. I am impatient to get back to my duchess, but there is one last thing to discuss. "How does our mission prosper?" asks Liora.

Ah, our mission. The reason why we were sent here and not banished to a prison camp at Falora. I raise a brow at her. "Your guess, Liora, is as good as mine."

It is Simor that puts a brave front on the matter. "I do believe, with the establishment of the first passenger steam-powered railway between Stockton and Darlington, that we are on the cusp of a great shift. It will be the start of an industrial era which will herald great improvements."

"I hope you may be right, Simor," I reply glumly. "Yet it still seems a very long way from the sort of development that is required if humans on Earth are to make contact with the people of Uvon."

Simor is the most blithe and insouciant of us all. His youth at the time of our banishment has inured him to the resentments and hardships the rest of us still suffer from. He sits back now and stretches his legs before him with a laugh. "And the

Uvonians are still a very long way off from creating the stable wormhole on which is predicated this high-speed corridor between our planets. I would not worry myself too much about it, for all these things are bound to happen well after we are cold in our graves."

"What about our family's name and the possibility of a pardon?" wonders Horis. "If we do not show tangible progress in our mission, will they not withhold these from us?"

I glance at my brother curiously. "Would you wish to return if you could?"

He shrugs. "I do not know. I do not like to ask myself such a question as all it would do is put false hope in my breast."

"A wise outlook, Horis," I respond gravely. "As far as we are all concerned, our exile is a permanent one. To think anything else is a recipe for disappointment and unhappiness—Gav'ox being the case in point."

There are murmurs of agreement. I rise to my feet, ready to conclude matters and seek Jane out. I stride out of the drawing room where we have been congregated and make enquiries as to Jane's whereabouts. I am told she retired to her bedchamber and has not been down since. This information, I greet with a frown. Why is she hiding upstairs? Is she doing what I told her not to, wallowing in shame? Well, we shall see about that.

I take the stairs up two at a time and dash to her chamber door. After a perfunctory knock, I turn the knob and push it open, stepping decisively into the room, then come to an abrupt halt. She is not there. Perhaps she is in the washroom. I look to it but the indicator light is not on to show it is occupied. A feeling of deep unease begins to spiral within me. No, it cannot be. She is somewhere in the house.

I turn around and head out of the room, marching to the opposite door, which is Chloe's chamber. Again, I knock briskly before entering, and again the room is empty. I tap the device on my ring to connect with Wolkan. At his reply, I grit out, "Where is the duchess and her daughter?"

His voice is puzzled in response, "They are up in their bedchambers, I believe."

"No," I bark. "They are not. Search everywhere for them. Now."

As I speak, I am striding out of the room and flying down the stairs again, heading this time towards the play room in the east wing of the house. Perhaps Jane is there with Chloe and Wolkan's daughters. But I do not make it there. A buzzing of the communicator on my signet ring heralds Galok's voice, brimming with urgency, as he tells me one of the horses, Jane's mare, has disappeared from the stable. And then I know. The feeling is eerily familiar. First it was Mother, then Tarla, and now Jane. All three of them deceiving me. All three of them treacherous. Only this time, the betrayal feels much worse. I roar my pain, to Galok's shocked ears. Then I am biting out instructions for him to saddle my horse. I will find the perfidious duchess and bring her back kicking and screaming if I have to.

I go to the main hallway and pull on my boots, then I am out of the door, all the while thinking rapidly. There is no time to go to my control room and fire up some probes to find Jane. There is one of two directions she could have gone—towards Bodmin or westwards towards the village. With a small child in tow, I am betting she has chosen the shorter journey west. Grimly, I mount my horse and flick its reins. A moment later, I pass through the main gates and turn left, heading towards the village. I urge my horse to a fast gallop, and the young stallion obliges me, eating up the distance with its sleek and powerful legs.

I keep my eyes sharp ahead of me for any sign of Jane, but still I do not see her as I reach the approach to the village.

Damnation! Slowing down, I think quickly. Will she have continued on to Newquay or stopped at the village? There is no inn there, just a grocer's shop, a miller and a blacksmith. To make certain, I canter down the main thoroughfare, looking for any sign of her brown mare. I even stop briefly and ask a boy that works as the blacksmith's apprentice if he has seen anyone pass by in the last hour. At the shake of his head, I thank him brusquely and turn my mount, heading out of the village and back onto the main road to Newquay. Then, I pick up my speed again.

As I ride, a cold anger grips me at Jane's treachery. How could she join her body in mad passion with mine, all the while knowing she was going to do this? "Trust me," she had begged. And I very almost did. Never again will I fall for such lies.

I am three miles out of Newquay when finally, I catch sight of her. With a raging cry, I urge my horse to gallop even faster, my body bent forward to pick up as much speed as I can. I see her glance back and her fearful reaction. Will she be foolish and try to outrun me? At first, I think that is what she will do, but then my horse gains ground on hers and I know, she has given up the race.

Soon, I pull up beside her and reach over for her reins, which are wound around her body and Chloe's, clearly to secure the child. She does not protest as I bring both our horses to a stop. And then I face her with a sardonic hiss, "Going somewhere, Duchess?"

CHAPTER 27

JANE

The game is up. My heart pounds rapidly in my chest as I hear Broek's approach. Soon, he is at our side and reaching over to claim the reins. I do not do anything foolish to stop him. Then once we pull up, he addresses me coldly, "Going somewhere, Duchess?"

I am saved from a reply by Chloe, who cries out gleefully, "Broek!" Then my little minx of a daughter is holding up her hands in the air, in happy expectation of being lifted into his strong arms. This he does, after extricating her from the reins I had tied around her. "Broek," she says again, clasping her small hands around his neck. "We been on a 'dventure!"

The coldness disappears briefly from his eyes as he returns her embrace and responds calmly, "So I see. It is time now, Chloe, to go home."

She does not argue but lets him settle her on the saddle, one arm holding her securely to him. Then we turn our mounts and begin the ride back to Reeves Hall. Chloe chatters blithely with Broek, who listens intently and speaks when required. To me, he does not address a word.

So, my brief taste of freedom is over. Back to my captor I go. What else is there to do? I cannot fight him here on a deserted road while he holds my daughter in his arms. I do not listen to the perfidious voice in my head that is glad he has found us, nor to the throb of my body as it remembers our earlier passion. At least I try not to, but it is no good. Much as I am disheartened that my escape has been foiled, I am also aware of an excitement thrumming through my veins at his presence. It is an excitement mixed with trepidation, for I know he is furious with me. I will have to face his rage once we are back at Reeves Hall and Chloe is no longer present.

We ride on at an easier pace, now that there is no longer a question of escape. Apprehension grips me as I wonder what lies ahead. Shall he tighten the noose around me? Lock my door at night and forbid me to leave the house? In his fury, anything is possible. Yet of one thing I am certain. He will not harm my person. I do not know why I am so sure of this. I think it is because I have come to know him. Despite the surliness of his disposition, violence is not in his soul. I know from the gentle care he takes of my daughter that we are safe, even though we are prisoners.

Nevertheless, I am fearful—not of violence, but of the depth of the betrayal I saw in his eyes. Knowing his history with Tarla and his mother, it must seem that yet again, he has been deceived. Trust, that rare commodity I had been craving from him, is now ever more elusive between us. I wish he could understand that my bid for freedom was not a betrayal but an imperative. There is no way forward for us without free choice.

These gloomy reflections follow me as we ride along the road back to Reeves Hall. We are nearing my old home of Penhale Manor when Chloe begins to grouse. "I need a chamber pot," she whines, then adds, "Hungry." She begins to fidget in the saddle, clearly in discomfort.

Broek scowls blackly at me, as if it is my fault that this has happened. I raise a haughty brow in response. His frustration evident, he comes to a decision and nudges his horse into the short drive towards the house. We ride to the front steps and come to a halt, then I am quick to jump down from my horse. I go to him, holding out my hands for Chloe. He passes her to me a moment before jumping off his own mount. A servant rushes over to take the reins from us. There are several of Broek's people here. A man by name of Stroxol is perched on a tall ladder, repointing the bricks. When we enter the house, I see another, whose name I cannot recall, busy replacing a floor board on the staircase—the one that had constantly creaked when I had stepped on it.

Without a word, I take Chloe to the washroom and put her on the commode. I see it is like the ones at Reeves Hall. Quite clearly, in the month since I lived here, Broek and his people have been busy updating the furnishings and fixtures of the house. I cannot complain about the improvements. Once our business is done, we head back out to find Broek waiting for us in the hallway. "Croris will prepare a light repast for you," he says shortly, then takes off in the direction of the front parlour. We follow him, Chloe grumbling about her tummy and being hungry.

"Hush now, Sugar plum," I tell her. "Food is on the way."

We seat ourselves on the settee in terse silence, broken only by Chloe's plaintive moans. We are not made to wait long. Soon, a young lad, whose name I now know as Croris, comes through bearing a tray with fresh fruit and Uvonian pancakes. There is fresh orange juice too, a delicacy I have become accustomed to in my time at Reeves Hall. Quietly, we eat our food and drink our juice while Broek watches us with a grim expression. When we are done, I murmur a *thank you*, then we stand to leave once more.

"I have ordered the carriage for the remaining journey," says Broek. I nod in gratitude. It will be a relief not to get back on a horse, for in truth my body is sore.

As we reach the hallway, we hear a commotion outside. I knit my brow in concentration. It sounds like a carriage has just come up the drive to the house—surely the vehicle that will take us to Reeves Hall. One look at Broek's face, though, disabuses me of this notion. This is an unexpected and unwelcome visitor, judging from his expression. There is a tension in him too, and it is all to do with me. Instinctively, I know what he is thinking. How will I react upon coming into contact with a person from outside his household? Will I beg for help in escaping my wicked captor? Of course, since he no longer trusts me, he expects me to tell all.

We make our way to the front entrance and look out to see an older gentleman step down from the carriage. I recognise him instantly. "Mr Oakley," I say under my breath. Broek hears my words and frowns. There is no time for more speech as the solicitor approaches us and bows gravely. "Your Grace," he greets.

I curtsy. "Mr Oakley, what a surprise. Please do come inside."

He follows us into the house, casting a curious glance at Broek. I make quick work of the introductions. "Mr Oakley, may I make you known to Mr Brook Reeves, my neighbour and also now my landlord as he is the one to have recently purchased Penhale Manor." I turn to Broek. "Mr Oakley is my solicitor," I say by way of explanation.

Broek exchanges a stiff bow with Mr Oakley, whose expression clears, as he exclaims, "Mr Reeves, a pleasure to make your acquaintance, sir."

I guide my guest to the drawing room, and in my capacity as hostess, request some refreshment to be brought to us from Croris. I also send Chloe to keep him company.

Once we are settled in our seats, Mr Oakley explains the reason for his visit. "Your Grace," he says, "you will pardon me for being a trifle concerned when I learned that you were no longer to purchase the cottage in Frome and wished to remain in the house you had sold to Mr Reeves, especially as I was to understand the difficult situation you were in with regards to funds. It was an unusual request and caused me to wonder if all was well. In the end, I decided it would be best if I came here and discussed these matters with you in person."

I look down at my joined hands. I could, of course, tell Mr Oakley the truth, or some part of it, though it would be hard to convince anyone that I am being held captive when I am supposedly in my own home. At the very least, I could pretend that I have changed my mind about renting Penhale Manor and ask for Mr Oakley's assistance in escorting me back to Somerset and securing another home. Mr Oakley is my ticket to freedom, and by the tense way that Broek sits beside me, he knows it too. For a very small instant, I am tempted. This could be the end to my troubles, but this ticket to freedom comes with a heavy price. *Trust.* It is that word again, that precious commodity that is at stake.

My bid for freedom earlier today eroded the fragile fabric of Broek's trust in me. Now I must mend things. There can be no possibility of asking for Mr Oakley's help without destroying this fragile tendril of trust forever. I look up at the solicitor and smile warmly, "Mr Oakley, it is most generous and kind of you to make this journey to ask after me. I do acknowledge that events the past few months have not gone in the direction that I had planned. I must tell you, Mr Oakley, that this house, when first I arrived, was in an intolerable condition—overgrown with ivy, damp and rodent infested. It was a severe blow to my constitution to discover that my new home was in such a shocking state."

"Your Grace," says Mr Oakley looking distressed. "I am most grieved to hear this. Had I but known, I would have advised a different course of action."

I incline my head. "I am sure that would have been so. In any case, shortly after my arrival, I met with Mr Reeves, who made me a generous offer for the house." I glance at Broek who is staring fixedly at me, bracing himself for the betrayal that he expects but that will not come. Then I resume my speech. "I will tell you now, Mr Oakley, that it was pride that made me refuse it at first. I had an ambition, you see, to overturn this misfortune through my own labours. However, a few weeks into this task, it became clear to me that the transformation of this house with my limited funds was beyond even my strong-willed endeavours, and so I accepted Mr Reeves's offer. I had also by this time received the particulars of the cottage in Frome that was for sale. It seemed a sensible decision to sell Penhale Manor and move to that cottage."

"Yes, quite," nods Mr Oakley. "May I inquire what occurred to change your mind, Your Grace?"

Broek sits up beside me and I can feel the tension emanating from him as if it were a tangible thing. I rearrange the folds of my gown and very subtly shift my legs, tucked most properly under me, an inch to my right until they touch the edge of his trouser-clad thighs. The contact is slight, hardly worthy of attention, but that light touch is enough to send electrifying pulses throughout my body. And judging by Broek's reaction, he feels it too. His fists clench. His countenance darkens.

With a deep breath, I continue. "I received a letter from Drummonds Bank in London with some new and disquieting information. It seems I was left a significant sum of money when my father passed away. As you may know, Mr Oakley, I went to live with my uncle then, a Mr Robert Price, who was appointed my guardian. I was made to understand that I was taken in as charity and that I had no funds to my name—a false claim as I have now discovered. I have also since learned that my uncle and aunt took the quarterly interest that was paid on my funds and kept it for themselves rather than spending it on me."

"Oh my dear," Mr Oakley murmurs, clasping his hands in consternation. "I had no idea. A shocking abuse of trust."

"You may understand then, Mr Oakley," I go on, "why I no longer had any wish to reside in proximity to the family that had so abused my trust."

"Of course, of course," he nods.

I turn to face Broek with my next words. "When Mr Reeves heard of my distress, he immediately and very kindly offered to rent out Penhale Manor to me until I could make further plans as to my future. And as there was a need for a great deal of building work on the house to make the necessary improvements, Mr Reeves most generously invited me and Chloe to stay at Reeves Hall with his family as a guest until Penhale Manor was in a liveable state. That is where I have been residing this past month, though I shall soon be able to return here as the improvement works are very nearly complete."

Broek's dark eyes burn fiercely with a myriad emotions as they rest on mine. His fists unclench. Across from me, I hear Mr Oakley pronounce, "To be sure, that is a generous offer." But my attention is on Broek. I urge him with my eyes to see the truth of things. I have willingly sacrificed my opportunity to flee rather than betray his trust. Although his stance has relaxed, there is still tension in his body, as if he does not quite believe the danger is over.

I turn back to face my solicitor. "So you see, Mr Oakley, that your concern was misplaced, though it is most appreciated. I do thank you for coming here."

"Your Grace," he replies, "I am glad to have my concerns put to rest. I shall set out for London in the morning with my mind at ease, but I will ask you to please write to me should you wish any further assistance with regards to securing another house."

"Of course," I murmur.

Mr Oakley clears his throat. "Your Grace, I wonder if I might enquire. Is there a suitable inn I can put up in at Penhale village? I fear it is much too late in the day to journey back to Bodmin."

It is Broek that now responds. "I am afraid not, Mr Oakley. The duchess and I were about to take our leave, having come to inspect the progress on the house, but you are welcome to stay here for the night if you do not mind a few discomforts. I can have the servants make up a room for you upstairs."

Mr Oakley smiles gratefully. "Thank you, Mr Reeves, Your Grace, that is most kind."

The matter resolved, we now stand to take our leave. "Mr Oakley," I say. "Thank you again for your kind concern. I wish you a safe journey back to London."

He bows. "My pleasure, Your Grace. Good day now. Good day, Mr Reeves." Then Broek takes hold of my arm possessively and guides me out. He pauses a moment in the hallway to issue instructions regarding Mr Oakley's stay and to summon Chloe. Soon though, we are settled in the carriage and on our way to Reeves Hall.

As the vehicle rattles over the rutted road, I soothe a fractious and worn out Chloe, while Broek treats me to his usual scowling scrutiny. Eventually, I face him. The look we exchange is charged with meaning and mystery. I cannot quite fathom what he is thinking. His rage has abated and so has his combative tension. In its place is something else that is difficult to gauge. It is not, as I would hope, a forgiveness for what I have done nor a friendly disposition towards me. A reckoning for today's events is still to come.

CHAPTER 28

BROEK

We drive back in the carriage to Reeves Hall in tense silence. Poor little Chloe is tired and irritable after today's adventures. Jane pacifies her with gentle words and caresses. All the while I watch them, deeply perturbed. Earlier, I had thought Jane was about to betray me, like she did when she ran away. Why, then, did she lie to Mr Oakley? Why did she not beg him for help to escape from the ogre that was holding her captive? I cannot quite reconcile that behaviour with the cunning escape she had attempted earlier.

I long to hold her, but instead I flee to my control room as soon as we are inside the house. The aching pain in my chest which conflagrated on learning of Jane's deceit has not quite abated. As I enter the control room and take a seat in front of my console, I rub my chest, trying to ease the constriction I am feeling. Why did Jane not speak out when she could? Why did she not ask the solicitor to escort her away from here in his carriage? She had wanted to leave. She had made a brave bid to escape. Yet now she has come back with me willingly. Has she changed her mind?

I fire up the console and go through the latest data, taking in the information with half a mind, the other half thinking of Jane. After I took her on the couch in the parlour, I was so sure that she was mine. It was inconceivable that she should give her body and soul to me in such passion, and then leave. That damned duchess is messing with my mind. *And my heart.*

How could she have left? I was set to offer her marriage and all the freedoms she had craved. Instead, she got on a horse with her daughter and galloped away. I stand, unable to concentrate a minute longer on the data in front of me. It is time for dinner, in any case.

I arrive in the dining room to find my family congregated around the table, and Jane sitting quietly, her eyes cast down. Throughout the meal, she avoids my pained gaze. Conversation is stilted. My siblings are uncomfortable. They had grown easy in Jane's company, but her mad dash to escape has changed things. Their hackles are up and so are their suspicions. I know how they feel. And they don't even know the half of it, for I have not yet recounted the events with Mr Oakley today.

At the first opportunity, Jane excuses herself. Once the door shuts behind her, my siblings turn their gaze to me. I am not in any mood for conversation, but quickly, I fill them in on the latest developments. "It is as I thought," nods Simor when I finish. "You do understand now, Broek, that Jane is not a threat to us. She will not talk of what we do here to outsiders."

I sense he is right, but still I have doubts. "Yet at the first opportunity, she fled," I say flatly.

"Well, of course she did," laughs Liora. "It is what any sensible person would do. How long do you think she was going to accept being a prisoner in this house, Broek?"

I look away, annoyed and frustrated. "I was going to set her free just as soon as she married me," I reply gruffly. "Why could she not have waited a little longer?" *Why did she leave me?*

Liora sighs sympathetically but does not reply.

"She is not Tarla," Simor says, bravely mentioning the name that must not be spoken.

"I know," I grunt, rising to my feet. It is time to have a reckoning with the duchess. Without another word, I leave the dining room and hurry up the stairs to my chamber. I will wait until we are settled in bed, then speak to Jane via our communications link. It is sometimes easier for us to speak our minds that way, I have found.

I enter my chamber and sit on the bed to remove my shoes. As I do so, I catch sight of something on my dresser. Abruptly, I stand and fetch the item—a folded sheet of paper addressed to me in Jane's hand. When did she leave this here? Just now, or before?

With impatient hands, I break the seal and unfold the sheet, then read the contents.

Dear Broek,

Today, I am breaking free from my captivity at Reeves Hall. Please understand, I cannot be free to love you when I am a captive. Do not think this as a betrayal of your trust. After all, Broek, you have left me no choice other than to escape. My repeated assurances to you that I would not reveal your family's secrets were not enough for you to set me free. I have come to the conclusion that the only way to earn your trust is to prove my word to you.

I will never betray you, Broek. I shall not go far, but seek the nearest suitable accommodation. Should anyone enquire about your family, I shall speak of your generosity, express my gratitude for your help to me, but I shall not disclose any other detail about what goes on at Reeves Hall. Perhaps then, you will begin to accept my word.

But I must go, Broek. It is the hardest thing to do, especially after what happened between us today. But I am weary of having to stay hidden in this house while you all go out to church, and having a guard escort me each time I wish to walk outside. I cannot live like this. And though you say I will be free to do these things once we marry, that is not the right way to go about things. If and when I marry you, Broek, I want to do it out of choice, not necessity. I wish to face you at the church altar and promise myself to you from a position of freedom, not captivity. I think from this you must realise how much I have grown to care for you.

I do not wish this bid for freedom to be the end of our story, Broek, but to be a new beginning—the breaking of the impasse. If you still want me, come and find me. I shall await your next move. And Broek, if I am to marry you, then I must be courted and receive a proper proposal.

Yours,

Jane

I re-read the letter, my mind in turmoil. As for the ache in my chest, Great Yol, it feels like my heart is about to explode. I glance across the room to the door that separates me from Jane. The washroom indicator light is on. She is taking a bath, as she likes to do every evening.

With a sudden burst of energy, I stand and begin to tear off my clothes. The infernal cravat goes flying in the air, landing I know not where. My shirt soon follows suit. Then I am ripping at my trousers and yanking them down my legs. Drawers and stockings are next. Once I am fully bare, I march to the washroom, open the door and enter.

CHAPTER 29

JANE

I sink into the warm embrace of the water and let the ravages of the day leach away. I cannot help but fret. *Will I forever be trapped in this house?* I had the chance to escape, but I could not take it, not without betraying Broek. And now, I wonder if he will ever forgive me. In weariness, I close my eyes and try to empty my mind of this misery.

Time passes. I am drifting into a semi-conscious reverie. Then the washroom door opens. I blink my eyes and see a naked Broek stride into the room. He gives me a cursory nod and marches to the rain shower, sliding the glass door shut behind him. A moment later, warm jets of water rain down on him.

I turn my head in shock to watch him. He has his back to me and is scrubbing his body vigorously, then washing his hair with soap, for all the world as if this is a natural thing to do in my presence. I cannot help but admire his body. The strong muscles of his back ripple with each move and the firm roundness of his buttocks have me ache to touch them again. Oh my! What is he doing? Does this mean he has forgiven me? I do not understand.

The rain shower stops and a moment later, he is sliding open the glass door and stepping out. Without a care, he rubs a towel briskly over his body to dry himself, then drops it on a chair. As I gape at him, he comes towards me and enquires, "Enjoying the bath?"

"Erm, yes, thank you."

He nods again and turns to the wash basin. He takes out a small contraption that I have noticed before but not cared to investigate. He pours a thick liquid over the brush-like implement then puts it into his mouth, whereupon it makes a strange, buzzing sound. He moves it around his mouth, and I realise this contraption is for cleansing teeth. Ha! My tooth powder and brush achieve the same without all the unnecessary effort. Scientifically advanced or not, I believe my method is superior.

I lie back in the tub once more and watch him from the corner of my eye. He finishes with the contraption and spits the liquid, then washes out his mouth with water. Finally, he pats his face dry with a cloth then turns to face me, hands on hips. "So, Jane," he says gruffly, "you wish me to court you and to gallantly propose."

I sink lower into the water under the intensity of his gaze. "If other conditions are met first," I squeak bravely.

He nods thoughtfully. "That can be achieved," he says on a grunt. "As of now, Jane, consider yourself free. Take the carriage out whenever you wish." With a quick smile, he adds, "Enjoy your bath. Goodnight." Then he walks away, shutting the door quietly behind him.

I follow him with my eyes, too shocked to speak. Relief, elation and some much deeper emotion wage war within my breast. On impulse, I rise out of the bath and briskly dry myself with a towel, throwing it down when I am done, much in the manner he just did. And then, with determination in every step, wearing not a stitch of clothing, I march towards the door that leads to his chamber. With no hesitation, I open it wide and walk in.

He is sitting in bed, the covers loosely gathered in his lap. I go towards him and with an imperious flick of my hand, pull the blanket off him and throw it to the end of the bed. An instant later, I scramble over him to straddle his lap, planting my hands over his shoulders. His eyes are liquid fire as he stares into mine. "You promised me satisfaction every night," I taunt. "Now show me."

Barely have I spoken than with a groan deep in his throat, he has me gathered to him and is tumbling us over on the bed so his body covers mine entirely. A moment later, he claims my lips in the wildest, most possessive kiss that has ever existed in the universe. Our hands claw greedily as we attack each other, rational thought gone, only a deep instinctual need driving us to act. Lips and tongues seek then find, legs entwine and hips press together in a rhythm driven by elemental passion. "Fill me, Broek," I moan against his lips. "Fill me."

"I will, my heart, I will," he grits in between desperate kisses. His hand flies down to cup my mound, then suddenly he is shifting down the bed to replace his hand with his mouth. With big, strong hands, he raises my hips to his lips and feasts on me, like he once promised he would. I gasp at the sensation, jerking uncontrollably as his tongue licks a long path from my opening to the small nub of joyfulness above it. He rains wet kisses on this most sensitive part of me, interspersed with laps of his tongue. He nips gently with his teeth then sucks. He devours every inch of that secret flesh with a hunger that leaves me trembling and undone. No part of me is left untouched, even the crevice between my buttocks is lavished with the wet stroke of his tongue. I moan. I cry. When his strong mouth clamps on my pleasure nub and sucks, I shriek. "Broek!"

He looks up, his face smeared with my lustful juices, and palms his huge, swollen member. "Will you take me now?" he growls desperately.

"Yes! Yes!"

Already, he is notching his male shaft to my entrance, and then he is pushing in, slowly but inexorably, until all his length is sheathed within me. No sooner has he filled me than he begins to move, pounding in and out. He leans over me, bracketing my body with his elbows as his mouth captures mine again. I taste the muskiness of my scent on him, but I do not dwell on this, for I am lost to powerful sensation as he drives himself deep within me while he possesses my mouth. Deep, oh so deep, he plunges, over and over, melding us together until I cannot say where I end and he begins.

I run my fingers through his soft locks and grip his head tight to me, wanting his kiss, wanting his possession of my body to last for the rest of time. I feel him shift his stance and lift my knees, then he is back to thrusting his shaft into me, his lips never leaving mine. Now with each thrust I feel him stroke a part of me deep inside that throbs at his every touch, driving me wild with need. "More!" I demand, and he obliges, plunging rapidly and deep as I begin to feel that build-up of sensation that will soon drive me to the precipice.

He senses I am close to it, for he redoubles his efforts, groaning with each powerful thrust. "Come, Jane!" he roars, his desperation lighting a fire that finally sends me hurtling to that pinnacle. With a loud moan, I lose myself in pulsing ecstasy. Broek follows me over the precipice, pulsing his shaft as he spends his seed inside me.

It is a long time before we are recovered enough from our pleasure to move. With a gentle kiss to my lips, Broek pulls out and drops onto his back beside me. We lie side by side, staring at the bed canopy and coming back to our senses. I have behaved wantonly, but I do not seem to care. What Broek and I experience when our bodies join is so profound a feeling that it can only be a gift from God. I am certain of it. That does not mean, of course, that we should not be plighting our troth in church at the soonest opportunity, only that I cannot find it in me to feel shame for what we have done.

Broek turns his face to me. "So, Jane, have I satisfied you tonight?"

"Indeed you have, Broek. I thank you."

I hear his quiet chuckle and smile to myself. A moment later, he is on his feet. "Stay," he commands as he strides to the washroom, returning soon after with a wet cloth. He uses it to cleanse us, then deposits it in the washroom again. When he returns, I am sitting up, readying to go to my chamber.

"Where do you think you are going?" he snarls.

I raise a brow. "Back to my chamber, of course, unless you wish to give me more satisfaction tonight."

"I may do so once I have regained my strength." He is now at the bed and lifting me easily in his arms before tossing me onto the other side of it. A moment later, the blanket is thrown over me. "You will sleep here from now on," he pronounces, settling under the covers beside me.

I frown. "But we are not yet married."

"Jane," he says impatiently, his usual scowl making a reappearance on his countenance. "We have experienced all the intimacies of a married couple. Do not balk at this now." He places a possessive hand on my hip then grunts, "Lights out." A moment later, we are in darkness. "Sleep," he commands. Dictatorial man! I should put up some resistance to these managing tendencies, but not tonight, I think as I emit a loud yawn. Instinctively, I burrow close to his large body and breathe in his heavenly scent. Tomorrow, I think sleepily. We can resolve everything else then.

CHAPTER 30

JANE

I wake gradually to a most pleasant sensation. My sleep-filled mind is slow to determine the source of this delight. It only knows that it does not want it to end. I breathe deeply, releasing a contented moan. "Hmm."

A large hand is roaming over my body. It stops at my breasts, easily engulfing them in a warm clasp. Fingers strum the throbbing tips, making them stand like stiff peaks. Then the hand carries on its journey, drawing slow serpentine strokes over the smoothness of my belly, the soft flare of my hips. On it goes, travelling lower still to my hair-covered mound, resting over it with proprietorial warmth.

I am seduced by the comfort of Broek's hand stroking me. It soothes a troubled part of my being that came to life the day I was taken in, orphaned and penniless, by the ostensible charity of my relations. Unloved and alone, I braved the challenge of each day with a stoic resolve that could not erase the void that had been left in my soul. It is a deeply entrenched need of every person in humankind to be encased in familial love. When that love is missing, some may fill the gap with a carapace of courage, a will to fight on. To the unkind world around us, we display a calm fortitude and pretend that all is well. But still, that need never subsides.

Then along came Giles, and I drank thirstily from the well of love he offered me. Dearest Giles. Yet even his tender ministrations could not shield me from the cruel words, the whispering, the snubbing. I was thrust into a world in which I patently did not belong and where all others understood that I was an upstart that did not know my place. Never have I felt, even in my father's home, a sense of truly belonging. My place was never assured. Perhaps it is this deeply felt uncertainty that has, over the years, fed the contrariness of my character. When thrown into deep water, the choice is either to sink without a trace or to swim vigorously towards the shore—even if that shore is never reached.

Yet now, with the simple act of this hand resting on the core of my body, I feel claimed. I belong. I feel it to my very marrow. No words of love have been spoken between Broek and me, though our bodies have proclaimed it so loud that we would be deaf not to hear. Broek lingers with his hand on my mound as if he too knows the importance of this touch. In this one instant, he calms my itinerant soul and locks it into the place where it belongs. I open my eyes.

Broek leans on one elbow as his other hand rests possessively over me. We say nothing, simply gaze deeply at one another, and I know I have made the right choice. My hand snakes up to the roughness of his cheek. With a gentle press I pull him towards me, parched for his kiss. His lips touch mine softly, almost reverently. This kiss is different from before. There is no passionate frenzy, yet it expresses just as great a need. Our lips come together repeatedly, feeding a mutual hunger for love that will never be sated.

Eventually, Broek pulls back enough to speak, his large palm still resting on the core of me. "Jane," he says, his voice gritty. "Marry me, please."

"You are supposed to woo me," I demur.

He expels a long breath and replies, a trifle irritably, "I am no good with words. You must take me as I am."

"I require some expression of your sentiments, Broek," I tell him, softening the rebuke with the loving touch of my fingers on his whiskery jaw.

"I would have thought my sentiments were clear," he grumbles.

"Ah," I say lightly. "So they might be, but for the clarification of any doubts, I would prefer a spoken expression of those sentiments."

He eyes me cautiously. "Would such words, if expressed, be similarly reciprocated?" he enquires.

"Naturally," I assure him.

"And what weight would such words have?" His tone is bitter as he continues, "I have heard them spoken before, long ago, poetic sentiments accompanied by soulful looks of the eyes. They were all for naught."

"I am not Tarla," I say very simply.

The hand at my mound pulls away, and I feel the loss instantly. Broek turns to lie on his back beside me, bleak eyes staring at the canopy above. "I know you are not her," he hisses softly.

"And yet you wonder why this between us would be any different."

A long silence then, "Yes."

I curse that wicked woman once more for the damage she has wrought, and wonder if it is possible for Broek ever to heal from the wilful destruction of his trusting nature. I conclude that only constancy through time can be a balm for this wound. There will be no quick cure for what ails him, and I shall have to be patient, trusting that what I sense in him is love, and that in the fullness of time, it will be expressed openly. Broek has taken the first, vital step of handing me back my freedom. Now it is my turn.

I turn onto my side, facing him, and place a hand to his groin in an echo of his previous touch. The tips of my fingers graze his stiffening member. In a clear voice, I tell him, "Yes, I will marry you."

He groans softly and places his hand over mine, guiding it over his swollen shaft. "Feel what you do to me," he grunts, and certainly, I can feel the magnificent solidity of him. "Ask me," he grits, and I know what it is he wants.

Looking up into his torrid eyes, I breathe, "Fill me, Broek."

"With pleasure," he grounds, then looms above me and spears my flesh with his. Thus begins the sweetly punishing rhythm that culminates in both our satisfaction. Afterwards, he takes me by the hand to the washroom and cleanses both our bodies under the rain shower. I am both wondrous and curiously at ease with this naked intimacy that has grown between us. It is as if we are Adam and Eve in the Garden of Eden before the advent of the evil serpent.

We step out of the rain shower and dry ourselves with the towels Broek possesses that are so soft and warm. Then, naked and without shame, we walk hand in hand to my own chamber, where Broek watches me as I take out fresh garments to wear. He stands and observes each step of my toilette. One time, he assists me with the laces of my stays, dropping a kiss on the tip of each breast before it is covered by the stiff material.

When I sit at my dressing table and pick up the brush, he takes it from me and runs it gently through my hair. When that task is done, he studies me intently as I gather my locks into a knot at the back of my head, leaving a few loose curls to fall at my temples. And last of all, I take the bottle of cologne and place a small drop of the fragrant liquid on my wrist, rubbing it into the flesh. He lifts my hand and sniffs deeply, making a humming noise of satisfaction.

It is by mutual consent that I then accompany him back to his chamber and watch him as he goes about his daily toilette. I am, of course, intimate with the undergarments of a gentleman, yet still I observe him in fascination as he pulls on drawers, stockings and trousers, covering the delightful bulge at his groin that refuses to soften in my presence. His shirt comes on next and then the cravat, with which he grapples imperfectly until I take the fabric from his hands and tie it neatly for him. It is something I used to do for Giles, so I am a quick hand at it. Broek watches my deft work in some surprise, then mutters, "Thank you."

I smile benignly and rise on my tiptoes to drop a kiss on his lips. "My pleasure," I reply. Then I am assisting him with his tailcoat, brushing away a speck of dust from the shoulder. I step back to admire him and nod in approval. My husband-to-be is an exceedingly handsome man, even if it is myself saying so. I shall not be one to complain if this is to be my life from here on.

We leave his chamber side by side, visiting a sleepy Chloe and bidding her good morning, then descending the stairs together to make our way to the dining room. As we do so, I reflect on the tremendous differences one single day can bring. At this very time yesterday, I was plagued by nerves in anticipation of my flight. Now, I am calm, content and hopeful. "I think perhaps I shall go to Newquay in the carriage today, and shop for a gown," I tell Broek airily. He raises a brow but does not argue with this. "After all," I continue, "I shall need something new to wear for our wedding."

"Not black," he grunts.

"Not black," I agree.

In full harmony with each other, we enter the dining room. We are the first ones there except for Horis, who greets us with both a timid and curious gaze. Broek pulls out the chair for me, dropping a kiss to the top of my head before sitting at the table beside me. He serves me coffee, eggs, a few slices of beef, and of course, Uvonian pancakes. I eat hungrily—our recent exertions having built my appetite—as one by one, Broek's other siblings troop into the dining room.

Our meal is a convivial one, though Broek himself does not contribute much to the discourse. He watches me with the predatory eyes of a hawk, and I bask in his hungry gaze. Once or twice, he cannot resist reaching forward and running a hand over the bare flesh of my arm, or tucking a loose strand of hair behind my ear. His attentions do not go unnoticed. "I see the two of you have made up," observes Liora.

In response, I state baldly, "Broek has agreed to restore my freedom. I shall be going out in the carriage today to visit the shops in Newquay."

No word of protest comes from the family. Liora merely replies that she has a few items she requires from town, and would I mind very much if I picked these up for her. I voice my acquiescence, pleased at this normalisation in our relations.

I finish breakfast in a jubilant mood. It is not every day, after all, that one becomes engaged to be married. And when in addition to this, one's freedom has been won after over a month of captivity, I would think it quite natural to feel some self-congratulatory sense of achievement. Each heated look Broek sends my way, each solicitous gesture, each tender touch brings forth in me a sense of joy along with a feverish excitement. I do believe that, were it not for the proper decorum, I would be hauling Broek back to the bedchamber for some further satisfaction.

CHAPTER 31

JANE

I set down my knife and fork, replete after my fine meal. Broek is on his feet, about to assist me to mine, when the dining room door is wrenched open forcefully and a red-faced Wolkan rushes in, garbled words pouring forth from his mouth.

Sadly, I have yet to learn the Uvonian language, though I promise myself that I shall set to that task at the first opportunity, for in this instant, I very much wish that I could understand what is being said. Everyone in the room freezes in shock, followed by urgent action as they hurry out of the room. Broek answers my befuddled stare with a quickly thrown remark, "A communication has come from Uvon." Then he too is heading out of the room. Determined not to miss out on whatever news this brings, I follow at his heels, not an easy task with the differences in our gaits. I arrive in the family parlour, huffing slightly at the exertion.

As I enter the room, I remember briefly the passionate happenings that occurred here a day ago, but this memory is soon dispelled as I take in nearly the entire household gathered tensely in anticipation of reading this communication. I wait for a letter to be proffered and for Broek to read it out loud to his flock. But that is not what happens. Of course, I should have known that the Uvonians, with their superior scientific knowledge, disdain the paper missive in favour of vision and sound on the screen.

Soon after our arrival, the large screen on the wall comes alive, and I see a lady address us in their language. She is dressed peculiarly, in a bodice that dips deep into her cleavage. The satiny fabric of her gown, a rusty shade of bronze, flares loosely down her hips to gather at the ankles, almost like billowing pantalettes. She is not young, though her creamy skin is flawless and free of any wrinkles. It is the eyes that betray her age, beautiful but knowing eyes of deep sea green fringed with long lashes. Her hair, a burnished golden red, is gathered in an intricate knot over her head, flowing wisps artfully set free from that knot. Her voice, as she begins to speak, is mellifluous and hauntingly compelling. I am captivated by her. Who could this lady be?

My eyes fly to Broek, and I see him stand to stiff attention, fists balled tightly at his side. Could it be? No! But it must be. The frozen grimace on his face is explanation enough. Yes, it is her. Tarla. I turn back to the screen and listen to her speak, not understanding the words but aware of their import. Her speech over, the screen dims and all of a sudden, there is commotion, voices speaking one over the other in their tongue, and the palpable sense of something momentous taking place. Gav'ox, one of the guards here, has his hands clasped together in febrile excitement. What is this news that Tarla has just imparted?

Through it all, my eyes stay fixed on Broek, who has not moved nor said a word. I want to go to him, but the rigidity of his stance does not invite my touch. Then, before my eyes, I see him take charge of the situation. In a booming voice, he silences the crowd, addressing them with short, sharp words. A moment later, he stalks out of the room, a pandemonium of voices breaking out at his departure. People talk excitedly among themselves. Some are embracing, tears of emotion running down their cheeks. Nobody notices me nor cares to enlighten me as to what has happened.

Finally, I see Liora, a look of awe on her countenance, begin to make her way to the door. I go to her quick and touch her arm. "Tell me please," I beg. "What is it?"

She casts me a surprised glance, as if only now recalling my presence. Her voice tight with emotion, she murmurs, "An official pardon has been granted to us all. We may return to Uvon should we wish. The ship arrives for us tomorrow." With this, she nods mistily at me and leaves the room. Others follow suit, a loudly chattering exodus. I am left alone in the parlour to gather my thoughts. So, the Reeves clan will be returning to their homeland on a ship that arrives tomorrow. I wonder how it has sent a communication to us here when it is still out at sea, then I wonder no more. If Broek has nanoprobes that can fly to all parts of the world, then surely the advanced civilisation of Uvon has its own speedy methods of communication too.

Will this ship dock at Newquay? Not if it wishes to keep its presence a secret. Most probably it will keep its distance out at sea, perhaps sending a contingent here in small boats in the darkness of night like smugglers do. Soon after, the people here will want to leave Reeves Hall and return at long last to their true home. I am sure they are already busy packing their belongings. And as for me? I look down at my hands to find that they are shaking. What can this mean for me? I do not know. Will Broek take me with him to his homeland as his bride or will he leave me behind in the knowledge that our two worlds cannot meet? Would I even have the courage to leave these shores to live in a faraway land among a people whose way of life is so very different to mine and who speak in a tongue I cannot fathom? It is too much to contemplate.

I bury my face in my hands and try to calm my anxious heart. I pray for patience and fortitude. All will be revealed in due course. I am sure Broek will find me once he knows his mind. He has a great many things to occupy him at present, and I must wait patiently. I must also prepare myself for the worst. Should he decide it is best to break our engagement and leave without me to return to his homeland, then I shall not cry nor burden him with my heartbreak. I am pulled back once more to that feeling of old, the one where I am alone and not assured of my place. The sense of belonging I felt earlier with Broek was merely a fanciful delusion. I know it now, and I am also familiar with what to do when I find myself in troubled waters. I make the best of things. I swim in the direction of the shore with resolution in every stroke.

With this last thought, I get to my feet briskly and take a deep breath. There is no point now in journeying to Newquay to purchase a wedding gown for a ceremony that may not take place. Instead, I seek out Chloe. I find her with Betsy.

"Have you heard the news, Your Grace?" she asks unable to suppress her excitement. When I nod, she continues animatedly, "Velnas has told me all about Uvon. It is a wonderful place full of scientific contraptions even better than the ones here at Reeves Hall." She clasps her heart, happiness shining from her eyes. "Velnas wants to take me there. He says we can seal our union and have it blessed the Uvonian way—it is their form of marriage!"

No doubts there as to her future, I think sourly. I am envious. Velnas was quick to clear up any uncertainty she may have felt. Together they will go. As for me—limbo awaits until Broek deigns to remember my presence.

As I try to distract and calm my excitable daughter who has sensed the frenzy in the air and is fairly bursting with it, I decide to go and find him. He must be in his subterranean room. Leaving Chloe in Betsy's capable hands, I take the stairs down to the basement and present my face to the red beam that alerts Broek to my presence. Then I wait, and wait some more. The door does not open. Reluctantly, I step back and retrace my steps upstairs. Broek, it seems, is not ready to speak to me.

In my chamber, I pace back and forth in frustration and worry. I decide there is nothing for it but to go for a ride until my mind is clearer. I am free to do so now, after all. And they will not want me here. I take my cloak and charge back down the stairs, then without waiting for a guard or for any permission whatsoever, I step outside the house in the direction of the stable. It is deserted, apart from the horses quietly shuffling in their stalls. Quickly, I set about releasing Daisy and attaching a saddle to her back. It is not an easy task, but I am a resourceful person. Soon, I have her ready. I lead her to the mounting block and hop up into the saddle. Then, I guide her out towards the front gate.

There, I am met with a young guard whose name I do not recall. He casts a wary glance at me then taps the communicating device on his ring. I hear him speak in his tongue and Broek's curt reply. A moment later, the young man nods and opens the gates for me. Broek has kept to his word, and I am free to go. I leave the gates of Reeves Hall and set towards the village of Penhale, gathering speed and letting the wind whip at my cheeks a I lead Daisy into a gallop. I have no clear objective for this journey other than to ride free and rid myself of the nervous tension in my being. Much better this than waiting anxiously in my chamber for Broek's pronouncement. The longer his silence, the more I suspect he is preparing to leave me.

I soon reach the village and slow down to a decorous trot. Though I have money in my reticule, there is not anything I require from the few shops here. My material needs are more than adequately met at Reeves Hall—though for how much longer I do not care to think. Despite my continued nerves, I consider going back. Perhaps Broek will speak to me now. It is then my eyes land on the spire of the village church. If there were any time when spiritual guidance was needed, then that time is now. With a gentle pull of the reins, I guide Daisy towards the church and dismount, securing her to a nearby post beside a water trough. Then, I walk inside.

It has been over a month since I was last here. As I enter, my nose catches the faint scent of incense. The large hall is empty and silent, a candle burning at the altar. I step forward softly. In the quietude of this space I sense an almost tangible peacefulness. Tears prick at my eyes.

I go to a pew and kneel, pressing my hands together in prayer. Head bowed, I silently pray. *Oh Great Lord, what am I to do? If Broek deserts me, where am I to go? What is the path that will lead to a secure and content existence? And if Broek desires me to accompany him to Uvon, should I go? Great Lord, give me the strength to do what is right for all of us.*

So many supplications pour forth from my splintered soul. I do not know how long I stay thus, but finally, when my prayers are exhausted, I rise to my feet. As I begin to walk up the aisle, I notice a man sitting at a pew a few rows behind, observing me. It is Reverend Edmund Horton. He stands as I approach. "Your Grace," he says gently. "It has been many weeks since we last saw you in Penhale. I was told you had returned to Somerset."

"Yes, I had plans to do so," I say, my mind working quickly to formulate an appropriate response.

He raises an enquiring brow. "And yet here you have remained. At Penhale Manor?"

I shake my head and decide to give a version as close to the truth as possible. "My daughter had an accident and I was obliged to stay with her at Reeves Hall. As you may know, Mr Harry Reeves has a great skill in healing. He has been tending to her."

The reverend's face falls. "Your Grace, I did not know. How dreadful! Is your daughter recovered?"

I give a small smile. "Yes, she is well now, Lord be thanked."

"Indeed, Lord be thanked. And will Your Grace be leaving once more for Somerset?" enquires the reverend.

"I—I do not believe so." At his frown, I elucidate. "The cottage I had hoped to purchase in the town of Frome has gone to another buyer, due to the delay in my arrival. In the meantime, Mr Brook Reeves has kindly agreed to let me have the tenancy of Penhale Manor. As you can see, reverend, the kindness and generosity of the Reeves family abounds."

He smiles sagely. "I do not know the family well, for they keep to themselves, but what I have seen of them chimes with what Your Grace says." He pauses. "Please forgive me, but was there something else, some other trouble, that brought you here today? If so, perhaps you may wish to speak of it with me." He smiles kindly as he says this.

Of course, the perspicacious vicar has observed my distress, but I cannot tell him all. I look down at the polished floor. "I have been left in difficult circumstances, Reverend," I murmur. "Not only am I a widow with a young child to care for, but I am also an orphan, and the only family I have left—an uncle and aunt—have been less than kind towards me. I am fortunate to have sufficient funds to live comfortably, and for that I am immensely grateful, yet my future lies uncertain."

Reverend Horton nods thoughtfully. "These are difficult circumstances, Your Grace, and you were right to seek sustenance from the good Lord. It is at those times when we feel forsaken and alone that we must remember Jesus's eternal love shines for us bright and strong. Keep with the prayers, Your Grace, and trust that in time, the future you fear will become less uncertain. And of course, I am here, should you wish a sympathetic ear."

"Thank you, Reverend. It is very kind."

"Not at all, Your Grace. It is what I am here for."

I nod and make a curtsy. "Good day, Reverend."

"Good day, Your Grace."

In a calmer mood, though anxiety still gnaws at me, I return to my horse and set on my journey back to Reeves Hall. I am let through the gates and ride towards the stable. There, I am met by Galok, who assists me to dismount and takes Daisy in to rub her down. As I walk to the house, my stomach gurgles and it is only now I realise that I have missed luncheon—though perhaps, with the great commotion of packing for the upcoming journey, there was not time for anyone to stop for a meal. I let myself in through the servants' entrance at the back of the house and look in on the kitchen, hoping to forage for something to eat.

There, I find Velnas, stirring a pot of meat stew. A delicious smelling pie bakes in the glass oven, firing up my hunger. He turns to me and exclaims, "Ah, you are back! Dinner will not be served for a few hours, but perhaps I can cut Your Grace a slice of meat pie?"

I shake my head. "No, Velnas. I simply need something I can take to my chamber."

He quickly goes to do my bidding, handing me slices of bread and cheese wrapped in a linen napkin. I thank him and take myself up to my chamber, where I wolf down the snack and refresh myself in the washroom. I look in on Broek's chamber, but it is deserted. With a sigh, I head back down the stairs in search of Chloe, who I find in the play room with Betsy and the other two young children she has befriended. I stay with them until it is teatime for Chloe, all the while telling myself that I have the faith and fortitude to face whatever lies before me. Why won't Broek talk to me? Is it because he is preparing to leave me, and won't say it to my face?

I leave Chloe with Betsy to eat her meal and return to my chamber. There is still an hour to go until dinner, and there is one thing that always seems to melt away my cares—a hot bath. I start filling the tub and undress. A short time later, I lower my body into the fragrant heat of the water and sigh with relief. Whatever happens, I shall be strong. My heart can take this, even though it will feel pain. For here, in the solitude of the washroom, I can confess to myself the truth. I have fallen in love with Broek Reeves.

I close my eyes, then open them again as the man that has captured my heart walks into the washroom. Grim-faced, Broek stares at me for an eternity, then gruffly declares, "Jane, we need to talk."

CHAPTER 32

BROEK

Am I in a nightmare or a dream? It is hard to fathom. A burden lifted from my shoulders when I heard Tarla tell us we had been pardoned. I had not realised just how much of a weight it had been on me to hold this treasonous guilt.

Beautiful as ever, poised and captivating, she spoke to us with her emblematic warmth as if we had parted only as sorrowful friends. She told of her battle with the governing body over several years to win us a pardon, and how at the last she—for the glory was to be hers—had managed it. She spoke of her wish to see us return and reinstated to our positions. She even addressed me directly. "Broek," she said. "I have missed you dearly. All that happened then is forgotten. Come home, dear love."

Ten years ago, I would have longed to hear her say this. Now, though, I feel nothing. It was all a sham. I do not love her. All delicate feelings for Tarla were killed long ago. And never do I wish to resurrect a relationship with the poisonous viper that she is.

But still, a decision must be made. I saw the joy on the faces around me. Our exile has been a penance, and many of us are keen to return to our old life. No matter how hard I have strived to build a good life for us here, it has not been enough. In this, I have failed. It is not just my servants that wish to leave. I saw it on Liora's ecstatic countenance, and a little on Horis. They have both suffered here, living a life apart from society. I have failed them most terribly too.

One thing was immediately apparent to me. Whatever the decision is to be, stay or leave, it must be a unanimous one. Our family cannot be split in two, with one half here and the other back on Uvon. If we are to return, then we must all go. And if we are to stay, then all of us must remain. And what of Jane? I forced myself not to glance at her. Until I know my siblings' mind on the matter, I cannot chart a way forward. I cannot prevent my family and servants from doing what they have longed to do for ten years. But how can I leave Jane?

Over the hubbub that broke out around me, I spoke with all the authority I had. "Silence! Clearly each of us has a decision to make—stay or go. No one will be judged harshly for the choice they make. All I ask is that you inform me by ten o'clock tomorrow of your decision so that we may make the appropriate preparations. I shall leave you now to reflect on the matter. Liora, Horis, Simor, my control room. I shall wait for you there." Then, careful not to lay eyes on Jane, though I sensed her confusion, I strode out of the room.

I feel a pounding at my temple and in my racing heart as I now go down to the basement and go through the security scan to enter the space below. Once at my console, I sit and stare blankly. Home. What would it be like to return? I shall hardly be welcomed as a hero. I would have to start over and rebuild our fortunes there. To our great ancestral palace we would go. I envisage my private apartment there that I had so lovingly appointed. Undoubtedly there would be greater comforts to be had there. But I could not go without Jane.

My heart stops. Will my wilful little duchess accompany me to Uvon? She does not even know yet that our home is on a distant planet. I am sure she thinks we shall be riding the seas on a ship to journey there. Space flight, or any flight for that matter, is something outside her comprehension. Will she even be able to start a new life on a completely different planet? It will be a shock for her to learn the truth. And with a young daughter to protect, would she ever consider setting foot in a machine that flies high up in the sky?

I sink my head in my hands, overwhelmed with despair. Great Yol, but you are testing me! It is then I hear the knock at my door. I rise to open it and let in Liora, Horis and Simor. We sit in a circle and wait. The silence presses on me. I must speak. "Let us freely express one by one what is in our minds," I say. "Liora, you go first. Do you wish to return to Uvon?"

She hesitates then blurts, "Yes."

"I thought so," I tell her with a touch of sadness.

She picks up on my melancholy. "Broek," she says quickly, "I know you have tried your best to help us build a good life here, and what we have achieved together is commendable. But you cannot change the way English society views women. We are chattels, at the mercy of men. And because of this, I have been condemned to remain here at Reeves Hall, hiding my true self from society. In Uvon, I can be free again to have a career, affairs of the heart, and perhaps in time to find a suitable mate to form a union with." She finishes sadly, looking at me, "None of these things I can do here."

My heart sinks, but I nod in understanding. "I hear you, Liora." I turn to my middle brother. "And you, Horis?"

He swallows thickly. "I am unsure, Broek. I am comfortable and used to my life here now. However, as a physician, it is nigh on impossible to practise my craft except within the confines of Reeves Hall. Look what happened when I made the decision to treat Chloe. I know it put us all in danger. Thankfully, that danger did not materialise, for Jane is unlike most people, and we have come to trust her. But if such a situation were to arise again, I would be put into that intolerable position of knowing I have the means to save a person's life and knowing too that I risk our lives by doing so."

I nod again. "Your logic is indisputable, Horis." Then I turn finally to my youngest brother. "And what of you, Simor?"

He glances at us uneasily then sighs. "If you decide to return to Uvon, then of course I shall come with you. However, I will have you all know that I would not mind staying on Earth. I was very young when we left our old home, and my memories of it are not as clear as yours may be. I will admit that I have grown comfortable here. It feels like home to me, and I have made friendships with people outside of Reeves Hall. I would be loath to leave that behind."

I press his shoulder. "Your feelings matter as much as ours do, Simor. Thank you for telling us your truth."

Simor eyes me narrowly. "It is your turn now, Broek. Tell us what you wish to do."

"Side by side with the fact that we will get a greater quality of life on Uvon is the reality of having to confront Tarla again, something I have no wish to do," I say heavily. "Be that as it may, I have one consideration that troubles me the most."

"Jane," murmurs Liora.

"Yes, Jane. She has agreed to be my wife, but she does not know that Uvon is a planet in a distant galaxy. I fear… I fear that when she learns this, she will not agree to journey there with me."

"And if she does not?" prompts Horis.

"Then I would wish to remain here with her," I say with finality.

"You have fallen in love with her," states Horis.

I do not reply. If I am to disclose my sentiments, then Jane must be the first to hear them. Instead, I say, "So, it seems we are split on the matter. I think I speak for all of us, however, when I say that we cannot split our family in two. We must either all go or stay."

Liora nods furiously. "If there is one thing that I have learned since our exodus here, it is the importance of family. We *must* stay together."

Everyone else murmurs their assent. "In that case," I decide, "we shall put it to a vote. And we must agree to all abide by that vote."

"What if it is a tie?" wonders Horis.

"Then we vote again, and this time, I will withdraw from the matter. With only three votes, it will be impossible to have a tie."

"That is hardly fair," frowns Simor.

"It is as fair as I can make it," I bite back. Softening my tone, I say, "whatever you three agree on, I will abide by." A heavy cloud descends on me as I know what that could mean. Just then, as if I have conjured Jane from my mind, the alert sounds on my screen. Someone is at the basement door, and though I put the screen on visual to see who it is, I already know. For an endless moment, I stare into Jane's hazel brown eyes. Then I take a deep breath and dismiss the alert, turning to my siblings to get back to the matter in hand. "Are you ready to vote?" I ask them gruffly. They nod. I hand them each a tablet and instruct, "Write your vote, stay or go, then on the count of three, hold up your tablet."

We all begin to write on our tablet. I countdown three and we all show our vote. My heart pounds madly in my chest. What if the decision is to leave? I feel as if I am standing at a precipice. Then, bracing myself for what I am to see, I check each of my siblings' votes. It is a three to one decision to stay, Liora being the lone voice wanting to return to Uvon. I expel a sigh of relief. If the vote had gone the other way around, I would have had to convince Jane to come with me, leaving behind all that is familiar to her. And what if she had refused? I begin to realise now that I could not have left Jane, even if it meant breaking up the tight unit of my family. Thank Yol, that is not a decision I now need to face.

"So," I say with finality. "We stay."

Liora stares down at her feet, her body held stiffly. I sense her acute disappointment. Without a word, she rises and leaves the room. My brothers too are quick to leave. And then I bury my face in my hands, emotion overcoming me. I remain in this state until I am interrupted by a call from Or'ots, one of the guards, who is on duty at the gate. "The duchess is on her horse and wanting to leave the estate," he says hurriedly. "What do I do?"

For a brief moment, I am tempted to withhold my assent. I want to keep her close, never let her go. But I gave my word. "Let her go," I bark. The line disconnects as Or'ots goes to do my bidding. Without thinking, I fire up my console and programme the nanoprobes to fly out to the main gates. A visual comes up on the screen. She is on her horse, looking tight lipped. I instruct the probes to follow her wherever she goes and sit back to watch and listen.

I see her urge the horse to a gallop and the wind whip at her face as she rides out to freedom. Her expression eases with each mile until she reaches Penhale village. There, she slows to a trot and looks around her pensively. Her eyes spy the church, and I know, even before she guides her horse in that direction that this is the place where she will go. I have deprived her of access to this holy place for over a month, I think with a heavy heart. Of course, it is where she will want to go.

I see her dismount and secure her horse to a post, then walk hesitantly to the church doors. The hall is empty as she enters and takes a deep breath, no doubt inhaling the unmistakable scent of beeswax and incense. Then she walks to a pew and kneels down to pray. I watch her for endless minutes, reading the pain and confusion in her countenance as she says her silent prayers. We each worship a different god—or perhaps it is the same entity with a different name—and yet I wonder if the words of her prayer echo my own private incantations not long ago.

After a while, I notice that she is no longer alone. Someone has entered the church hall and is observing her from a pew three rows behind. It is Reverend Horton. He sits calmly and watches her. I straighten up in my seat and turn the volume higher so I can hear whatever words are spoken.

Eventually, Jane finishes her prayers and stands to leave. That is when she notices the reverend and goes to him. I listen to their conversation. Of course, he is curious about her presence still in Penhale when all had supposed her to have left. Jane replies cautiously. I see in her eyes that she is thinking rapidly about her response, but I have no fear that she will betray us. I know my Jane, and I am proved right. She concocts a story that is close to the truth without revealing the secrets of Reeves Hall.

But then the reverend asks if anything is troubling her, and she pierces my heart with her reply. "Not only am I a widow with a young child to care for, but I am also an orphan, and the only family I have left—an uncle and aunt—have been less than kind towards me. I am fortunate to have sufficient funds to live comfortably, and for that I am immensely grateful, yet my future lies uncertain." *I will take care of you, Jane. Never will I leave you.* I send the promise out into the ether, but I doubt that she can hear me.

Then she is out of the church and mounting her horse again, riding back like the wind. I do not let up my watchful vigil, even as she enters the house and goes to the kitchen, searching for something to eat. I realise I too have eaten nothing since breakfast hours ago, though in the agitated state I am in, I do not think I could consume a single morsel. She goes up to her chamber, finishes the slices of bread and cheese, then enters the washroom. I see her open the door to my chamber, a hopeful look on her face that quickly disappears when she finds it empty.

She collects herself, hides her disappointment and goes to find her daughter. It is then I disengage the probes and leave her alone. For the next hours, I keep busy speaking with members of my household to ascertain their wishes. I am surprised by just how many of them decide to stay on here. Catana, thankfully, is not one of them. I know it is her that aided Jane in her escape. There is no room in my household for such perfidy, and I make that clear to Catana when we speak. It is no surprise then that she elects to return to Uvon.

Finally, I can stall things no longer. I need to find Jane. I head to my bedchamber and it is then I see the indicator light on the washroom door. Jane is inside, and I know she must be in the bath. The time has come for her to know the whole truth about me. I enter the washroom and declare, "Jane, we need to talk."

She sits up in the bath, the wariness in her expression turning to confusion as I begin to disrobe. Once I am naked, I step into the tub and pull her into my lap. For this conversation, I want her in my arms, my hand to her chest, feeling the beat of her heart. She does not resist as I draw her close and drop a kiss to the soft nape of her neck. "Jane," I murmur into her ear. "There are important matters I must reveal to you, but first, I have this to say." I kiss her temple, then take a deep breath and speak. "I love you with all my heart and wish to spend the rest of my days with you."

CHAPTER 33

JANE

I hear the words my heart has been yearning for. Broek holds me close, a hand splayed to my chest while he murmurs into my ear. My heart swells. When he told me we needed to talk, I had prepared myself for the worst. But this is unexpected in the best of ways.

I turn in his embrace, suddenly longing to see his face. I place my hands to his cheeks and search his eyes which glitter with the force of his desire. "I have said the words, Jane," he growls.

I smile lovingly. "Yes, you have."

"You promised to reciprocate," he prompts, brows knitting into a fierce scowl.

"So I did."

He waits impatiently. "Well?"

I press a kiss to his lips. How I love to do that. A quick thought flashes through my mind that from here on, I shall be privileged enough to do this every day of our lives. At least I hope so. I kiss him again for good measure. "Jane," he rumbles.

"Yes, Broek, I am getting to that," I say placatingly. Placing both hands to his chest, feeling the springy hair beneath my palms, I tell him what he wishes to hear. "I love you with all my heart, Broek, and wish to spend the rest of my days with you."

He sighs in relief, yet his next words bring a fresh bout of apprehension. "Good, but there is more I need to tell you."

I take a moment to settle myself in a straddling position above him, keeping my palms pressed to his chest. "Tell me," I say quietly.

"You may have gathered that we have received a pardon and have been invited to return to Uvon," he begins. I nod encouragingly. "Liora, Horis, Simor and I took it to a vote," he continues. "Before doing so, we all agreed that we would abide by the majority decision. Either we all go back to Uvon or we all stay."

Now I know my doom is come. He means to leave me behind. "The majority decision was to stay," he states matter-of-factly.

I let out the breath I have been holding. Yet I am still filled with doubt. "Do you not wish to return to your home?"

"My home is here, with you."

"So, it is not just your siblings? You too elected to stay?" I ask uncertainly.

He kisses me softly. "I voted to stay — with you. We are going to be married."

I nod in relief. He searches my face intently. "If my siblings had elected to go," he asks, "would you have come with me to Uvon?"

"Yes," I say with no hesitation. I have been pondering it the whole of today. I have prayed and reflected. I have dwelt on the reverend's words. *It is at those times when we feel forsaken and alone that we must remember Jesus's eternal love shines for us bright and strong.* In this moment, I know that even in a distant land foreign to me, I would not be alone as long as I keep my faith strong. And looking into Broek's eyes, I realise also that I would not be alone as long as I have his love. "Yes," I say again. "If you ever wish to return to Uvon, then I shall go with you."

He releases a breath, but I see we are not done. There is more. "What is it?" I ask quickly.

"Where do you think Uvon is, Jane, and how do you think we would be getting there were we to go?" he queries.

I stare at him in confusion. Slowly, I say, "I am not sure exactly where it is, but I know it is far away across the seas."

He huffs and draws me close so my head rests on his shoulder. "It is much further than you can imagine," he says softly, "and it is not across the seas."

I pull back to look at him. "But Liora said a ship will arrive tomorrow."

"A ship yes, but not one that travels by sea."

My brain is sluggish today, for I cannot think what he means. "I—I do not understand."

He strokes a wayward strand of hair back from my face. "It is a ship that travels in space," he says, watching me intently.

"In space?" Still I do not understand.

"Up above in the sky."

I am trying to picture what he says in my mind. A scientifically advanced society must have developed means of travel more rapid than we have here at present. My brow clears. "A ship that flies in the air like a bird?"

He laughs gently. "We have those too, but the ship I am talking about is not quite like a bird. It flies even higher than a bird, beyond our atmosphere, and travels through space to other planets."

He sees my continuing confusion and kisses me softly on the lips. "I believe it is best if I show you what I mean on the screen," he says. Then, speaking in his tongue, he raps out a series of instructions. A moment later, the screen behind me lights up. He turns me in the water so my back rests on his chest and I can see what is being displayed. The screen shows a night sky of a dark blue and in the midst of it, a blue and green dappled sphere. "What you are seeing," he murmurs above me, "is planet Earth from space." He points with his finger and a small red arrow appears on the screen. "See there, is the Atlantic

Ocean and there—" his arrow points to a thin area of green, "there is Britain."

I gaze in marvel. "So this is what our world looks like from the heavens," I say wonderingly.

"This is what it looked like from the ship I was on seven years ago, when we arrived here."

"And Uvon," I whisper in wonder. "Where is it?"

He kisses the top of my head. "I am about to show you on the screen the journey to Uvon. Bear in mind that it is greatly speeded up, for in reality, it takes up to three years to reach my world."

Three years? Lord almighty where is this homeland? Hoarsely, I say, "Show me."

So, he shows me a journey through the heavens, passing by countless constellations, some bright, some a dark red, some with rings around them, then a long stretch of black sky, then more celestial bodies in fiery colours. It is a very long time, long enough for the bath water to cool though miraculously it does not, before the voyage ends at a sphere that looks remarkably like the one where this journey began, almost a twin of planet Earth. "That is Uvon," says Broek speaking very softly. He points with the arrow to a green mass of land beside a large ocean. "And there is Luxzuc, my home city."

He goes on to show me pictures of a fantastical city with tall buildings that kiss the sky, surrounded by sloping valleys through which winds a long river. It is beautiful, magical even, and oh so foreign. I always suspected that Broek came from a country much different to mine, but I had not known just how different. And there is something else that I am beginning to realise. "You are not from my world, Broek," I say shakily.

"No, Jane, I am not. I come from a very distant planet in a different galaxy."

I breathe deeply, trying to calm my racing mind. "You are from an alien world," I breathe, "yet you look the same as us."

He laughs softly. "You were ever the perceptive one, sweet duchess. Yes, we look the same for we are all of the same human race. Will you believe me if I tell you that my family was not the first from my planet to visit Earth? Many hundreds of thousands of years ago, my people discovered your planet. They gave it the name Strahmek 2 and decided it would be a fitting colony to ship off our criminals to. There was talk also of creating a high-speed corridor between our two planets, but it came to naught when my world became embroiled in a long period of war, during which time that colony of criminals was forgotten."

I wrinkle my brow. "What happened to them?"

He chuckles. "Eventually, after a very, very long time, they formed civilisations, then nation states. You, my dear, and every other human on Earth, are direct descendants of those men and women that we shipped here all those centuries ago."

I turn to face him in horror. "Do you mean we are descended from criminals?"

"It was a very long time ago, Jane," he reminds me gently.

"What you say is unbelievable," I state firmly.

"Perhaps so, yet it is the truth." With a sigh, he adds, "We had best come out of this bath before your skin wrinkles like a prune."

He pushes me up gently and we both step out of the bath. I stand docilely as he fetches a towel and dries my body, then quickly does the same for himself. "Come, Jane," he says. "Time to dress for dinner." He leads me to my chamber, where I set about getting dressed. He disappears out the door and comes back a few moments later holding forth a pile of clothes in his hands, then begins to dress in company with me.

I sit on the edge of the bed and pull up my stockings, attaching them with a garter. As I do so, I mutter, "I am not the descendant of criminals."

"Have it your own way," he humours me.

I pull a chemise over my head. He helps me with my stays. Then I march to my wardrobe to take out a gown to wear. "Not black," Broek says firmly.

My fingers hover over the black muslin then pass it to reach a gown at the far end of the wardrobe, in pale blue silk. I take it out with hands that shake. Broek nods approvingly as he finishes fastening his trousers. He comes to me and helps me with my petticoat, then the gown. "Very pretty," he says admiringly, patting the folds down.

As he goes to put on his shirt, I stand in front of the mirror and examine myself. There is relief, finally, in divesting myself of the black. A symbolism too. I will always remember Giles fondly, but my time of mourning is over. Now is the time to start anew. I go to my dressing table and pick up the brush. Broek takes it from me and begins to dress my hair, running the brush through my locks then expertly pinning them as if he has been doing it all his life. Once he is done, he raises a brow in enquiry, as if demanding praise.

I merely stand and fetch the cravat, tying it expertly for him, then raise my own brow. "Excellent work," he murmurs. As he pulls on his tailcoat, he asks casually, though I know the question is anything but casual, "So, Jane. Now that you know that I come from a distant planet, that I am not from Earth, will you still marry me?"

There is not a shred of doubt left in my mind. I place both hands on his chest, close to his heart. "Yes, Broek. I will marry you." He draws me to him, and we both take comfort in the closeness of our bodies. Then he releases me, and we go down to dinner.

CHAPTER 34

JANE

Next morning, I wake once more to that possessive hand roaming over my body. I can see that this is going to become a habit for my husband-to-be. I can have no complaints. Broek's hand comes to rest warmly on my mound and again, I feel that sense of certainty that I belong—with him.

My husband-to-be, my mind thinks sleepily. And then comes another thought, which I voice out loud, albeit in a low croak, "When shall we get married?"

"I was just about to bring the matter up with you," he rumbles at my side. The hand that covers my mound moves lower, and I startle as fingers probe the soft flesh beneath.

"Ah, that tickles!" I groan.

"Hush, Duchess and be still," he admonishes. His fingers continue their wicked exploration, and I groan once more, though this time more in pleasure than surprise.

"About the wedding," I remind him breathlessly.

"It will happen today," he states decisively. "After breakfast, we shall all go to see Reverend Horton."

I laugh despite myself. "That is not how it is done, Broek." I speak with a degree of expertise in the matter, having walked down the aisle before. "One must first call the banns. By all means let us see the reverend, but we cannot marry for another three weeks."

"We shall marry today," he repeats stubbornly. I wriggle helplessly as the hand at my mound finds my joyful nub and begins to rub it gently.

"But Broek—"

He covers my body with his. "Shh, no more talk," he chides, then fills me with one determined thrust of his male shaft. Next moment, his lips claim mine and all thoughts of a wedding fly out of my head.

Later, as we dress together in my chamber, I think to quiz him on the matter some more. "Jane," he sighs wearily. "Do pay me the respect of knowing what I am about." At my mutinous expression, he adds, "I took the precaution, on my last visit to London, to obtain a special license. We can and will get married today."

"Oh," I say, pausing with a shoe in my hand. "You had thoughts to marry me all that time ago?"

His look is searing. "Duchess, I reached the conclusion that you must marry no one but me the day after our dinner party."

I am doubtful of this, flattering though it may be. "Yet you were at pains to get me to sell Penhale Manor and leave."

He comes to me then and takes my hand, placing a gentle kiss to it. "Humans are not always logical beings, Jane," he says gruffly. "My head told me you had to leave, but my heart knew you were mine." He leads me out of the chamber, saying as he does so, "Besides, even had I let you leave, I would have continued to keep my eyes on you. Sooner or later, I would have come to claim you."

And so, later that morning, we arrive at the church, Broek, Liora, Horis, Simor and I. My dictatorial husband-to-be takes Reverend Horton aside and speaks to him. I do not know exactly what is said, but it must convince the vicar for a short time later, Broek and I stand at the altar and exchange our vows. As I speak these words once more, I am struck by how much truer they are, second time around. I had loved Giles in a gentle way and was grateful to him for plucking me out of my life of servitude. My feelings for Broek are anything but gentle. I love him fiercely and with the possessiveness of a tigress.

When it is my turn to say the words of the service, I do so with a fervour missing in my previous marriage ceremony. "I, Jane Eleanor Cavendish take thee Brook Phineas Reeves to my wedded Husband, to have and to hold from this day forward, for better for worse, for richer for poorer, in sickness and in health, to love, cherish, and to obey—" I ignore Broek's raised brow and carry on, "till death us do part, according to God's holy ordinance; and thereto I give thee my troth."

Throughout the rest of the proceedings, I am aware only of the warmth of Broek's hand on mine and the burning flare of his dark gaze. The reverend concludes the service, with the words, "I pronounce that they be Man and Wife together, In the Name of the Father, and of the Son, and of the Holy Ghost. Amen." A final blessing is given, then we sign the register, give our thanks to the reverend and return to Reeves Hall as man and wife.

LATER THAT AFTERNOON, we gather on the moor to bid farewell to all those that have decided to return to Uvon. They will be flying up in a machine called a shuttle to join the ship that awaits them in space, high up in the sky. Broek explained it all to me, though I confess I did not fully understand what he said. There are a dozen people leaving today, including that glowering Amazon, Catana. I cannot but be relieved to see her go. Someone who I shall not be glad to say goodbye to, however, is Betsy, who is leaving with Velnas to make a new home for themselves on Uvon.

We have left Reeves Hall via the back gate and traipsed for a half-hour over scrubby land. Now Broek stops and points ahead of him. "There it is," he says.

I follow the direction of his hand and see nothing but empty moor before us. "Where?" I ask. "I do not see it."

"That is because it is cloaked. Its exterior mirrors the environment around it so as to hide it from view."

I am puzzled. "Then how is it you see the shuttle?" I ask pertly.

"It is subtle, but I can tell the grass does not sway with the wind way yonder," replies Broek.

I look again and see what he means. It is so small a thing as to be unnoticeable unless one is clearly looking for it. We resume our walk towards the shuttle. A few moments later, we reach it. I cannot see anything before me except for grass and sky, but when I hesitantly extend a hand forward, I feel the cool touch of metal. It is like magic. This then is the contraption that will fly these people high into the sky. It is unfathomable to me how it can be done, but I do not doubt Broek's words.

A door slides open, and I watch as trunks, furniture and other baggage are loaded into the shuttle. Keeping hold of Broek's hand, I peer inside. I see a large circular space with leather seats and a luggage bay to one side. There are some flashing buttons along a panel on one wall. I say a silent prayer that I shall not be one of the people travelling on this contraption today. Perhaps ever, though if Broek decides one day that he wishes to return to his homeland, then I shall gather my courage and go with him.

Then it is time for farewells. There is Gav'ox, one of the guards, who likes to get drunk on some brew called krilk. Stroxol is leaving too, as well as Croris, the young lad who served us our food at Penhale Manor the other day. There are several more people whose name I do not know, and Catana.

And then of course, there is Betsy. We embrace tearfully. She has been with me since my marriage to Giles, and I shall miss her dreadfully. We say our goodbyes, then one by one, they enter the shuttle. The door slides shut. Broek pulls at my hand. "Time for us to move to a safe distance, sweet duchess," he coaxes, guiding me several yards away. From this distance, I can barely see the shuttle, but I hear the loud roar of its engines as they start up. The air around us trembles with the force of it.

I shiver in fright and sensing this, Broek draws me close to his body. "Shh, duchess," he whispers in my ear. "There is nothing to fear."

The roar becomes louder and louder, and through the shuttle's cloak, I notice licks of orange flames gathering at its base. The sound becomes unbearably loud, almost like a piercing whistle. And then it is quiet once more. "That's it," says Broek. "They are gone." He stares at the spot where once was the shuttle, his look almost wistful.

"Do you regret not going?" I ask uncertainly.

He huffs and gathers me tight. "There are times when I miss my old home, Jane, but never in a million years will I ever regret staying here with you. Do not doubt that for even a second. It is done now, so let us return to the house."

We begin our walk back to Reeves Hall, along with the others who have come to say their farewells. I look sideways and spy Liora, walking a few paces to our right. Her expression is somewhere between glum and irate. The Reeves siblings may have voted overwhelmingly to stay on Earth, but not Liora, I suspect. Her eyes meet mine and for an instant, I see fury in her regard before she looks away and marches off. Broek follows my stare and sighs, "Liora had wished to return to our homeland. She chafes at the restrictions to her freedom here."

"Another captive at Reeves Hall?" I scoff.

"Not a captive, no, but as a female here in England, she is not free to live her life on equal terms with men, not like she would on Uvon."

I ponder this. I had not given much thought to the fact that men have a greater power than women in our society. I just accepted it as the way the world was. But having lived in subservience for many years in my aunt's household, I can sympathise with Liora's plight. I am glad though, that she did not have it her way and convince her brothers to travel back to Uvon. "Well," I say after a moment of consideration. "She shall simply have to find a way to win her freedom, much as in the end, I won mine."

"Perhaps so," smiles Broek, and we resume our journey to the house.

EPILOGUE

JANE

One month later

The day has finally come. Broek and I have talked it over and we are both agreed. It is time to destroy the nanoprobes, along with any information that would allow another person to replicate them. Playing God with them has served us well, but there is danger in their continued existence. We both understand that very well.

There is no more need for the probes now, nor for the information they provide. We are established at Penhale Manor and Broek's mercantile business continues to thrive. We have more wealth than we could ever want. Our position in society is becoming more secure with each day. Just last week, we hosted a dinner party in our new home, and this morning, I received an invitation to dine with the Drakes in a few days' time. All is well in our world.

So, it is time. This evening, a month after our marriage, we wait for the return of hundreds of thousands of probes from their journey across different parts of the world. We are in the garden at the back of the house, a large metal bowl before us. Broek has instructed each probe to return here, to this spot in the garden, at exactly six o'clock. I am beyond understanding how such a thing can be done. It is yet another of the miracles of science.

Broek checks his pocket watch once more. I glance at it to see the time is five minutes to the hour. He puts the watch away and stands, staring fixedly at the horizon. I inch towards him and put my hand through his arm. "It pains you to destroy your creations," I say softly.

He says nothing at first, then replies, "I spent thousands of hours perfecting their design."

"They are a wondrous creation," I assert. "Without them, I should never have known that my aunt and uncle were swindling me."

His mouth twists bitterly. "They are both my finest and my worst work in equal measure."

The juxtaposition of good and evil has ever been so. And though the nanoprobes were of a great help to me, they also pose incalculable danger to humankind for the power they bring to the person who wields them.

"You are doing the right thing," I say quietly. He simply nods.

We wait together, arm in arm. There is a dark cloud up ahead foreshadowing rain. I wonder if we should not go retrieve our cloaks, though the weather on this July evening seemed fine when we came out a few moments ago. As I watch the horizon, the dark cloud grows closer. It is then I realise this is not a cloud. It is a swarm of nanoprobes flying at speed towards us.

I shrink back in horror. Beside me, Broek squeezes my arm and holds me close. "They will not harm you," he says in a low voice. I watch in fearful fascination as the swarm swoops down towards us, emitting a peculiar buzzing sound. One by one the probes descend on the metal bowl before us, crackling and popping on their descent as if they were live creatures rather than machines. I shiver inwardly, glad of the comfort of Broek's arm.

For several minutes they continue to arrive, a dark cloud of dust that dives into the bowl, filling it nearly to the brim. And then it is done. All the probes, some three hundred and fifty thousand of them, are in the bowl. "How shall we destroy them?" I ask.

From a small box on the ground beside him, Broek brings out a metal contraption with sharp edges and a small rotor. "We shall crush them to a fine dust," he says grimly. I watch as he places the contraption in the centre of the bowl, then covers the whole thing with a large cloth. I suppose that is so none of the probes flutter out of the bowl as they are being crushed. He then presses a button on the metal contraption, and next moment, I hear a grinding noise coming from within the bowl. We continue like this for some time, until Broek presses the button again for the contraption to stop. Carefully, he removes the cloth and the contraption. Inside the bowl, there is now only a fine black dust.

"What now?" I wonder.

"Now," he says solemnly, "we give them a ceremonial burial." He goes to fetch a spade that is leaning against the wall and asks, "Where shall we do it?"

I point to the ground beside a rose shrub. "How about here?"

He sets about digging, not too deep, just around ten inches into the ground. Once he judges the hole large enough, he drops the spade and picks up the metal bowl of crushed nanoprobes. With great care, he pours the dust into the hole, then takes the spade again. This time, he passes it to me. Without a word, I scoop up some soil and sprinkle it over the hole, doing this repeatedly until all the nanoprobes are completely covered.

I step back, observing my work. "We should say some words to mark the occasion," I decide.

His lips curve. "Go on, Jane."

Breathing deeply, I pronounce, "Dear departed nanoprobes, wondrous fruits of Broek's labours, it is with sadness that we say goodbye. You served us well, yet to everything there is a season, and a time to every purpose under heaven. A time to be born, and a time to die; a time to plant, and a time to pluck up that which is planted. A time to kill, and a time to heal; a time to break down, and a time to build up. A time to weep, and a time to laugh; a time to mourn, and a time to dance. A time to cast away stones, and a time to gather stones together; a time to embrace, and a time to refrain from embracing. A time to get, and a time to lose; a time to keep, and a time to cast away. A time to rend, and a time to sew; a time to keep silence, and a time to speak. A time to love, and a time to hate; a time of war, and a time of peace."

As I recite these familiar lines, Broek regards me quizzically. "Ecclesiastes 3, verses one to eight," I say by way of explanation. I am a churchman's daughter, after all, and have been well instructed in the scriptures.

"Very apt," he murmurs. He releases a breath, as if relieved of a burden, then in a stronger voice he says, "Quite right too. There is a season and a time for everything. And now, Jane, I believe the time has come for us to love. Let us go to our bed, my heart."

"But how about dinner?" I demur.

"We can have something sent up to our room later. To bed, now," he growls. I have vowed to obey my husband, so of course, I let him lead me up to bed without complaint. We go to our chamber, whereupon Broek locks the door, and it is not long then before our clothes are thrown off and we find ourselves in bed.

Our bodies close, I look into Broek's dark eyes and breathe, "Fill me."

"With pleasure," says my husband, and proceeds to do just that.

AFTERWORD

Dear reader,

I hope you enjoyed this first in the series *The Reeves of Reeves Hall*. Next is *My Masquerade With the Duke*, Liora's story, in which she falls in love with a handsome duke while masquerading as a man. You can read an excerpt from it in the following pages.

Stay in touch

Want to hear about new releases, sneak previews and special offers? Join my reader list on my website:

→ **mw-author.com**

May I ask you for a small favour?

Reviews are the life blood of independent authors. Please could you help spread the word about this book by submitting a review on Amazon, Goodreads or any other book reader platform.

Thank you again for reading, and I hope you'll return to Reeves Hall with me soon.

M.M. Wakeford

ABOUT THE AUTHOR

M.M. Wakeford lives with her husband and son in a London terraced house that gathers dust while she loses herself in her writing. A lifelong reader of romantic novels, she writes in many genres including contemporary, sci-fi and historical romance.

Her stories capture that heady feeling of falling in love, with emotionally rich characters whose journey to a happily ever after is lined with dilemmas, desire and difficult choices. If you're looking for a page turning romance with high emotion and a good dose of spice, you're in the right place.

To be the first to hear about new releases, sneak previews and exclusive extras, sign up for M.M. Wakeford's mailing list at <u>mw-author.com</u>.

MY MASQUERADE WITH THE DUKE

A Steamy Regency Romance With a Sci-fi Twist
(AN EXCERPT)

THE REEVES OF REEVES HALL
– BOOK 2 –

M.M. Wakeford

PROLOGUE

⊰ ⊱

A NOT SO INVIGORATING CUP OF COFFEE

July 1821, London

AS HE WOVE his way through the busy thoroughfare of Lower Thames Street, ignoring the clamouring cries of street vendors peddling their wares, Jos could not shake the conviction that he had made a grave error. He walked on, following the path of the river in a westward direction, and reflected on the matter. Yes, it had been a mistake to confront the man as he had done, making loud accusations and threats.

At the time, Jos had thought that a show of determined strength was the way to resolve this intractable problem. Now, he could see that his approach had not only failed, it had also exacerbated the situation. Soon, he would have to come clean with his master and tell him just what a mess he had made of things. He hated the idea of it. For more than three decades, Jos had served the Reeves family diligently, earning their trust and working his way to the position he now held. What would they think of him now? Would he be stripped of his duties and sent back to Reeves Hall in disgrace? All because he had underestimated this enemy and played into his hands.

Some minutes later, he arrived at his home on Barton Street. The elegant townhouse belonged to the Reeves family, but Jos and his wife, Esa, who worked as the housekeeper, had been assigned generous quarters on the top floor. His heart heavy with the burden of his failure, he traipsed up the stairs and let himself into their private parlour, where Esa waited for him as usual, a pot of tea and a slab of cake on the table. Without a word, he removed his shoes and set them neatly by the door, then went to his armchair and sank gratefully into its timeworn depth.

His wife gazed at him in concern. "Long day?" she enquired.

"Yes," he replied. "Long day." That was all that was said. In their long years of marriage, the two had learned the art of unspoken communication. He did not need words to tell her that something was bothering him, and she did not need words to bring him comfort. Instead, she poured him a cup of tea and cut a slice of cake, placing them on the small table beside him. He grunted—his version of a thank you—and drank the hot brew.

Perhaps, he reflected, the situation was not so dire. On the morrow, he would go to plead his case again, maybe use some of his precious store of coins to grease a few palms. Yes, that was what he would do. On that hopeful thought, he retired to bed and sought solace in the familiar embrace of his wife.

But there was to be no chance to plead his case.

Early the next morning, he trudged down to the kitchen, and as was his habit, ate a thick slice of buttered bread with a wedge of cheese. Their maidservant, Nessie, brought him a steaming cup of coffee. He liked it bitter and black, with enough strength to invigorate him for the day. He drank from it, enjoying the sharp, biting taste, and smiled gratefully at the young lass. She was new to the position, having knocked on their door a few weeks previously in desperate need of employment. His master had done a good deed in giving her a job, and she had repaid them in kind.

He got to his feet, his head beginning to spin a little. He steadied himself with a hand to the back of the chair. There was no time to lose. Matters were pressing. He took three steps to the kitchen door, which opened onto a narrow side alley, then another half dozen steps, only to collapse on the cobbled stones of Barton Street.

CHAPTER 1

A FAMILY OUT OF THE ORDINARY

THAT AFTERNOON, FOUR people were gathered in the large parlour of Reeves Hall. One gentleman leaned a hand casually on the mantlepiece as he spoke. Another lounged on a graceful-looking armchair, a leather-bound volume clasped in his hands as he listened intently to what was being said. The third man in the room stood at the window observing the extensive grounds, though it was clear from the stiffness of his stance that his attention was also fixed on the words being spoken.

The final occupant of the room was a lady. Tall and slim, with walnut brown curls and fine, intelligent eyes, she sat ramrod straight at a chair by the fireplace, her gaze alternately set on the gentleman speaking and down on the floor.

A cursory look at this scene would impart nothing out of the ordinary—four well-dressed persons of quality convened in an elegantly appointed parlour in a prosperous-looking country house. But if one looked a little closer, one might notice some strange things about this room and these people.

On the far wall, at waist height, there appeared to be a small square of light continuously flashing green and then red. Higher up on that same wall was a small rectangular grille through which cool air wafted into the room, keeping the temperature low even on this hot July day as the sun speared the windows with its powerful rays. And a closer inspection of the leather-bound volume in the seated gentleman's hands would show it to be not a book but an unusual contraption with a flat glassy surface on which different symbols appeared and then went.

This was no ordinary family, for the Reeves of Reeves Hall had a closely guarded secret. They were not from this world — not from England, nor from Great Britain, nor from the continent of Europe nor from any nation on this great sphere called Earth. The Reeves family hailed from a world called Uvon two million light years away. On that world, their name had been Reevas, but this was changed to the more English sounding name of Reeves shortly after their arrival in England.

As might be expected from a society able to engage in interplanetary travel, the world of Uvon was highly evolved and far more scientifically advanced than England in the year 1821. One might wonder then what such a family was doing living in a country estate in the heart of the Cornish moor. How had they got here and why?

Quite simply, the Reeves family had been banished from Uvon and sent into exile to the only other habitable planet in the universe: Earth. This was a planet that had been colonised by Uvonians hundreds of thousands of years ago, in the early phase of their space exploration, with the hope of forging some mighty, interplanetary empire. With this in mind, thousands of felons from Uvon's overcrowded prisons had been shipped to Earth as a first step towards building a new and enlightened civilization there. The plan had failed; the distance between the two planets far too great for such an ambition — and the stranded felons soon forgotten, left to fend for themselves in a land populated by large reptile creatures.

Over the many centuries that followed, Uvonians had sent the occasional unmanned missions to orbit Earth and gather data, but nothing more. From this data it was known that the felons and their descendants had ended up building civilizations, though whether these were enlightened was debatable. And it was to one of these civilizations, to England, that the Reeves family had been banished.

Why this happened was a story as old as time and all to do with an insatiable lust for power. The matriarch of the Reeves family, a high-ranking member of Uvon's governing body, had been involved in an unsuccessful plot to seize permanent control of the government. Found guilty of treason, she had paid the ultimate price with her life and that of her husband. All four of their children—Broek, Liora, Horis and Simor—had been spared death but forced into exile. With heavy hearts, the bereaved members of the Reeves clan, their ages ranging from fifteen to twenty-three, had left Uvon, accompanied by a retinue of devoted family servants, and embarked on a three-year journey in space to this distant planet that was to become their new home. They had arrived in England in the summer of 1814, discreetly and without fanfare, and set about establishing themselves as members of the landed gentry; their new seat, Reeves Hall.

It had been a derelict estate some six miles east of Newquay which they had purchased and upgraded to their Uvonian standards, installing a security system around the perimeter to prevent outsiders from entering. Its location in the midst of uninhabited moorland, the sleepy village of Penhale a mile away, was perfect for their needs. Of necessity, the family had to keep their true origins to themselves and to guard against anyone finding out about their way of life. Whatever knowledge Earth humans may have once had of their true Uvonian ancestry had long since been lost in the drifts of time. The people of England had no inkling that there existed a planet, impossibly far away, on which lived their brethren humans. And they did not know that secretly amongst them, there lived a family of humans come from that planet on a spaceship, with scientific capabilities beyond their wildest imaginings. They could not be allowed to discover such a fact. This then was the closely guarded secret of the Reeves family.

This secret was a weight on each member of that family, not least on Liora, the lone female among the four siblings and the lady seated ramrod straight in the parlour of Reeves Hall that day. In the years since her arrival in England, Liora had had to contend not only with the loss of her ancestral home on Uvon, but also with a reversal of her status both within the family and in society at large.

For Uvon had been a world where women had an important role to play, not merely be wives and mothers, or chattels of their husbands. Liora had been on the cusp of adulthood when tragedy had struck. All her life up until then, she had been groomed to follow in her powerful mother's footsteps. It had been expected that she too would one day rise to a prominent position on Uvon's governing body. To that end, she had received the best education that money could buy. From early childhood, she had learned to speak fluently all the dialects of her world so that she could address the people she was one day to rule. She had been schooled in every facet of the law, as one day, she would be promulgating new laws of her own. She had studied her people's long history as well as science, for the leaders of Uvon were expected to be steeped in deep knowledge. In short, Liora had been poised for a magnificent future. Faster than the blink of an eye, all this had changed.

Banished from her planet, the bright future mapped out for Liora was suddenly gone, but she had adapted. In the course of their long journey to Earth, she had tried to prepare herself as best she could for her new life. A proficient linguist, she had applied herself to learning English. Knowing that a career in jurisprudence or government would be out of the question for her in England, she had pragmatically set to studying engineering systems, a skill that would prove useful in the setting up of their new home. However, no amount of study could prepare Liora for the reality she had found in England.

Here, she could no longer live as she had before. Her freedom was abominably curtailed. She had to adhere to the strict rules that English society set for women from the clothes she wore to the preservation of her virtue and reputation. For someone who had been used to leading a carefree life, answering to few people but herself, this had come as a profound shock.

Again, she had tried as best she could to adjust to her new circumstances. To all appearances, she had succeeded in doing so, living a quiet life at Reeves Hall and letting her brothers take precedence when it came to external matters. But it rankled. Even after several years, the resentment had not been totally erased. This might help to explain why she acted as she did that afternoon on hearing the news of Jos's sudden death.

Standing by the fireplace, Broek, the eldest sibling, was saying, "It is imperative one of us goes to London as soon as possible and takes over the running of the shipping business—at least until we can appoint a permanent replacement for Jos." He looked around the room, casting meaningful glances at his two brothers. It was usually Broek that dealt with business matters, but he did not wish to do so this time. Newly married and still in the early period of domestic bliss, he was reluctant to subject his new bride to a likely stay of several weeks in London. His brothers could take on this responsibility for a change. But before either of them could do so, Liora spoke up. "I will go," she stated firmly.

Her announcement was greeted with surprised stares and a growing scowl on Broek's face. In stern tones, he addressed her. "As capable as you are, Liora, I'm afraid it's a man's world out there."

She was not to be fobbed off with that excuse again. Oh no! Seven years she had spent in subservience at home because she was told England was a man's world. No more.

Raising a stubborn brow, she lobbed back, not thinking the matter through, "Then I'll have to become a man, won't I?"

MY MASQUERADE WITH THE DUKE

On her home planet, women command power. On Earth, she must pretend to be a man to gain her freedom.

What you'll find inside:

- ♥ A steamy Regency romance with a science-fiction twist
- ♥ A hidden-identity heroine in disguise
- ♥ Road trip tension and *only one bed* proximity
- ♥ Opposites attract with a cinnamon-roll hero
- ♥ A murder mystery woven through the romance

"Once I started reading, I couldn't stop… a THOROUGHLY enjoyable story to read." ★★★★★ Reader Review

"I thoroughly enjoyed it. The chemistry and love Liora and Marcus have for each other is so beautiful to see." ★★★★★ Reader Review

ALSO BY THIS AUTHOR

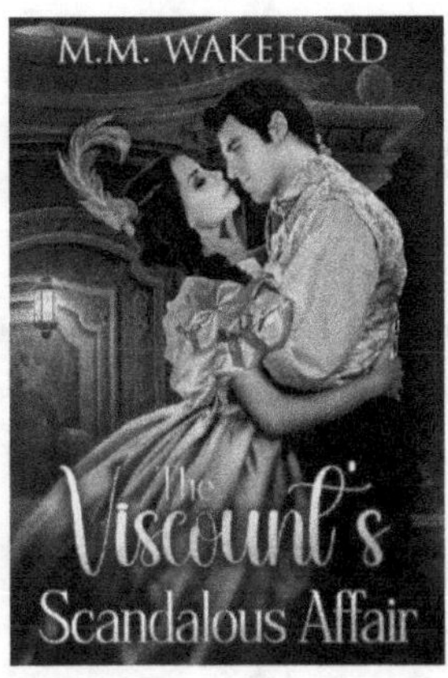

THE VISCOUNT'S SCANDALOUS AFFAIR
Book 1 – The Stanton Legacy
– Series Complete –

A high-heat, open-door Regency romance about a scandalous affair and unexpected love.

"Why not have a short dalliance with me? In the cold desert of my spinsterhood, I assure you I will not treasure my virtue half as much as the memories of sensual pleasures with you."

Charlotte Harding has little to expect from life. Orphaned, penniless, and painfully aware that society finds her forgettable, she survives on the charity of kindly relatives.

Then she meets the Viscount Stanton—handsome, wealthy, and entirely out of her reach. He barely notices her… until one reckless night changes everything.

Charlotte accidentally witnesses the viscount in a secret liaison, and her silence is bought with a single, unforgettable kiss—one that awakens a longing she never dared hope could be fulfilled.

And when later, an opportunity presents itself, **Charlotte does something truly scandalous: she makes him an offer.**

→ A discreet, temporary affair
→ No promises. No future
→ Stolen weeks of pleasure—memories to sustain her through a lifetime of spinsterhood

But the viscount soon discovers the quiet, overlooked woman he never noticed is the one he cannot forget. Desire deepens, and both must decide whether society's rules are worth denying their hearts.

The Viscount's Scandalous Affair is the first book in *The Stanton Legacy*, a completed Regency romance series. Each book features a full romantic arc, explicit open-door love scenes, and a guaranteed happily ever after.

Praise for The Viscount's Scandalous Affair:

"A beautiful story... and the ending was perfection." ★★★★★ Goodreads review

"A stunning read and a great story... compelling and very steamy." ★★★★★ Goodreads review

"Excellent book to curl up with and enjoy. What a way to start a new series. Would strongly recommend." ★★★★★ Goodreads review

"Charlotte enchanted me completely... a superb romance with twists and turns and a stunning HEA." ★★★★★ Goodreads review

"It's hard not to fall in love with Charlotte... This was a charming book and I loved every second of it." ★★★★★ Goodreads review

"I loved reading this book! Right from the beginning I was invested in the story. The writing style is not rushed, so detailed and so well executed. I loved being immersed in the story of how the main characters fell in love." ★★★★★ Goodreads review